I0741173

8th DEADLY SIN

CHAMP HAGAN

WWW.KULTUREKINGS.COM

ISBN: 978-0-578260-4-1 (Paperback)
Library of Congress Control Number: Pending

Editor: Dolly O. Amsk
Proofreading: Frank Williams
Interior Design: Jennifer Houle
Cover Design: Angie Ayala

Published by:

Kulture Kings Publishing
Valencia, CA 91355
www.kulturekings.com

Printed in the United States of America

DEDICATION

First, I'd like to give my Highest Praise to My Divine Creator. With gratitude and humility is what I try my BEST to walk with daily; thank you for my life, thank you for the lite at the end of all my Darkest Hours!

To my Mother, who has always supported me throughout everything: You are amazing, and I could not have asked for a better you!

Dad, we know the deal, and we know what's understood; it doesn't need any more understanding.

Champ and Zy, I'm praying y'all see that I'm trying my best. And I hope this makes you both just a little bit more proud to be a Hagan one day . . . !

Kim, You pushed me . . . ! You believed in me..! You are remarkable . . . !

"Leah, R.I.P!" If it weren't for you, I would not know writing even mattered. You are the most talented person I've ever seen with a pen and paper, hands down . . . !

Freak-O, Wish it was different, wouldn't change a fucking thing . . . I got your back little brother, no matter what . . . !

This book is also dedicated to all the family and friends I haven't spoken to in some time. Life is short, so I thought y'all should know that my prayers and love of heart are with you all always . . . !

Last yet not least . . .

De'Shawn Lionel Johnson . . . ! Nonnie Scott . . . ! Jan Hagan . . . ! Patricia Lowe . . . ! Kenneth Artel Miles . . . ! Damien Henninger . . . ! Christopher Butler . . . ! Gone but not forgotten . . . We love y'all . . . Make sure you hold us a spot . . . !

PROLOGUE

I'm The Biggest Dog in This Dog Eat Dog World!
Who Am I?

THE EIGHTH DEADLY SIN

Sin is seeded by seven roots that make up a stump. Greed, envy, pride, lust, wrath, sloth, and gluttony are the vines that makes me the Almighty Tree. The eighth sin, which is me, is what you call the Money Tree.

Still, most already know that man will subside to me, and woman can't deny me, and no human will defy me. Yet most would die for the sake of trying me.

I am *the* almighty, powerful, dollar bill.

👿 *If I could talk, then this would be my story.*

Though, it's a terrible shame that this must be another tale of schemes, deceit, envy, and greed, not to mention a few more attributes that go with being born into poverty. Mix that with the lack of resources and people's slothful ways, and this is how life unfolds.

You've seen this all before!

People accepting me as their divine ruler. People implementing me as their only means to an end. So much so that I often become their sole purpose for living, and I'm often their reason for dying.

In their eyes, I'm an inspiration. I represent success. I'm the pinnacle that shows obstacles have been hurdled. More often than not, I define who they are, their self-esteem, and principles, amongst other things. The conduct of their character often turns into a quasi-fascist-like facade whenever I'm involved.

In fact, usually the more they attempt to possess me, the more outlandish they act.

And that's exactly why the more they lust to obtain my soft flexible texture, the more calamity I create in their world!

Granted.

They yearn for me even though most people know that I'm the devil in a material form. And in spite of the fact that they know chaos is always not far behind me, they're still comforted by putting me in their pocket or wrapping a rubber band around me or securely snuggled in a money clip.

See, my master knows how to lurk and wait. His plan is to begin devouring you right after you put me in your briefcase or toss me into that Louis Vuitton duffle bag. Because after all, all you want is this bag.

So, we exploit the simple one-track mindedness that makes you an easy target. Sometimes too easy!

He oversees me, and I control you. I just happen to be the tool he uses to get the job done.

It's a fucked-up chain of command.

But we all know that shit floats downstream and people just like you are always at the tip of the ravine.

Now don't get me wrong, I do good things for good people, who do good by me, so in essence, I'm not all bad.

But I'll be damned if you trick, abuse, manipulate, steal, rob, kill, destroy, or use any other of my worldly almighty father's devices to obtain more of me and think you're gonna' get away Scott-free.

Whatever moral you live by in getting me, will be the same guilt turned on you, in losing me. But of course, you remember the universal cliche, "what goes around comes around."

Now I understand that common sense ain't common, and I been trying to make this as simple as possible, but Imma go ahead and dumb it down to make sure you're keeping up with what makes the world go 'round. Which is the same thing that will eventually tear the world down.

IT'S ME!

Yen, dineros, cash, moolah, pesos, etc. On the streets, they call me "money bags" but depending on what region of the world you're in at the time, will determine the title people use to describe me.

I'm the answer to all your problems!

I can make that super sexy woman want to know your name. I can get you to mingle with the rich and famous. I can even get you the finest of cars, clothes, and all of life's other luxurious accessories. They can all be laid right at your feet.

But first—

You'll have to solemnly pledge your soul to making ME the most powerful entity in your life. And secondly, you have to take an oath that my father's tyranny is what you swear to obey.

Once you do that, then I'll be happy to fulfill every wish that your little money hungry heart desires.

"Oh, hell no you say, huh?"

Yeah, that's what they all say until I let them see what they're turning down.

—but not you. I can sense you're different.

Someone must have installed ethics like hard work, and fortitude in you. I see someone has already tricked you into believing that material things aren't as important as the world would make you believe they are. It's only obvious that you've already been brainwashed into believing that a pork chop is the same as steak.

But hey, I admire your type.

Though you people are an endangered species, you still try to fight a good fight for what's right. And even though I'm my father's right-hand man, I still respect that.

No biggie, tho, your just one in a billion.

In fact, to prove my point, I'm going to tell you a story that happened not long ago. This story even has a few people just like you in it. The kind that swears up and down that they're not puppets to my bullshit? Let's just say that I gave them an opportunity to reveal what lies dormant in their money hungry hearts.

And you know what? It didn't cost us that much.

Now I usually don't do this, but because you look like you can keep a secret, Imma go ahead and show you how my father uses me and has no empathy for the people we destroy!

So please, keep up. And if you have any questions, just ask, and I'll break down the play for you, right here from the press box! 😈

ROME. RITA. DALNESHA.

ey sis. Why are you sitting out here on this porch wearing that long face?" Rome questioned his big sister, Rita, as he stepped onto their porch and out in the sunny Southern California sun.

"Ain't nothin', I'm good," Rita responded with her eyes still locked on something on the floor as she spoke.

Rome and Rita were as close as a brother and a sister could get, Rome could feel Rita's sunken spirit, so he decided to probe further. "After all these years. How about you miss me with that cap shit, you should know by now that I know you better than I know Little Boosie lyrics and you know I know Boosie shit."

Rita gave a smile at that because it was no doubt, she knew Boosie Boo was Rome's shit. He gave her a slight nudge as he sat next to her.

"It's tuition," Rita said, "I was supposed to make the Dean's List and be covered for my last two years of school, but something about them needing a third exchange student on the Dean's List so it didn't look like the university was being ethnically biased."

Rita exhaled her frustrations as she finished, then Rome cut in. "So what you're telling me is, so they don't look like racists, they're going to give away your honors money to someone who's family can probably afford to buy the whole damn college?"

Rita looked over in her brother's direction and nodded her head.

"How much is it?" Rome asked.

Rita answered with defeat surrounding her words, "It's thirty thousand for my last two years."

Rome whistled in amazement.

Her head went down again trying to avoid her little brother from seeing her cry. Ever since Rita, Rome, and their little sister, Dalnesha, lost their mother in a car accident when Rita was sixteen, she was forced to assume the role of a parent to her younger brother and sister. Rita instantly enrolled in home studies and started working for the local grocery store to pay bills and support their other necessities. Luckily, their uncle Nate was there to fend off child protective services from breaking up their family.

They had already lost their mother, which was devastating, but to lose each other would have been earth shattering. Somehow the good Lord pulled them through, between the money their mother had hidden, Rita's checks and uncle Nate's disability, they'd seemed to maintain for five years often, without a dollar to spare.

Rome rubbed Rita's back trying to help her find some sort of solace. He could see the disappointing look of defeat in Rita's mannerisms, which was something he had never witnessed in his superwoman. That was the name Rome had given Rita, since their mother had passed. In all his 19 years of life, one thing he had never seen was his big sister break down. To him she was like Robert Horry in the clutch. In the final seconds with the game on the line, just give it to Rita and she'd hit the game winner, eyes closed.

But today was different, her bionic powers seemed to be fading, like her tank was on empty, and the fuel she needed to push on was being guarded in a faraway country by a terrorist rebellion group. Rome in that moment made a pact with himself that it was time to pay homage to big sis, and the only way to do so was to make sure Rita was able to receive her dream of a higher education.

"Don't worry, girly, school doesn't start until next month, it's nothing for God to fart out a miracle and turn this into a success story. Just put your head down and send your prayer up and let him do the rest. Ain't that what mom used to say? Put your head down and send your prayer up," they both finished their mother's adage together, " . . . let him do the rest." They both smiled, remembering their mother.

That was what Rita needed to hear and the spirit boost Rome had intended to give. "Thanks, little bro," Rita said with a smile, "I'ma take a walk and clear my mind. Stay here and keep an eye on your little sis till I get back."

As Rita was leaving, Rome's hand came out as if to say babysitters get paid. "In the famous words of E-40, the only things Imma pay yo ass is no mind." Rita slapped his hand as she skipped down the porch steps.

Dalnesha emerged out the front door and onto the porch beside her older brother. "Hey, where's superwoman going?" Dalnesha asked one of her typical nosey questions.

"To clear her head, she's kinda in a slump," Rome answered.

"I could tell she's been stressing, what's wrong?"

Rome looked up at her with an annoyed look and said, "Grown folks' problems, something a teeny bopper wouldn't understand."

Dalnesha popped her gum and leaned on her brother's chair, all undeveloped twelve years of her. "Must be an issue that only a bag full of money can solve." Then she pranced off as Rome starred in her direction.

Again, utterly amazed. It never ceased to astonish him how much his little twelve-year-old sister understood about life.

JAMES

James and his oldest friends stepped out the side door of Red's garage headed for James' porch panorama. Both men remained silent as they stepped stride for stride to the curb, both prepared for whatever ambush may have laid in their wait. James squeezed the Gucci shoulder bag that contained his winnings from the all-night dice game that Red commonly held on Friday and Saturday nights, only for certain privileged dope boys of course.

They both were elated about last night's scam, they pulled out the old-school tricks on those new booty youngsters by using magnets that were strapped to their thighs as they worked a pair of lead loaded dice. Red, whose job as the house man was to simply keep the discrepancies down while monitoring the game and collect his $100 every time a six hit the dice. No one ever expected Red to be rigging the game because most people thought him a bona fide hustler from the old school with a spotless reputation, not your typical con man with honest eyes that were full of deception.

James take on the night was four hundred fifty thousand dollars, and that was after he paid Red his eighty thousand dollars for setting it all up. As he walked to his car, his bag was tucked tightly under his arm while his other hand firmly held his cocked 10mm in his pocket.

Red also held his all black sawed- off Mossberg shotgun to his side as he watched their surroundings closely while James jumped into his car. They both knew that even though the early morning sun had already begun to light up the sky, these young goons would run up on the President with a cap gun if they thought he had three hundred dollars stashed in his sock. So, you could imagine what stupid shit they'd try to pull for some big boy bread. And there was no way James was going out like a nobody if anyone thought they could take what he had scammed all night for. James wasn't a baby, and his money wasn't candy. So, taking it would not be easy.

As James found the leather seat of his Panamera, entered his key, and pushed the button to start his ride, the duo scanned the scene carefully. They shared a few jokes and a homie type pound before James pulled off and left Red to stand in his driveway watching him safely drive away.

Feeling on top of every cloud higher than nine, James reached in his Gucci bag and retrieved a rubber band bundle of 100's and put it up to his nostrils. "Fuck, I love the smell of big money!

James spoke aloud to himself, feeling like the statement was a personal stroke from him, directly to his ego.

Rounding the corner of Red's block, James', white leather on white paint on white rimmed, Porsche came to an immediate halt.

Hey, it's me, Mr. Money Bags. Now I know I'm interrupting, but before I can keep giving you this storyline, I've got to explain to you the affinity between me and my guy James. See, James and I go way back. He saluted me when he was about 10 years old! I remember it like it was yesterday.

One day after James' uncle Reggie had just won in a dice game at the local park. It was early evening and time to head home when James spotted the ice cream truck and asked his uncle Reggie could he have a dollar?

"No!" said Uncle Reggie.

He thought this was an appropriate time to teach James a life lesson.

James' sadden face turned into a pout. After some time of them walking and Reggie continuing to count his winnings, James finally worked up the nerve to ask why his uncle had denied him a dollar when he'd had so many.

"Money is the most important thing in this whole wide world," Reggie began his lecture while opening his arms up as wide as he could. "We need money to do any and everything," Reggie told James who listened

intensely. "To buy food, clothes, and go to the movies like you love to do. And nobody is going to just give it to you just because you're a handsome little guy."

Reggie banked a playful punch off his nephew's chin, "In this world, nephew, you're either a working square or a man with a hustle . . . like me. But whatever you do, you've got to get up and go get it. Can't have your hand out like that guy who stands in front of the corner store, or you'll be just like him. You've got to get up and get money, nephew, you've got to think it, dream it, and if you really care about your dollars, your dollar will be about you—just like Uncle Reg."

Hell of a message, for a thirty-something year old uncle and guardian to teach his nephew, but Reggie was merely offering all he had known and learned in his own life. But to an impressionable child who idolized the man that spoke those praises of money so openly to him, that was all it took.

That day was the day James had been awoken. And even though before that day James was familiar with what money was and did, until that day, he never realized how it was the only necessity that truly mattered.

Every day after that, James watched his uncle closely, attentively taking note of all the monetary transactions that occurred. And that's when James became conscious of just how results were established when dollars exchanged from fist to glove.

Standing in the doorway of his uncle's bedroom days after they had that conversation, James spoke to me, and said, "I want money. No matter what, I don't want ice cream or cookies or candy anymore. I don't want to play my video games. I want to be like my uncle and make lots of money."

The next time that James and Reggie locked eyes, Reggie could tell there was something different about James, "Show me how to make money," were the simple words that plastered a proud, sinister smile on Reggie's face.

That's the day I became James' mentor. I used Reggie to turn James into the slickest little conman on the West Coast. He showed James his first successful scam.

The plan went like this:

James was to go into his elementary school's bathroom right after recess, throw some water on the floor, cut the back of his head with the small razor Reggie had put in his pocket. Then as was instructed, James was to lay in a puddle of water where he supposedly slipped and cry hysterically.

"Let them take you to the hospital. I'll be there shortly afterwards to take you home, then it's cha-ching up in this bitch." Was the exact word's Reggie had used to coach James just as he had climbed out of Reggie's car that very day.

Of course, Reggie's tactless plan worked like a charm on the clueless school district, and ever since then for James, it's been scheme-scheme, plot-plot.

But don't get it backwards!

I've gotten James shot for trying to rig a pit bull-pit fight. I've had him beaten within half an inch of his life, for getting caught trying to drug a boxer right before a semi-pro fight.

There was also the time a few car club members threw him out a four-story apartment building window. They found out the day after James won forty-thousand dollars betting against their driver that someone had majorly tampered with their racer. One of the members remembered James having close access to the car, because a member had known him, and invited him in, as a prospective club member. The way it happened it should've been a world class movie.

When they asked the club member how they could locate James, he told, and they were at some pale foot bimbo's apartment in Dallas, Texas in no time.

When they kicked open the front door, James saw their racing logo from their trademark patch, he'd known right away that his evil deed had been found out. That's when James bolted from his reclined chair in front of the T.V. and dove directly out the window headfirst. Like an Olympic diver off one of those concert platforms.

It was beautiful!

Lucky for James, he landed on the hood of someone's car. His assailants, still thirsty for blood, went to give chase. James' second stroke of luck came when the patrolman parked across the street and saw the whole thing unfold. At the end of the day James escaped with his life, two broken legs, a broken arm, three broken ribs, and a concussion.

It's been close, but no cigar.

But Imma get his ass one day. I can promise you that. 

"Hey Sexy-face, where are your pretty little feet carrying you to?" James asked, still holding the rubber band stack of money in plain view under his nose.

It was Rita. She was crossing the street.

"Oh, hi James. How you doin'? I was just headed to the store for my daily V8 juice." She stopped momentarily to be polite, but she knew this scene all too well.

First, James would make some small talk, while at the same time, trying to flash his baller status. Then he'd follow up with a heavy dose of flirting, that's when she'd brush him off and be on her merry little way.

"Hop in, I'm going that way"

Rita rolled her eyes as she replied through a tight smirk, "James, you a good con-man, but a terrible liar."

Rita was a very beautiful young lady. She had the kind of sex appeal that no man could deny. Her brown almond eyes always seemed to dance with a glimmer as they invited you into her innocence. Her caramel hue complimented her lighter toned full, plump shaped mouth, which left the illusion that they'd never been kissed and her button nose, small and in the center of her oval face. While her thick eyebrows and eyelashes were perfectly shaped to outline her almost doll-like features. At only 5'2", Rita's tall crop of thick, straight hair fell a tad past her midsection. Her flat belly was shadowed by her full, c-cup breast line, and her small waistline was accentuated by a pair of full hips. Tiny enough to be seen as that little helpless girl or stacked enough to stand beside Serena Williams and hold her own. Rita was an uncharted prize, lusted over by every baller around the city.

Her less than impressed attitude made grown men chase her even more.

James could only laugh at the fact she'd seen how transparent his bullshit was.

"Legit, legit, look . . . I'm feeling on top of my boss right now and I wanted to talk to my favorite—you. The circumstances couldn't be more right and you look like you could use a dose of my flattering charm right now. So, stop acting like I just asked for your bank card pin number and get yo'ass in this car so I can take you to the store."

She didn't really want to foot it all the way to the store and, she figured she could use some of James' pointless gratifying praises for a recharge of her self-assurance as a bonus along the way.

"Fuck it," she whispered to herself before stepping from the curb to get into his car.

James reached over and grabbed his money bag. He concealed it on the floor next to his left leg as he unlocked the door so Rita could occupy his passenger seat. Turning down Rick Ross, "You're the Boss," to a whisper as she shut the door and he hit the gas.

They rode in quietness for a little way. James didn't want to seem rushed or anxious to shoot his punchlines. He figured the soothing leather and powerful engine would contribute to moistening Rita's wet spot.

James knew that all these boppers wanted to fuck the man behind the wheel of a $90,000 foreign car, with hopes that they could someday accommodate the steering wheel. He looked over at Rita, her head back but bobbing to the rhythm, eyes closed in a daydream.

Always works like a charm, James thought. He couldn't help but to smirk. He had always wanted her as his own sexual conquest. Yet he'd also known that this "cat and mouse" game would eventually run its course. Rita was playing hard to get, but only for a short while. Over time he had learned that all pussy had a price tag, and coming from where they were from, unlike most, this one was probably worth every red Abraham Lincoln.

"Feels good to just ride and think a little, huh?" James said, opening his game book.

"Yeah. Kind of just what I need to take my mind off things, you know?" she replied still in her reclined relaxed position.

"Nah, ba' girl, this is just to make sure you ride in comfort from spot A to Z. Now see, trips to the Caribbean are what we do to get our mind off things."

Rita exhaled with a reply, "I could only dream!"

"Actually, Sexy-face, you can get that," James quipped.

They were perched at a stop light. Her head leaning in his direction as they looked upon each other.

"From me and every other money machine boy in this city. I'd like it to be a plan for us since it was my idea, and I've fantasized about you and those tropical waterfalls for the longest."

She smiled at how James was coming correct, she felt like this was his first real attempt at pursuing her interest.

He continued, "I've really got respect for you and how you move as a woman because you've been on your grown women tip since like forever and a day. Taking care of your brother and sister, working, and doing your school shit. I'm just impressed, and liking that, and needing that, and wanting that."

James witnessed a small mood change at his last mention of school, but she tried to hide it with her genuine smile at the playfulness of his last words.

"You know, this is the first time you've approached me like I'm a woman you could be into instead of just some woman you're trying to get into. I never thought you cared or took notice of what I'm about or much less, what I go through. At least you don't see me as some ditzy jump-off."

Rita patted James' thigh to show warm affection for his thoughtfulness.

"So, tell me what got you in the trenches. Eternally you seem founded and grounded. Internally, I think you're frustrated like no one's business?"

Rita looked over at him. "And what makes you think that?" She asked curiously.

"Just call it a hunch." James replied vaguely.

"Well on top of my little sister starting to get half out of control, and Rome not knowing what he wants to do now that he's graduated school, I might have to give up on my dreams because school may not be an option next semester."

Parking and turning the car ignition off, James said, "Tell me why that is?"

"My problems are a long story." It was Rita's opportunity to be vague.

"Well luckily for you pretty lady, I've got a long attention span."

Rita grinned back at James, released a loud sigh, then she gave him a rundown on her tuition situation. To her, he seemed to have a keen ear as she rambled, but, he could only think of her silky thighs around his waist.

"Can you believe that shit?"

His lustful mirage was broken.

"They want me to come up with thirty-thousand dollars in four weeks or the last four years is a complete waste," Rita finished.

"You want my advice, pretty lady?" It was a half question.

"Maybe," she said, trying to playfully restore joy to her spirits while still looking out the window at nothing.

"Your sister's just young and going through that sassy stage. Your brother is good, he's not out here selling meth or robbing or painting a target on his back by hanging a rag out his pocket. Give little folks sometime to navigate his next course, he'll make the right decision."

James went silent for a split second before continuing.

"But those are family issues, and for those, all I can offer is sound advice. But as far as your dilemma goes, I can offer a solution." James tossed something into her lap.

Almost in tears, she began to blot her eyes while looking down in her lap as she simultaneously asked, "What's this?"

Once her eyes landed on what her hands held, she was more than astonished, more than shocked, she was speechless.

Not even an hour ago, she had prayed for such a miracle, asked God with every authentic fiber of her God-fearing soul for a blessing that would help further her education. Sitting in her darkened closet, she prayed with so much vigor that she could have sworn the Lord himself placed his hands on her shoulders and promised her deliverance from her issue's. She protested in that quiet closet that she'd do and give anything if she was granted what she wanted and sincerely needed.

And here was her answer, exactly what was required to continue down her driven path to better her life's fortune. She needed this money more than a hog needed slop.

"It's like this my girl, I'ma keep this part of life all facts with you," James spoke as Rita gawked at the epiphany of her heart's requisite.

"I'd spend that money on taking you to the Bahamas, getting you diamonds, even wining and dining you, all in the end to fulfill my own sexual gratification. But to be honest, instead, I'd rather you take that money, and do yourself some good with it. So how about I give you that thirty thousand and we go to the nicest Air BnB we can find. And I'll pay and pleasure you all night, I can guarantee you that!"

James' arrogant look displayed just how ready he was to back up every word.

Now, Imma take this time out to holla at you while Rita's thinking over how she never thought her goodies would go so pricey on the street market. But one thing I can say. At least she's thinking about having some virtues and discretions about herself.

Cause Shit . . . !

80% of you mothafuckas would have sold your mother and or daughter, if not both, at the feel of that money on your lap.

Hell . . . if I know the hearts of men like I do, then 80% of you dudes would have taken 30" of dick yo damn self for that thirty thousand dollars.

But I get it though. You can front while no one's looking. Even though you and your God, and me and mine, all know the real prerogative.

And you ladies? Boy oh boy. Y'all ain't no better.

It's a fact that 85% of y'all would have sucked and fucked thirty condom-less sick dicks in thirty minutes, all on a stopwatch, for thirty bands by now.

Not you, huh? Bitch stop lying.

But it ain't about you right now. We'll get around to testing your texture sooner or later, you can bet that!

Right now, it's about Rita's high strung, better than Pookie's girlfriend on New Jack City acting ass. Trying to have principles, and not get caught up in the exploitations of the ghetto's deteriorating mind sets of sex, drugs, and violence.

This bitch really thinks she's better than us. She thinks she can make it out of my chaotic cycle of destruction. She seems to be under the impression that she can beat the drugged out, childbearing, sexually used statistics of where my father and I run shit.

See, Pops and I had to wait on the perfect time because Rita's not as easy as most ratchets. She's not impressed by cars or clothes. The beast that lives inside her isn't motivated by envy, greed, or hatred. And to add injury to insult, her worldly desires are minimal and her superficial wants somehow don't consume her.

She's a rare animal that's risen beyond the basics but she, too, can be enslaved. Rita's demons can also be activated just like you all. It's all about timing and the right angle of approach. And we've waited patiently for this avenue to unveil itself.

Come to find out, if you threaten Rita's family, dreams, or well-being, that's when she becomes just as disenfranchised and vulnerable as every other naive red-blooded human being.

So, do you think you've worn her down to just the right size, or do you think she's going to pass on this opportunity of a lifetime? Hell, if it was you, would you pass up this chance to have a chance at a better future, to achieve your goals of being a college graduate, if all it took was for you to sacrifice your beliefs for one night.

I'm sure we both know the answer to that!

But anyways, how about we get back to it. And I hope you're paying attention, because I ain't no rapper like Mike Jones, so I don't repeat myself!

This is a no brainer, Rita thought as she contemplated his proposition. *This fool dropped thirty G's in my lap.*

Rita's mind turned over more tumble routines than an Olympic gold gymnast. She thought, *if an admirer is willing to pay thirty thousand dollars to panty pump a little, a bitch supposed to get my money, right? An old friend obliges you with what you need in your time of need, then it's only right that I should show my gratitude by letting him taste this Cali Peach, right? Shit, the dick might be long, and strong. How can I turn down getting paid to get my orgasm on? The boy might eat this pussy like the Cookie Monster eats chocolate chips. Then, too again, he might have the mosquito needle dick syndrome. His rotation might be straight trash- but who cares. I can't turn this down . . . it's my future, my life, my only shot!*

James interrupted her thoughts.

"So can we head for the W for the day and get our room service on or what . . . ?"

As James spoke, he peeped over at Rita. She wet her dry throat, then tightly shut her eyelids to the reality of what she was about to do.

This decision would probably change her life's aim, but oh well. It was what it was.

Rita looked over at James and said, "I'm flattered but you got Rita way past fucked up."

James' jaw hit his lap at the same time the stacks of money he had just given Rita did.

"It's like this, boss, this kitty doesn't get jumped off, not even at that expensive ass rate. A corporation or enterprise can buy my mind, and put me on their employee payroll, but my body is attached to my soul. Unlike these women, those two things simply aren't for any price with me. You want to use my body tonight, but I'm not okay with how that might have me feeling in my heart and mind in the morning. Sorry, my guy, but money doesn't make me thirsty."

She pushed out of the car. "Thanks for the ride, but I can walk home," Rita shot over her shoulder as she shut the door behind her.

James lowered his window and said, "I was just trying to help."

"I know and thanks, but no thanks . . . " Rita said as she disappeared into the store, proud and empowered, yet still broke. But somehow, she still possessed enough self-respect not to give a damn.

Now that's a real woman! Don't get me wrong, I'm the most sought after entity in this shallow universe, but I can't lie, this lady is just my type! When they don't chase me, it makes me want them even more. And she was flawless with her conduct. I salute her for that.

See, my creator is a bonafide hater, but me, I give accolade's where it's due. But try not to repeat that to anyone, especially him.

I really thought we had her handcuffed and ready to be put on the team. But it's good, we lose one in every million! But please don't think I'm done with Rita though, 'cause I got more games than a little bit.

Just wait and see.

CHAPTER
2

JAMES. RASHEEDA. ISAIAH.

Papa," Isaiah yelled at the top of his three-year-old lungs as he began to run toward his grandfather. Kneeling on one knee, while jacking up the slack in his jeans, James set the bags he'd been carrying with him down to the side. He opened his arms and captured his grandson, as if he was Julio Jones catching a Matt Ryan 50-yard touchdown pass.

"How's my little Prophet?" James asked as he hugged his only grandson.

"Good," Isaiah or "Prophet" as James loved to call him, answered in laughter, as James took off chasing his grandson around the front lawn.

James and Isaiah adored one another to the max. They shared a spiritual and mental likeness that was beyond explanation. In most ways, they even physically resembled one another, despite the huge difference in age. Their look and walk were so identical so much, that unless you asked, you would have thought that Isaiah was James' seed straight up.

James put Isaiah down, "Prophet, go get those bags for Papa and bring them inside, 'k?"

Isaiah took off like a pocket rocket.

Walking into his daughter's, Rasheeda, home, James surveyed the unclean mess that was her abode, and shook his head. Stepping over clothes, couch cushions, and an alcohol bottle or four, he grabbed the TV's remote and turned down the amplified Nicki Minaj uncensored video.

Rasheeda emerged from the back, "Hey James, how long have you been here?" She blurted her question while in stride to the kitchen, no "good to see you daddy," or kiss on the cheek like most daughters greeted their fathers.

"About five minutes ago," James answered as Isaiah came crashing through the screen doors. Rasheeda rushed back down the hall holding a plate. She didn't even look to acknowledge her son.

"One more, Papa," Isaiah said then dashed back outside.

It hurt James to the core to see the neglect, lack of structure, and improper guidance Isaiah was receiving from his ghetto fabulous daughter. It also disturbed James that his daughter was truly a product of her environment to the fullest degree. In 25 years, she had three children. But now, she was only in custody of one. Ambitionless, she kept her hand out to anyone who would fill it with something. And that's how James pegged his one and only daughter.

The government, James, and whatever random boyfriend that was in her life at the time were her main hustles.

Over time, she'd shown her revolving door of boyfriends more attention and affection than her own son. And like clockwork, every Friday she had her nails, hair, and a fashionable new dress on for the club. Even if Isaiah had to eat a cup of noodles and drink water, Rasheeda was on her "all about me" swag in life. That was where she was, and most likely would always remain.

😼 *"LOL," guess I don't have to tell you Rasheeda's been a cat in my bag since she was a kid, just like her father. It's true that the apple doesn't fall far from the tree, but Rasheeda was rotten with worms, way before she fell and hit the ground. Yeah, I been fucking her figuratively and literally for the longest and she's hooked "LOL" watch . . .* 😈

Isaiah and James sat at Rasheeda's small dining room table fiddling through bags and trying on new clothes. They were having a private ball as Rasheeda popped up out of nowhere. "Look Mami, I got shoes just like Papa," Isaiah enthusiastically told his mother.

"That's nice, Izze, did you ask Papa what he bought for your Mami?"

On cue Isaiah asked, "Papa, did you buy Mami anything?"

James cast his eyes to Rasheeda but answered Isaiah, "No, Prophet, only good boys and good girls get presents from Papa and your mammi knows that."

Just like Rasheeda tried to use Isaiah to see what she could sucker out of James, he used Isaiah to subliminally scold her for not being a better mother.

"Mami—" Isaiah said.

Rasheeda abruptly cut Isaiah off, "I heard James just fine, Isaiah."

Isaiah sensed the agitation in her tone and went back to focusing on his new toy.

Rasheeda rolled her eyes with attitude and went to clean up her upkept home, trying to restore some tidiness.

"Looks like you threw a party for the whole week up in here," James said while looking at the multiple blunt stumps in the ashtray.

Rasheeda didn't respond immediately. She glanced out the window and saw the brand-new Benz truck parked on the curbside. One look and Rasheeda had just confirmed the talk of the circle she ran in was true, James had hit for some big money. She no doubt felt untitled to her thirty-three and a third percent for being his closest blood relative.

Cut and dry. Plain and simple.

"Daddy, I need some money."

Her question sounded more like a demand to James, and he'd known it was bullshit from the word "daddy." Rasheeda only acknowledged James by his parental status when she wanted something. He decided to see what kind of good reason Rasheeda would have for wanting to spend his money.

"How much do you need and what do you need it for?" James never took his eyes off his beloved grandson.

Rasheeda let it roll off her tongue without any regard, "About $10,000."

James didn't bat an eye.

"My car is tripping and it's old and worn down. I'm a little behind on bills and I want to go on a vacation. I've been stressed and I really need some time, you know? The Jay-Z and Beyoncé concert is in L.A. next month and I need some new clothes," she said.

"Please, Daddy, I really need it. Then we can call it even for my birthday next month."

Rasheeda never looked her father's way as she made her outrageous request, and James was appalled that his daughter had just broken cardinal rule number one—never bite the hand that feeds you.

James was about to make Rasheeda pay for her treason.

"How's your car trippin'? I just bought it, brand new off the lot two years ago. I even took it to the shop not even a month ago and had it serviced."

He stood up, 'cause his arsenal was now locked and loaded. As James spoke Rasheeda just kept right on cleaning.

James' blood was boiling.

"Ain't shit wrong with that car! You just see these bags and tags and that new truck out there. Now you all big eyed and in play for 'what you can get' mode. You ain't got no fucking bills, this is your grandmother's house and it's been in the family since the 80s. And look at how you've handled what my mother left me."

James slapped an empty beer can from the table in Rasheeda's direction.

"If it wasn't for him," he pointed to the floor where Isaiah was busy playing, "I would have kicked your ass out a long time ago. You think every time you see me with something new, you're supposed to get kicked down, like I'm bonded to pay homage to you for being my child. Money hungry, self-absorbed simplest. I didn't raise you like this."

Rasheeda was frozen at her father's outburst.

But James wasn't finished.

"Niggah's running in and out yo 'house and you don't think you're not setting a low standard to Isaiah. Trying to pimp on your family's pockets so you can trick everything off on these low budget muthafucka' s habits. Taking them to see Jay-Z! Bitch, you just sad."

Rasheeda was open-mouth, captivated by her father's frank acrimony. He kept right on plowing.

"You don't ask for $10,000 for a CD investment or a trust fund for your son. Hell, from the sound of it, you didn't have a plan to spend not one dime on that baby." James kept scolding his daughter as he moved for the front door, "You party all night and sleep all day. You not teaching or taking interest in your son what-so-ever and these worthless niggah's get to use your body, fuck over your house and all that for the free. But you want to tax me like I'm the one fucking you! You got me fucked up, baby girl!"

As he turned to leave Rasheeda's home she stood there holding a couch pillow tightly to her chest. To call her stunned, would have been an understatement.

"Papa, Papa, can I come with you?"

Isaiah chased out the house on his grandfather's heels, almost knocking him down. James turned and once again kneeled with a sympathetic understanding in his eyes for Isaiah.

"No, Prophet, not this time but next time. Ok?!"

Isaiah's disappointment made him hang his head down as he began to pout.

"Hey," James said in his most cheerful voice, "Papa will come back tomorrow and bring you some ice cream. How's that sound?" Instantly he stopped sobbing and dove into James' chest, wrapping his arms around his neck.

Again, but now in the doorway, Rasheeda stood there to observe as Isaiah and James hugged so firmly that water couldn't have passed between the two.

James stood as he told Isaiah, "Gimme a pound?" Isaiah smiled as he slammed his tiny fist atop his Papa's.

James looked up and locked eyes with his daughter for a long second before he reversed his pivot and walked away.

"Come inside, Izze,." Rasheeda told her son as they both stood there looking after James. One looking on at his leaving in fondness, the other watching him depart in sheer envy.

She closed the door behind them, poured herself a double shot of Patrón® and immediately went into a rant.

Standing in her kitchen, Rasheeda vented irately aloud, "muthafucka gone come over my house on his boss tip, but he doesn't want to pay boss fees." She downed another shot. "He got new cars and new toys for Izze, but I'm his daughter and I ain't got shit coming. Then, he wants to talk to me like I'm throwed away. At least I didn't lie about what I was going to do with the money, you know?!"

Her glass was refilled yet again. "But he wants to play a bitch, like he can't throw me that, like I don't know he hit for all that bank. Like I'm a slow bitchin' these streets!" She drank what she had just poured and went right back to ranting. "That niggah got long money, always has, but he acts like all I'm worth is a few cars and this bullshit house. I don't ask that niggah to do shit for Izze. Then he comes in here disrespecting me and talking like I don't do right by my son."

She walked to the couch where Isaiah rested and leaned down to pull the cover over his shoulder.

"I ain't letting that shit ride. We're gonna get his ass and we know just how to do it. Ain't that right, Izze, baby!"

Her rhetorical question to her sleeping son was simply her inner seeded envy towards her father, it was something she had to speak aloud, but something she truly did not want anyone to hear.

😈 *So, what do you think? Can you see the bullshit coming, or are you just as lost in my sauce as my girl Rasheeda? LOL. I got to tell you, I really like shorty, she's been one of my many loyal concubines for quite some time now and, when I say she'll do anything to please the autocrat who uses me to get you to hells domain, I really mean every word! When I'm in the scenario, and people like Rasheeda know about me, then it's best you check for those who could be envious, because envy usually secretly grows first in those who share your very own bloodline. Just watch MY bitch, Rasheeda. She's going to show you all about it.* 😈

"Muthafucka wants to hold out on me when he's got Brinks truck money. I'ma hit his weak ass in his heart," Rasheeda mumbled under her breath as she tossed the butt of her Newport on the living room floor before smashing the almost burning filter with the heel of her shoe. "Mark my words, Dad. I'ma get yo'ass."

Rasheeda meant every word.

The next day James decided to return. This time he drove a freshly painted old school Lincoln. It glistened underneath the California sun lustrously as he pulled up curbside across the street from Rasheeda's house. After parking, his driver's door swung open. Dressed more casually than usual, his Jordan 12 covered feet hit the asphalt.

Isaiah played happily in the front yard with every toy his Papa had bought, as Rasheeda sat on the porch side waiting on James to pull up. James walked past the two giant bush pillars and into his mother's front yard, Cold Stones ice cream bags in hand.

Isaiah had his back turned as James snuck up behind him. He turned and hoisted him in the air, spinning merry-go-round circles with Isaiah in his arms until they were both breathless.

"Here, hug this," James said while pulling out a cup of Isaiah's favorite flavored ice cream. Isaiah's eyes sparkled like a flawless diamond that had just touched his hands. As James popped the cup's top, Isaiah flopped to the ground, hands wide open. Once his granddad handed him the frozen treat, Isaiah dug in and looked up at his Papa with approval.

Then James smiled and picked his bag up, before taking a seat beside his daughter. They both stared straight into the front yard where Isaiah ate his ice cream, neither looking to recognize the other's presence. They were both aware of the feeling that the only reason for their being together was the small guy in the grass, scarfing down his ice cream.

After some time, James wanted to make amends for giving his daughter the insulting truth about how she was living, so he reached into his bag and pulled out another two-scoop cup of Cold Stone's ice cream with all the trimming and pointed it toward his daughter.

Rasheeda hesitated, then reached out and took the cup acquiescing with a half-smile on her face. They sat in silence, both taking savoring bites of the tasty dessert before James broke the monotony.

"About yesterday," James began as her eyes were glued to the cup in her lap," I'm not good with apologies." As he paused, Rasheeda stole his train of thought.

"No need for apologies. You meant everything you said and insinuated about who I am and what I've become." Her chin never left her chest as she held her eyes closed.

James was all too aware that his daughter may be intentionally trying to unnerve him. So, he decided to tread this conversation with as much delicacy as possible.

"I don't mean to hurt your feelings, Ree, but I've been trying to school you. I give you instructions on how to get past these fucked up obstacles this shabby ass world throws a black woman's way. It's like, you've been doing the exact opposite of everything I've told you and it seems like you do it on purpose."

James kept on; his ambivalent inner self always ran effusive when it came to his daughter. That was because his love for Rasheeda was absolute and pure, a concept that was abstruse to Rasheeda.

"We used to be tight, Ree, before your mom left, and ever since she left, you've been sending your hate and hurt in my direction. I'm sorry for the pain she put you through when she walked out on us. But I've been here trying to raise you right and set a good example. All these years you've rebelled towards me because of your resentment towards her. And It has been pushing you down a self-destructive path."

James took a minute to clear his throat.

"So yes . . . you're right, I meant what I said about who you're becoming, but I know that's not who you are. That's what's disappointing to me most."

James had spoken his heart's thoughts with hopeful anticipation that something he said might have touched her core, but it had been all to no avail. As Rasheeda pressed talk on her cell phone, she looked over to James thinking devilishly to herself, that it was now her turn to go on her fake emotional spill. It was time to draw this drama to her vantage point, just before it was timed to reach its plot.

"You think it was all Mommy?" Rasheeda said with a gust of fury as she bounced to her feet. "When she left, you changed to, you jumped on your little Wayne, I love bitches and money shit".

Rasheeda's fist balled up tightly as her eyes began to water, her believable act somehow tapped into her true feelings. It was then while hearing herself talk, that Rasheeda had finally uncovered why she had been so numb and on her self-preservation tip all these years.

"I may be seen you once a week after she had walked out on us. It felt like instead of me just losing one of you, I'd lost you both."

Rasheeda's eyes spilled tears as she spoke, "But you came through with all kinds of cash, clothes, and toys for me, just like you do your hoes. I see your money more than I see you. Shit for the longest time I thought Benjamin Franklin was my real daddy. You made money yours and my priority when she left. Now you look up and see Ree hasn't turned out how you would have liked, and you're disappointed. Mama told me that there's nothing's more important to you than money."

Rasheeda poked her finger at her chest. "When she left us high and dry for whatever happiness she was chasing, you told me that money comes in a close second when it comes to priorities in life, you even showed me that by chasing it with ninety percent more of your time then you spent with me. Now you want . . . "

Rasheeda's eyes went away from James toward the front yard where Isaiah was playing with a frightened aghast look plastered pale over her brown skin. "God! No!" Rasheeda muttered as James followed her helpless expression to where her vision rested.

"God! No!

Almost simultaneously the vans tires screeched beside James' Lincoln, stopping directly in front of their house. In mere seconds, Isaiah began yelling, as a man rushed into the yard and snatched him up. Scrambling backward to the van as fast as possible with Isaiah's flailing body in his arms.

Instantly, James sprang free from his seat while raising his Ruger from his waistline and dashing for the street behind the van that held Isaiah hostage.

"Papa, Papa, Papa," James could hear his grandson screaming as he aimed to shoot. The ski masked assailant held Isaiah in front of him, like a shield, as the van's side door slid open. James lowered his weapon as the abductor stood behind his grandson and grinned at knowing he was totally in control.

"We'll be in touch, Papa." The masked man gave a horrible laugh as the door closed and the van sped off.

On the porch, Rasheeda still stood there, hollering God's name, and crying with every hysterical topping she could muster at the top of her lungs.

JAMES. RASHEEDA. DAMIAN.

Rasheeda stood inside of her home fumbling nervously with her cell phone dial pad, more than hesitant to call the police. She felt it more believable to play the role that she'd rehearsed.

"Wait. Don't do that" James told his daughter as he caught her by the wrist to keep her from shaking uncontrollably, also to stop her from hitting those three digits on her phone's dial pad.

Rasheeda looked at her father wet eyed and puzzled.

"These are basic hood nappers. If we involve the police, we'll probably never see Prophet again. These muthafuckers are close to us, somebody who knows you, Isaiah, and me. They also know I love my grandson, and that I keep a little money laying around. He told me they'll be in touch, and they will, because they don't want us to do anything stupid or rash like call the cops."

As logic settled in, Rasheeda snatched her wrist from his grasp and flopped down on the couch with her hands covering her tear-soaked face. Her sobbing made James slump on the couch beside her. He wrapped his arms around her head, and shoulders, then pulled her into him. His attempt at solace immediately turned on him.

"Let me go! Let me fucking go," Rasheeda yelled as she kicked and swung in James's direction until they both were standing. He was silent, but still remained at least three feet out of her danger zone.

"They got my son because of you, James. They took my son because they want your fucking money." Rasheeda wiped her light brown cheeks and centered her tone so it held conviction. "They took my baby behind you, but you say I'm not a good mother, then what the fuck does that make you! Huh, Papa? My whole life your money has caused me more bullshit than anything. And now it's hurting my son. Oh God, they took my baby!"

She began to cry once again as James tried to move toward his daughter. The moment she sensed her father nearing her she again ranted in a hollering fit.

"Get Out!"

Rasheeda shouted as she pointed firmly for the door. James wanted to object. He wanted to console his child, to hug her and comfort her with the promise that he would get Isaiah back safely.

But one of his old lessons came back to haunt him, when Rasheeda was just a child, James had taught his daughter that any man's promise to a woman was just simply comfort for a fool.

As James walked out of his daughter's front door, he declared to himself that he would retrieve his grandson at any price, even if it cost him his last breath.

. . . 2 HOURS LATER . . .

James had been riding around the city for the last two hours making precautions and setting booby traps in the streets. In addition to putting feelers out via his expansive street network, he also put out that he would pay a $50,000 bounty to whomever found his grandson. He figured that kind of bounty would get the most discreet of snitches to tell on their mother. James figured that now all he had to do was to be patient and see what these streets could produce.

In the interim, James had called Rasheeda's phone at least five times and she had not answered. This concerned him because he didn't want her to resort to doing something that would jeopardize everything that he had already put into action.

Only a few blocks away from Rasheeda's house, James stopped at a Chevron to fill up his tank when a call came through.

"Daddy, I'm scared. I want to call the police." She cried on the other end.

Suddenly, out of nowhere, his passenger's door suddenly opened, and a man jumped into the passenger seat holding a 10-millimeter Taurus to his temple.

"Bitch nigga, check that shit in." James was frozen stiff.

He was so surprised he had been caught off guard, that his mind's mechanics had completely failed him. He couldn't believe a jacker was able to catch him like this, much less at a time like this.

Then, something aberrant and contradictory to what usually happens in James current circumstances, happened.

The gunman began to laugh as he tossed the gun on the dashboard. "I was just bullshitting James, I'm really not a robber. I just like to see people's faces when that pistol takes them from power to pussy".

The unidentified man began to laugh again as James upped his Ruger and swung it on the unarmed perpetrator. With total intention to make this fellow's brain apart of his Lincoln's interior design.

"Hold on," the man said, "If you kill me your little man's going to need to be fitted for two things, his last tux, and his one and only casket."

The culprit looked out the corner of his eyes at a bloodthirsty James who still held the muzzle of his gun barrel to the man's cerebral. After some time, James sighed deeply as he un-cocked his Ruger and lowered his weapon.

"Now that we've established that getting your little one back is way more critical than killing the one who took him, I think it's about time we get going," the stranger told James as he pointed in the direction he wanted James to drive in.

Once he retrieved his pistol from the dashboard and tucked it underneath his shirt, the kidnappers phone rang.

He handed it to James.

"Something just came through for you. Just an incentive to make sure we get your full cooperation," the man said. "Here, look."

Looking from Isaiah's abductor to the phone he had just been handed, there was a picture of a masked murderer standing behind little Isaiah. He held his head slightly back with a Ginsu knife under his throat.

James felt a ping of nausea ride from his stomach to his esophagus, but he fought back his vomit, he refused to let this dick head, who was holding all the cards, see him sweat. He tossed the cell phone in the lap of the man who occupied his passenger seat without consent.

"How much?" James asked while never allowing his vision to detour from the car ahead of him.

"See that's what I'm talking about, a man who's about his business in these streets. I'm really feeling your swag, my guy, and since I'm liking you so much, I'm only taking fo' hunnitk for your little booger of a grandson, instead of the half a million my counterpart says you're good for."

After the culprit finished, he reclined in the seat in a smugly arrogant fashion.

"Now what makes you think I got four hundred grand?"

The kidnapping blackmailer raised his fitted hat just above his eyes. "Come on James! Everybody knows you got little face fossil money. You probably got the first hundred you ever made balled up tight and stuffed deep in your sphincter as we speak." The man gave a light chuckle. "Well, all I want is the new hundreds. I figure minus the thirty-five bands or so you spent on this nice we're riding in, and the splurging you probably did between today and the other night, when you won those four or five hundred stacks. Yeah, I would say you should have about four hundred rubber bands left."

James' face went pale as his enemy patted him on his shoulder while sliding his cap back over his face as he rhetorically joked.

"How do I know you got that kind of bread, that's like asking me if Pinto is a car and a bean. You even got a sense of humor, you jokester. Now. Take me to my money!" In the kidnappers last sentence James could hear the threatening 'or else' innuendo loud and clear.

Welp! They've got to take a ride to Carson. So how about we take this time to get us a quick verbal in. I mean, that's a nice little bill for someone that ain't nothing but a bill, you feel?

Got to feed it, clothe it, bathe it, nurture it, and spend hella time coaching and guiding them crying little fuckers!

If you were Papa, would you pay the ticket, or be happy with the fact you don't have to buy not another Huggies® diaper?

LOL. What do you mean that's cold?

Shit, he ain't yours!

Oh yeah, I forgot you one of them old do-gooders, pork chops over steak is your order. I almost forgot! You a goofy just like that old sucker James, too much love to live lavishly!

I told you, I'm just as jealous as every other god! How dare a student of mine love anything over my instruction.

So, I giveth and I taketh from a half-hearted follower to a devoted servant expeditiously! Especially when they've forgotten who's putting butter on their white bread, the very bread they broke ass couldn't buy until I made it possible!

Now weak ass James thinks he can renege on our alliance.

But I'm going to show him!

This is just the intro to me breaking him down to his lowest compound. Hope he's made some nice investments or set up something so he can live off of some residual income. Hope he's got a decent amount of capital in a CD investment. Maybe some bonds or a piece of change very deep into the stock market, with his smart ass! LOL.

But I doubt that he has any of those kinds of assets that can be sold or generated into financial revenue from a property liquidated loan! After all, that's "upper-class-secure-your-future-businessman's" talk, nobody from the slums cares about monetary security for tomorrow, at least not on the prosperous legal agenda tip!

That's why when you're born in poverty, ninety-five percent of you stay in poverty. You don't think about your end game, and that's why you end up leaving your kids a bill and not a will.

Just like good old James.

It's time to make him wish he would have bought that $250,000 house. Instead of renting his $600,000 crib. All so he could keep big money in his pocket and be a slave to a monthly payment, versus staying within his means and owning his own shit.

Even those nice cars ain't paid for!

See, I've given so much of myself to James that it's created a false sense of security for him, he thinks I'll always be abundant in his life, he thinks that I'll always fall by the hundred thousands, at his right hand, and that's why he's never took preparation to make sure I'd be around permanently in his life!

Too bad for his bad, 'cause boy oh boy, does he have a rude awakening coming!

I'm about to strip him of everything!

He'll be broker than Tyler Perry before Madea and he'll be broker than those rich white people who jumped out of the World Trade Center in 1929 when the stock market crashed, before It's over, he'll be Job before God restored his life ten-fold. And you can bet my bottom dollar on that!

"It's all there, four hundred bands," James said as he climbed back into his car and tossed the bag in the lap of the man who was still reclining leisurely in his passenger seat.

Unzipping the bag, the kidnapper began to thumb through the money as he gave a whistle and a nod of approval.

"Let's go get your little man."

They rode in silence as James' passenger directed by pointing his finger. James drove for what seemed like forever, far outside of the city limits he was accustomed to. They eventually wound up forty miles away, in the city of Pacoima.

"What are we doing at the Hansen Dam Park?" There was a look of surprise sprawled across the face of the criminal that had taken James' grandson.

As always on every Sunday afternoon people cycled the enormous landmark park while others jogged, tossed their Frisbees and footballs, while others barbecued and enjoyed showing off their souped-up cars.

Everyone's attention seemed to be locked on their own festivities, totally oblivious of the ill-natured happenings that surrounded them.

"Pull in right here. Park and kill the engine," James did as he had been directed.

After sitting and observing for about ten minutes, the robber looked over to James and said, "Give me the gun and the keys to your car."

James looked him over with a 'kiss my nuts' expression written over his features.

"If you want your little man, give me the keys and the pistol," he stated again, with a 'quit trying to be tough you stupid niggah' look of his own.

As James turned over some more of his personal belongings, the abductor nodded his head in the distance.

"There's your grandson, about two hundred yards out, he's seated real cozy at that bench with my Reli."

Looking out over the park's terrain, James spotted his grandson and immediately bolted from the car in a dead sprint for Isaiah.

The man standing next to Isaiah pointed towards his grandfather and Isaiah also began to sprint as fast as his little legs would carry him, all while both kidnappers walked away from the scene with a gingerly calm stride.

"Papa, Papa, Papa!" Isaiah screamed until they reached one another's embrace with a rapture of joy.

Just hours ago, they had both feared they were lost to each other forever, but the fact that they held each other so tightly now renewed their faith in the other that everything would be fine. As they hugged, James' moist eyes fought back tears.

"Hey, James?"

He looked up to see the man who had just previously pointed his grandson in his direction standing by the Lincoln's passenger door.

"Come out of the park and walk south on Osborne, just over that hill. You'll run into a Seven-Eleven . . . you can't miss it. Your keys will be under the seat."

Then the man jumped in James' car and sped off. Again, James gripped Isaiah to make sure the reality of him being alive and well was not just a figment of his imagination. Isaiah did the same, and they both knew it was over.

"Come on Prophet, let's go home," James said as he placed Isaiah atop his shoulders, all while digging his phone from his pocket.

Dialing Rasheeda's phone, she answered on the first half ring. "James, where are you? It's been over an hour. I'm calling the police right now," Rasheeda said rapidly without taking a breath.

"Everything is fine, Ree, he's with me now," James informed her as soon as she allowed him to get a word in.

"Oh my God . . . thank you! Thank you so much, thank you James, Oh my God. Can I talk to him?"

James handed Isaiah the phone.

As Isaiah and Rasheeda spoke, James heard their laughter and gave a prideful inward smile. Isaiah knocked the phone against the top of his papa's head and laughed at his own playful handiwork. James snatched the phone while he chuckled at his grandson.

"Oh my God, James, thank you . . . bring him home please," Rasheeda pleaded.

"Yeah, Ree-Ree," James said into the receiver. "That's what the plan was, to bring him home. We'll be there as soon as possible. Over and out."

And, that's that!

I told you that the apple was rotten way before it hit the canvas! Damn shame how low a person has to be on values to totally disregard their father as family, so much so to get him robbed. Much less to use his grandson as bait to make it happen.

See, Rasheeda had known that James loved her unconditionally, and she also knew James' love for his grandson had just as much unconditional conviction.

At some point in Rasheeda's life she began to develop a disdain not for her father, but for his personal success.

As a child, Rasheeda was blessed amply with any and everything a little girl could want from her father, and though she longed for more of his affection and time during her adolescence, she learned to expect and cherish the short time her father was able to give.

Though that never stopped her from using the 'you could have spent more time with me' routine on her father. Rasheeda had known that her father's guilt would often make him vulnerable, too, and could be used to manipulate her wants out of his pockets.

In the depths of Rasheeda's heart, she held contempt for her father because she did not make the right decisions in her own life to be as financially prosperous as her father.

Rasheeda never possessed James smarts or good fortune, and for her lack of better, her heart had been enviously callused concerning her father for years.

Chris Brown told you these hoes ain't loyal, and now you've seen it in its rawest form!

A daughter robs her daddy for the almighty dollar, and you know you don't stand a fighting chance.

Better to be connected to me and know it's gain in it for you, than to be tied to all these spurious worldly people who plan to bust your brain for the shiny things.

Can't you see?

Without me, people feel like they don't have shit, like they ain't about shit, and like their lives won't add up to be shit! So, everybody's in my rat race, trying to weave through this rat chase, to get a small piece of my pop's cheese.

But you still ain't convinced, huh?

Well don't worry, cause I'm not done pitching my case!

In fact, I'm almost absolutely sure that by the time you reach the end of my story, there'll be no dispute as to who the omnipotent one is around this bitch!

So, with that said, how about we get back to my dilemmas, ladies and gentlemen.

And let's not forget!

Behind every great man, is undeniably, an even greater woman. 

CHAPTER
4

DAMIAN.

Have I not had your Victoria's Secret backside since forever?" Damian asked Rasheeda as they played footsies under the thick blankets of one of the MGM master suites bed covers. He tenderly scrolled his fingers through her hair's endings by brushing his fingertips across the nape of her neckline.

Rasheeda lay inactive atop Damian's chest, panting from the animalistic, no holds bar, breeding they had just performed. As he gently caressed her neck, she was resting, while trying to allow her a chance to return to it's regular rhythmic beat.

She answered Damian's question without thought, from the enchantment that left her lost in the aftermath of their current sexcapade.

"Yes, Dame, you've had my back since the opening credits."

He grinned inwardly. He knew his nine-inch—he had measured it at least a hundred times that year alone—*"Magic Stick"* had done its work.

Experience had him feeling himself, knowing that any woman, Rasheeda included, became stupefied and totally under his control, mind and body, the moment they began to make love. Just like it always had done since the opening credits of their relationship.

Clutching Rasheeda by the wrist, Damian rolled her onto her back, then

39

pushed his passion deep inside her womanhood. His swift, seize, and attack storm of the front entry, was both smooth and calculated.

"Um hmm," moaned Rasheeda as he took her from pleasure to euphoria.

As he continued imposing his manly power over her, his thoughts travelled to what he could get out of her. Knowing that her father had conditioned her to think that flattering words mixed with a little attention equated to love, Damian was sure it was the right time, and he was the right man, to squeeze blood from the ripe turnip that was Rasheeda.

Now, with her face and pussy balled uptight with pleasure, Damian knew this was the best time to subvert the extorter with a different kind of extortion. Rasheeda's mouth caught the swaying $15,000 diamond platinum chain she'd bought him the moment they touch Las Vegas soil. Her teeth bit down into the necklaces as if it was a horse's brittle specifically made for her.

"If you break it, you're going to upgrade me," Damian whispered into Rasheeda's left earlobe between his labored breaths and steady strokes.

He knew it was time to dominate the way Rasheeda loved to be controlled. Her muscles locked around his manhood as he took hold of her throat with slight force.

Her eyes closed as she grabbed his ass and pulled him into her bottom while convulsions and spasms made jets of climax squirt repeatedly.

Snatching himself free, he instantly lowered his head to her stiff crimson clitoris and began to tongue joust her vaginal nerve button. His technique only caused her to expel more sap from her body, making Damian fully aware of just how much she wanted more.

Now, I just need one quick second to take an intermission so I can school you to Damian's cupidity ass. That's unless, your prudent side is fading, and you'd like to indulge in the act of their lustful fornication a little longer?

DAMIAN.

LOL!

But seriously!

I got to tell you about this guy, Damian, because he's truly one of the lowest snakes slithering around the snake pit! He's the one who entices sinners to gather like a cult and wait on their opportunity to shed blood. Only to plunder the collection plate of his own syndicate of misfits once their backs were turned!

This fool honors nothing but this all mighty dollar. Fucking sellout! And you just don't know how much I love his two-faced ass. LOL!

Years ago, Damian dug his tentacles into Rasheeda's soft spots when she was only a naive 14-year-old little girl. He knew she would produce the day he'd first met her. And the moment he found out who her father was, that was all it took for Damian to make Rasheeda his. From that day, Damian began the small task of planting seeds in Rasheeda that would cause rebellion towards everything in the world other than himself.

Not to mention the fact that Damian was her first everything—friend, lover, confidante.

Hell! Even Rasheeda's very first child was all part of Damian's master plot to use her in the end.

Damian knew he was mostly responsible for Rasheeda not finishing Suma cum Laude at some university. He knew he was the reason she'd first smoked weed or dropped a molly. He even knew he was the reason she would never excel past his distorted view of a good life.

But the thing about Damian was his despise for women didn't just birth itself overnight, his disdain for the opposite sex was something rooted way back into his childhood.

It started way back when Damian's mother used to solicit herself for money. Her name was Lisa. She was a heroin addict who fed her addiction by turning tricks in their cramped apartment. Oftentimes right in front of a then adolescent Damian.

"A pussy is a wound that will never heal. The more you fuck it, the better it feel."

Was what Damain's mother used to tell him when he was just a little boy, just as she was walking some random John through their front door.

That's where Damian's despise for women had stemmed from. His disregard of his own mother's lack of sexual discretion, made her a woman of the night. So as an adolescent, it left Damian with a tarnished mindset, that women were objects to be used for the better of his gains!

The first woman a son falls in love with is his very own mother, so I'm sure you can imagine why Damian has the fixation that bitches ain't shit!

To him, women were nothing to be revered, but only used for a quick physical release, or as a means to meet his goal's end. 😈

"Stop, please! Oooh Damian please stop," Rasheeda begged him to stop lapping her swollen crown with words, but the way she arched her pelvic up to meet his face was a serious contradiction of actions.

With his fingers laced together as if he was Spider-Man casting a web, pinkies inserted deep in her sphincter's base, his index roaming deep in her canal, all while his thumb spread her thick lips so he could assault her tongue to clit. Watching Damian's technique sent Rasheeda past the acme of erotic bliss.

"I'm coming! Oooh . . . please don't!"

"So, are we going back to see the jeweler or what?" Rasheeda looked baffled at his question.

He buried his head deep back into her midsection. Almost immediately another climax came roaring.

"YES." She screamed as both a response to his question and to the orgasms she had just experienced.

Damian realized that there was no better moment for his request, then in her moment of ecstatic rapture.

...*LATER THAT EVENING*...

"I'm feeling the one that's got the bezels shaped like stop signs," he said to her with excitement in his voice, as he held the blue transparent diamond earrings up to his ear lobes as they reflected in an undersized counter mirror.

"What do you think, Bae?" Damian asked Rasheeda, in a don't you agree type tone.

"Yeah . . . they're nice, Bae, but $9,000? Don't you think you could get two pair with some change to sit on?" Rasheeda shot back only trying to make Damian see the obvious.

"Yeah, but I don't want two pairs, these bad blue bitches got Dame scribbled all over them. What, your man ain't worth it?" Damian spat questions at Rasheeda that were laced with reverse psychology.

He'd known her opinion of his value to her had always been infinite, and because of that, her natural reflex in response would be.

"Boy you know you're worth that times ten," she replied.

That's when he turned to face her wearing his biggest smile as he held the diamonds next to his beige skin. Showing all his teeth as he held the flawless diamonds beside his earlobes, Damian removed the diamonds from his ears, his smile jokingly turned into a frown as he poked out his bottom lip as if he was pouting like a saddened child.

"Okay! Okay, get the damn earrings, Dame," Rasheeda said as she rolled her eyes to the ceiling.

Setting the earrings down so the salesperson could register the serial number, Damian stepped behind Rasheeda to hug her stomach and shoulders affectionately.

"Stop boy, get off me," Rasheeda jokingly said.

"I love you, Ree-Ree." Damian continued to tickle his lips against her slender neck.

"Here boy," Rasheeda said as the rubber band bundle of ten grand came from her new Louis Vuitton bag.

"That's what's up, Ree, treat your man like a king just one time," Damian said all while pulling the money free from Rasheeda's outstretched hand.

Tooting her mouth up in defiance, "Dame, how about you just shut up one time. I'm going outside to call Izze. Meet me outside when you're done." Rasheeda kissed Damian lightly on the lips as she spun on her heels in search of the exit.

She walked out of the jewelry store, pulled out her cell phone and dialed James' number. Not once did Rasheeda ever expected her blackmailing scam to work itself out so oddly, and once it had, she did not know how she would be able to spend her money leisurely without arousing her father's suspicions.

Two days after her staged kidnapping, James called and told Rasheeda that he wanted to spend an undisturbed week or so with his grandchild.

That's when Rasheeda's mind instantly began to run rampant about all the fun she would soon have, to go along with all the thing's she'd planned to buy soon. The very second James told Rasheeda the news, her mind seemed to go as blank as an erased chalkboard.

Of course, for Rasheeda, James popping up couldn't have been better timing. She needed some free time to enjoy her spoils of war, and this would be her chance to turn up for sure.

So far it had been two days and James had not called, so Rasheeda wanted to at least play as though she missed the presence of her son.

"Hey Ree, what's up girl?" James' voice answered in an animated tone.

"Hey . . . James, where's my Izze?"

"Hey, Mama," Isaiah finally erupted into the receiver as he laughed. A jealous reminiscence sunk into Rasheeda's mind at how she and her father used to play and have times that were uncontrolled and remembered for months.

"Hey . . . baby boy, you having fun with Papa?" His giggles told her the obvious.

"Yeah, we jumping on the tramba, tramba," Isaiah responded. His vocabulary, not advanced enough to pronounce all his syllables.

"The trampoline," James' voice trailed through the sky until Rasheeda heard a loud splash of water in the background.

Isaiah cut back into Rasheeda thoughts on cue. "Hey Mama, we jumping off the tra- bam-or-lean into the swimming pool."

Rasheeda was happy that her son was having fun, and the fact that he tried to pronounce a 'big kids' word made her very confident that he was safe.

It was a foreign feeling for Rasheeda to experience the amount of pride she'd just felt toward her son. All she could do was smile.

"Well, be careful. Okay?" Rasheeda asked.

"Okay Mama," Isaiah shouted as his voice sailed away.

"Hello . . . ?" James came back on the phone unannounced.

"James, make sure my son doesn't get hurt trying to impress his dang grandad," Rasheeda blurted into his listening ears.

"Ree, this boy's almost four and fearless. Besides, I'm the one who's impressed. The boy swim like he's a little black Michael Phelps. You should see him."

"Yea, maybe I should." That was the irrefutable transcending thought that quietly slipped from her lips but spread throughout Rasheeda's conscience.

"Haahaa, what did you say Ree?"

She was glad James had not caught her reply. "I was just asking when you were bringing him home?"

She could hear Isaiah still parading and chuckling with laughter. Joy illuminated Rasheeda's core to hear her son's distant joy, to know that he was truly happy.

"He'll be home when he's done having fun and not a minute sooner. You just relax and take a load off for a few days. When I bring him home you and I are going to have a much-needed conversation about what we need to do to get our relationship back on track. Okay girly?"

Holding the receiver as she listened, Rasheeda could have sworn she was experiencing the first sting of guilt she had ever felt in all her days of swindling her father.

"Okay, Daddy. I'd like that," she responded from an instinctual place deep within her heart. It was a place she had buried over and over again after being lied to and let down so many times.

"Okay, Ree, I got to go, girly. It's my turn to cannonball. Love you, see you in a few." Then the line went dead.

Rasheeda stood there, in silence. Boggled. Staring at her phone, her screensaver was a picture of James holding Isaiah. Something internal told Rasheeda to turn her attention to Damian and the salesclerk inside the store.

"Is this fool really in there flirting with the help?" Rasheeda spoke aloud into the open air, as she pounded on the glass window. Damian and the white female clerk who had been helping them had become very friendly since she had left to make a phone call.

Rasheeda posed with pursed lips and a hand curled over her hip. Deploying attitude that only an angry black woman knows how, she went back to her growing internal thought, on how foul this whole situation really was.

Ain't this some shit! Is it me, or has Rasheeda jumped brand new as an Oregon University football uniform?

What's all this emotional vulnerability bullshit?

It's just disturbing how easily people think they can acquire me by breaking laws and ethics codes using underhanded mayhem. Only to become scruple after they make a deal with the devil. Somebody should have told you that once we become blood brothers, only death can do us part.

You live by karma, and you die by karma's boomerang, the vengeance that goes around will be the vengeance that will eventually come back around.

And I don't give a damn if you're no longer disillusioned by my superficial gratifications! Once you stand at the altar and vow your love, we're in a nuclear marriage with no prenuptial.

Commit adultery if you want, and I'ma leave your ass broker than a dropped antique porcelain china doll!

Facts!

Now this bitch, Rasheeda, talking like she wants to have a change of values on her guru!

So now I'm watching her ass like the C.I.A did El Chapo, and just like that snitching big, lipped boy in the movie Belly said, "I might have to drop a dime" to Pop's on this brand-new bitch. 'Cause I don't like that shit, no, I don't like that shit at all. 😈

To say that Rasheeda was pissed, would have been the biggest asinine understatement of the millennium.

"I'm hittin' licks out here with yo'ass. Twenty-five thousand dollar chains and earrings, backstage at the Jay-Z concert, and not to mention the crap tables. Then, as soon as I turn my back you up here in some white bitch's face. Like I'm a bopped-out flunky."

Rasheeda was yelling at the top of her lungs, her blood was boiling fire as she dug through her suitcase, counting the total sum of what they had spent in the last three days.

Damian sat on the opposite end of the suite's king-size bed and sunk in his own account, as Rasheeda took inventory, Damian's greed tainted eye's roamed undetected.

"It wasn't even like that, Ree, you acting like you caught me in bed with the bitch," Damian spoke meekly before his voice took on an acrimonious tone, as he rose to flee for the bathroom shower. But not before he left Rasheeda with some truth to digest.

"By the way, let's not act like you jacked your dad for me or some shit, like it was my idea to use Isaiah to blackmail him. Let's not forget without me and C.J., you never would have got paid. So, while you're sitting around here talking like you're tricking on me or something, don't you forget how you even got that bag."

Damian concluded before he slammed the restroom door, the sounds of the low music and the cascading water bounced off the walls and under the door's bottom crack.

Rasheeda's swelling deflated because defeat seeped into her veins at how genuinely abrasive Damian's words had been. Sitting on the edge of her suite's bed with a stack of money resting in her lap. Rasheeda fell into that meditative acumen that everyone does at least once in their lifetime.

An overwhelming melancholy settled over her like a lingering cloud, shameful regrets and guilt that harbored dormant since she was a child, all sprang to the surface.

The skeletons began to exit her closet. And that's when the tears began to fall uncontrollably.

Rasheeda cried for the neglect she had shown her son and for the lack of ability to provide for her family. She cried because she had lost to the system, and because she hadn't practiced temperance over the men she'd allowed in her body and around her son.

She cried for all the insidiously conniving scandals she had pulled on her father, but, mostly, Rasheeda cried because in all the things she was actually crying for, evidence of the fact that she was an underachiever whanged in the splash of every dropped tear.

Wiping her damp face with the back of her hand, it was all those ambivalent feelings that compelled the motive for her to want to change her life.

It was the sudden self-evaluation that seemed to have Rasheeda experiencing an epiphany that would ultimately transition her into an intervention. It was that turning point in life that only came when grown people saw their childish ways needed to be left behind.

Which was exactly what Rasheeda had planned to do. And she planned to start by righting her most recent mistake.

Damian spoke to the continuous speckles of shower head water that hit his body soothingly. His thoughts ran rapid just as Rasheeda's had been doing on the opposite side of the bathroom door at that very moment. Unfortunately for Rasheeda, his vocal undertone only made him audible within the confines of the bathrooms for walls.

"Bitch acting all funny and shit, like she doesn't know Damian's pedigree." Whenever Damian was lost in his alter ego he would speak about himself in third person. "Mad at Dame 'cuz I can bust a bitch in mid-air and make her panties fall off anywhere. Then got the audacity to get at me like she's splurging out on me, like she forgot she wouldn't even have that guap if I didn't make them wheels turn so she could even touch that money. Ask me, I think I'm really, owner of half those proceeds. Or better yet, I might just as well go ahead and get all that out her ass. She ain't going to do nothing with it but buy everything she lays her greedy little eyes on."

He continued, "Bitch ain't loyal to her own dad, so I already know she won't hesitate to steal from me."

Damian's heated and self-indulged thoughts transformed into a scheming plot.

"Fuck it, what better time to cut our ties then at the end of where I see dollar signs?" He smiled in amusement at his own rhythmic cliché.

"Will you hurry up please, I'm ready to go," she yelled as her eyes beheld her impatience.

Formatting his thoughts on how she had embarrassed him, acting brand-new on him, wasn't appreciative of the work he had put in, and was spoon feeding him what was rightfully half his, only amplified his 'take what's yours' conduct to the max. Before Damian could begin to piece the puzzle together, the bathroom door flew wide open.

Damian was playing it cool even though Rasheeda's energy obviously held animosity, he'd known he would have to think fast without anything seeming amiss.

"Where are we going baby? The Biloxi, or downtown Fremont for the show?"

Rasheeda was already retreating out of the bathroom while closing the door, as she answered over her shoulder. "Neither. We're going home."

The door shut just as her last word slid through to Damian's awaiting ears . . .

😈 *Now keep it real?*

If your woman and you just gamed the game for a lot of paper and out of the blue she jumped brand new . . . what would you do?

If your bitch started feeding you your money like a mother does Gerber baby to her newborn, then she puts you on the spot like she got shit in check because some random bitch drooling over your jewels, are you going to let that ride? I mean, this is the reason you put Shawty on the team from the start, because you knew someday, she'd be a Payday!

Who cares that they dealt with each other for years and that Rasheeda is his child's mother, the only reason he'd gotten her pregnant was to lock her in anyway? And besides, Damian hadn't seen Nichelle since the judicial system took her from Rasheeda for having barbiturates in her system the day she gave birth. So, what if that's his baby mama, the only reason you got her pregnant was to lock her in anyway.

And you can bet my guy Damian isn't going out like no wankster, because he already knows I'm semi-deity and he's already a part of my extended coalition.

See Damian and myself agreed a long time ago that if he aspired to be socko in this day and age, then he might have to stab love in its back. And that sacrifice to Damian was but a small drop of sweat compared to the amount of blood he was willing to spill to fulfill his greed.

Everyone knows that a greedy thief doesn't care who they steal from, they only care about their personal accumulation of treasure!

And that's where you gullible women and naïve men go wrong. To you people, the value of money has small merit over love, togetherness, and all that other blah, blah, blah!

But for some reason, these people still don't understand that I'm the biggest indifference between ethnic relationships. They act as if bills, vacations, stability, and the need for a constant cash flow don't matter much. Until the one they love leaves them for someone with a lot more money.

Or? Cash gets tight and what happens?

The woman puts pressure on her man and challenges him about his ability to provide. So, that toxic motivation encourages him to get a gun or do something wrong. Most likely it ends up in him adding himself to the recidivism rate!

Either that or, the man in the relationship has made himself appear to be of higher importance. Which in turn pushes his woman in the same state to be exploited, manipulated, belittled, and solicited for the attainment of that man's aim.

And of course, I'm usually the desire of those shallow people's aim!

Maybe later I'll take the time to elaborate on how I use people and show no empathy for you inner city ethnic couples. But right this minute, I don't have the patience to spend all my time burping you to all my devious traits. So, you're just going to have to learn some of this by ear and eye.

That's unless . . .

You'd like to kneel before the king and kiss the almighty money ring.

DAMIAN. RASHEEDA.

Not one word had been passed between the two of them during the next four hours as they drove back towards Los Angeles, California from Nevada. The tension in the air between them was thick enough to cut with a knife as their rented Lincoln Continental cruised along the California highway.

Damian broke first, about ten minutes outside the city of Barstow. "Can I ask you a question?"

His request caught her by surprise. She answered but never looked his way.

"Sure, shoot?" Rasheeda said blandly.

"We had already paid two more days in advance for the suite. Now it's over three hours later into our unexpected ride home, and you haven't said one word. Mind filling me in on what I did to rub you the wrong way?"

"You didn't do anything. I'm good," Rasheeda tried to respond convincingly in her passive and non-confrontational voice.

"You know what's crazy? I taught you how to lie and you're still lousy at it. What's the problem Ree? If I did something, just say so," he said.

Rasheeda was busted and had known that Damian wasn't buying the two buck throw off she was trying to sell him.

Hearing Damian abbreviate her name had got the better of her. It also helped Rasheeda to decide that it was pointless to continue playing the clueless blonde role. She knew that would only be pushing her luck.

Licking her lips nervously, Rasheeda exhaled before proceeding with caution. Her personal assessment of herself brought tears to her eyes before she even began to speak.

"The things I've been doing haven't amounted to shit. I haven't finished anything I've started in life but a blunt or a bottle. I haven't done shit with my life. I haven't excelled in raising my own kids. I got no career. I've even been out here stealing from my daddy almost my whole life because I'm jealous of his success. Who the fuck does that? I'm tired of me?" Rasheeda asked herself a rhetorical question that made tears soak her face.

Damian was quiet, not knowing what to say about her confession.

"Only the unintelligent bite the hands that feed them, and I've bitten off the arms of everyone who ever fed me. That's why I can't prevail in life. Karma is kicking my ass."

Pushing the tears from the corner of her eye's Rasheeda kept on.

"This doing wrong shit ain't getting me nowhere, and I'm just ready for a peace of mind. I'm ready to start being responsible and get in pursuit of making all my pipe dreams a reality. And I need to start by righting my wrong, by being noble and admitting to my fuck ups."

Still brushing the tears away from her cheeks, Rasheeda's attention went to the fact that the car had stopped, and the engine was off. She plowed forward with the conclusion of her heartaches.

"I hope you're not mad, but I'm taking my dad back his money, and I'm going to tell him everything that happened."

Rasheeda was prepared for Damian to be awkward, for him to refute every piece of logic she had just unveiled to him. However, to her astonishment, Damian did something unfathomable. He reached over to unbuckle her seatbelt, then he lifted her slender body from the passenger seat and cradled her tightly to his chest, while he held her in his arms. She began to sob uncontrollably as he gently rocked her back and forth.

"I know where you're coming from baby. I know what it feels like to want that devil off your back. I spent hella nights in my cell praying for the courage to turn over that same new leaf," he whispered gently in her ear.

Rasheeda was totally baffled by how Damian responded to her sudden change of heart. She giggled at not only his words, but at the feel of his breath as he spoke into her earlobe.

They kissed. It was long and passionate.

"Better?" Damian asked as they separated for oxygen.

She nodded her head, unable to speak.

"Good, now get your ass over there to that purse so I can get us some gas," Damian joked.

Rasheeda poked her lips out playfully as she gingerly slid from his lap and back into her seat. Digging in her Louis V handbag to retrieve a hundred dollar bill.

"You want anything?" Damian asked as he exited the car.

"A Brisk Iced Tea and a Kit Kat bar," Rasheeda shouted as Damian disappeared into the gas station.

After coming back out and putting gas in the car, Damian got back in the car and handed her the things she'd asked for.

"Hey, KitKat bar!" Rasheeda spoke as if she was a child anticipating a promised dessert.

"Damn! My bad baby, I completely forgot." As Damian spoke, disappointment seemed to take precedence over Rasheeda's lost excitement.

"I got the Brisk though." He handed over the bag and Rasheeda dug in to salvage the content.

"Damn! This is a blueberry." She held it up to his face, so he could see the label, all while sporting an 'ughhhh' look across her face.

"And just so you know, I hate blueberry Brisk." Rasheeda gathered her purse and took the door handle.

"Where are you going?" Damian asked as she opened her door to exit the car.

"To use the bathroom and get what I asked you for," Rasheeda said as she closed the door behind herself.

Inside the gas station, after she stepped from the gas station's bathroom, Rasheeda rushed down the candy aisle and grabbed two bags of candy, Sugar Babies for him and a KitKat bar for her. Then she headed down another aisle, Rasheeda snatched up her iced tea from the freezer before she made it to the cashier. She eyed the chubby, half bald brother before she put her purchases down.

"Let me get a pack of Camel Crushes?"

The man went for the cigarettes and rung them up with the rest of Rasheeda's items.

"That'll be nine twenty-four," he said.

When she handed him a fifty-dollar bill, the clerk used his money marker to check its authenticity. Satisfied, he began to pull her change free from his cashier drawer slot.

"Honey, can I ask you a question?" The clerk asked with a heavy hint of concern, verus, the perverted flirtation she was typically used to receiving from middle-aged brothers.

She was intrigued to hear what he had to say. Rasheeda gave him a look which signified that it was cool for him to ask a question.

"Well, I'm only getting in your business because you remind me of my daughter, and I pray that if another Christian man witnessed a man slandering my child behind her back so viciously, I'd hope that someone would drop a birdie in her ear, if given an opportunity," he said in a heavily accented southern drawl. He continued while holding his belt buckle just like a cowboy would. "Honey, I hate to be the one to tell you, but that man out there, he ain't the man for you. Unless he's your pimp and you like being called bitch and hoes, and all those other degrading names they call women of the night. I just wanted to say that I hope that's not the man you plan to marry," he paused, "And if you need a ride, or any help, you just let me know."

Rasheeda stared in with puzzled curiosity, all while thinking to herself, that statement wasn't close to a question, as the clerk dropped her change into her palm, and she turned to the door.

Still replaying the odd conversation that had just occurred between the clerk and herself as she moved towards the door and looked outside. What she saw stopped her completely in her tracks. The space where Rasheeda had left Damian sitting in the car was now vacant, unoccupied, abandoned, empty.

In fact, there were no other cars parked anywhere.

He had left her high and dry, just like the desert she was stranded in. Standing motionless, with her fingertips touching her mouth in foolish shock, Rasheeda could barely feel her own body. She now understood why the kiss they shared just minutes ago seemed so surreal, so special, so powerful, and so irreplaceable.

It was because that kiss was meant to be their last, bitterly marked and sweetly blanketed by betrayal. The kind you never forget, it was the kiss she'd use to change her life!

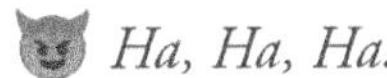 *Ha, Ha, Ha!*
Now, that's truly the epitome of
M. O. E.—Money Over Everybody!
First, you play the abductor in the staged kidnapping of your child's mother, then you play on her soft emotions for you. Which only keeps Rasheeda unsuspecting of your double-crossing intent so you can rob her blind!

Isn't it obvious by now that Rasheeda was love struck? Can't you see, she fell victim to the very thing her father tried to give, and she had taken for granted all her young life.

Rasheeda would have rather had the false comfort of the misleading words of a worldly man and her material vanities, than to practice things like patience, being forthright and staying diligent in her works.

But yet again, that's where the problem lies. You people are always in a rush to keep up with the Joneses, always thinking that these rappers, actors, athletes, and even hustlers are doing something you're not.

When in actuality, most of those rich and famous people with financial longevity aren't living up to the image they are betraying to you common folks. But y'all too caught up in my money green rapture to see the truth, or much less give a damn.

Most of y'all don't understand that there's a trade-off. The more I give them in wealth, the more I take from their souls. Major things like their privacy, life's internal clock, sense of right and wrong, and the value of true friends and loved ones, are often misplaced or forfeited by those who I've cursed to be opulent.

Not to mention, there's a bunch of other God-given luxuries of basic life that cease to exist once I become plentiful in your life.

Most don't know that those people with volume bank accounts are usually monitored on all different stages and levels. They're usually governed by a sect, cult, or some form of secret society that oversees where they go, what they do, who they mingle with, and how they spend their own personal earnings.

Eventually, they begin to crave the small things like simplicity, loyalty, and genuine love. But by then it's usually too late! They're usually broken and empty, and the greatness of my riches has usually stripped them of everyone and everything that's great for them by the time I'm done showing my natural green ass.

DAMIAN. RASHEEDA.

And It's at that point that I know I've done my job and I quickly move on to the next.

Damian's greed-stricken ass is headed for the same dead-end. Literally!

But the coldest part is that once he turned himself over to me, he gave me permission to orchestrate his entire life.

But I can tell you this—the one thing that Damian doesn't know, is that greed has a cousin named betrayal. And everywhere one goes, the other is almost sure to follow. Unlike the envious, the greedy are enthralled only by what they possess, but when I remove myself from their grasp, it's crazy how easily they lose all hope and control. 😈

DAMIAN. KEISHA. YOSHI.

Damian had now been back in Los Angeles for almost twenty-four hours. And in that time, he had checked himself into one of the biggest suites at the most expensive Hollywood hotel he could find. Once he was comfortable in his luxury suite, he decided to add to his relaxation by ordering room service, lighting some weed, and watching porn on the pay channel until he passed out.

Awakening right before dawn, the drinks he'd consumed from last night seemed to turn his whole body sweaty and chilled to the bone. Damian's first instinctive thought, the moment his eyes opened, was to dive from the bed to the floor, where the luggage bag that contained all his worldly riches lay.

Holding his breath deeply in his lungs until he unzipped the bag of cash and saw his reward for his latest dishonorable deed, Damian then exhaled his biggest fear into the invisible air.

Feeling the need to revamp himself, he headed for the shower to get fresh and steady his nerves and trying vigorously to wash away the nightmare from the previous night. In his dream, someone had pushed him back into his suite, then pistol whipped him until he lost consciousness, and made haste with all that he himself had swindled so hard for.

As the cold water from the shower began to awaken his senses from his drug and alcohol induced stupor, Damian remembered that today was the day he had to return his rental car. Which also meant that it was time for a change. He'd figured it was time to buy something fresh off the lot, for the first time ever in his life.

Quickly tossing dirt on his negative thoughts, he emerged from the shower ready to make it rain on himself, then maybe a stripper or two a little later.

XXXXXXXXXXXXXXXXXXXXXXXXXXXXXXXXXXXX

"Hell yeah, this bad boy got Pine-Sol written all over it," Damian said to Mike, who was a private car dealer with a nice inventory of foreign automobiles.

"Pine-Sol . . . I don't understand?"

Mike, a little Asian man who was constantly taking lessons in Ebonics jargon, was a cool dude who had gathered a little street cred from selling affordable luxury cars to people who possessed the cash value, but not the credit credentials.

"Means, when I pull up, all the bitches is going to be calling me Mr. Clean," Damian told Mike. They began to laugh profusely as Damian sat behind the wheel visualizing himself commandeering the sports luxury Audi.

"How much?"

"It's $47,000 with $5,000 down on leased or pre-approved credit, if you don't have good credit."

Damian cut into what Mike was saying by getting directly to the punchline.

"How much if I pay cash?"

Seemingly pleased by what he had just heard, Mike uttered a few short words in his language before saying, "$42,000, that's tax included."

Damian seemed to be in contemplation, which told Mike that this potential cash money sale might be slipping away.

"And I'll throw in a pair of twenty-two inch Mag O.E.M Crossfire tires with black interlining. It'll make the black-on-black that much more Pine-Sol."

Damian smiled up at Mike, held his finger to his lips, as if he himself was the thinking man monument statue, then he said without looking Mike's way, "Bring it down to forty k and throw in the rims, and we got a deal."

An hour later Damian rode off the lot with his name on the owner's papers of a brand new, black on black Audi.

Maneuvering his newly purchased horsepower through 101 Freeway traffic, Damian felt as though he was a superstar. His jewelry sparkled with luster threw the tinted windows he rode behind, and the shine from the gleam of his new ride made heads turn and mouths drool. For the first time in his life, he felt what his alter-ego had always told him he was—an unparalleled boss who deserved to live life freely, without fear of repercussions or need of anyone or anything.

Damian's next move was to find a place he could upgrade his sense of style. Even though Rasheeda had bought him plenty of new outfits, he thought it was time to switch his look from curb to corporate. And he knew just the place where they could fit him just right—Italian Tailored.

Once he hit the city of Burbank, it took him no time to pull into the parking lot. Entering the upscale retail shop, Damian was immediately greeted by an attractive middle-aged Italian woman named Arletha.

"How can I help you sir?"

Damian gave her a piercing look as he allowed his words to carry a heavy sexual orientation. "You, Cheri, can help me, so many ways."

Her rosy, red cheeks blushed as their gazes met.

"But first," Damian tossed her ten-thousand dollar's wrapped in a rubber band, "I need you to make me look like somebody's entrepreneur. The kind that would make your mouth water," Damian closed the distance between the two of them, all while adding sexual emphasis to his last words. "And other parts of you run rapidly wet as well."

Arletha never broke eye contact. She was impressed by him, she tried to show her prowess by matching the intense sexual energy Damian was sending, but her reserved upbringing and her repressed side caused her to shy away.

And for the next six hours while Arletha put all kinds of foreign trendy designer attire on him, Damian took that time to fraternize Arletha with charming jokes and sly but obvious compliments. Somehow, he'd flattered and flirted Arletha into a late-night rendezvous at his hotel suite later that night.

After lining up his late-night tryst with Arletha, Damian was finally pleased with his suit selection, and he left Italian Tailored with his bags in hand headed for his hotel, more than eager to show off what he thought was his new and improved self.

It was getting late and he wanted to make his appearance at this strip club called Kitty Cats in West Covina. Shiting, showering, and shaving before checking the radiance of his jewels and the suave of his demeanor all while in his Italian slacks and Gators, Damian was more than pleased with his self-appraisal and he was more than ready to let the world see him shining bright like a diamond.

Once Damian was en route, he decided to phone his big homie, Spoony.

The phone rang and he briskly answered on the phone's second ring. "Who is this?" Spoon's voice flooded the receiver.

"It's Dame, big homie, what it do?"

"Ain't shit around here, but my money bro. Can I get what's mine?" Spoony spat as soon as Damian identified himself.

Damian had owed him for several different business ventures they recently shared in their past. He'd been avoiding Spoony for the last three months, and now that it was possible, he figured there was no better time than the present to pay his debts.

"Damn! No, how have you been? Good to hear from you. Guess friendship doesn't mean shit when money's involved?"

Damian shot a question he already knew the answer to, but he thought it humorous to string Spoony along.

"Niggah, you know it's dollar signs over friends and family out here in this world. Don't act like you don't know."

Damian laughed. It was funny to him how some people never changed.

"Yeah, I already know. But anyways, meet me at that Kitty Cats spot you told me about. I'm going to put a little interest with your ends for you waiting on me. And Imma buy you two shots, a shot of Remy, and a shot of Coochie, so make sure your old ass pop's a Viagra on your way."

Damian knew mentioning that Spoony would be getting paid would only add pep to the old fool's step.

"Shit! That's gravity . . . I'll be there around 11."

The line went dead.

As Damian pulled into the parking lot and entered the club, he allowed his diamonds to reflect the aqua colors from the club's lighting. Taking a seat at one of the bar's counter stools, Damian ordered a single shot of D'Usse® and a Heineken® to chase his liquor down.

Waiting for his order, Damian spun in his barstool to check out the half-naked women and the live festivities. Either a dumb stroke of luck or fate itself had put Damian in that precise place at that precise time. Because, no sooner had he sat down in his chair and began to sip his drink, he'd locked eyes with what had to be one of the most beautiful women he had ever seen, in flesh and in fantasy.

They stared into each other's eyes, both trying to decipher who was the prey and who was the predator. And just as fast as they were tranced by the intrigue of one another, Damian's spell over the young temptress was temporarily broken when an uninvited hand reached out to steal the stripper's hips, and her attention.

"That'll be $30.50," the bartender said as Damian pulled a $100 bill from his Italian cut trousers. In the time it took him to look down and make sure nothing of green value had fallen from his pocket, the beauty Damian had been eyeing had vanished into the dim club and its overran crowd of bodies. In those lost seconds, the seductress had shed her would-be advancer and disappeared like only a prowler could.

Damian's sixth sense told him to steer clear, his instincts warned him that there were other fish in this sea with a lot less teeth, which were a lot less prone to biting.

But to Damian, the challenge and potential danger is what excited his inner animal, which caused him to reject his manly premonition to stay away.

Getting his change and giving the bartender a $10 tip, Damian asked. "Who's the copper-colored one walking around in the black one piece, with the fire red Mohawk and shaved sides? She has a big ass lion tattoo on her right thigh."

The bartender finished Damian's description for him. "About 5'10, ass and hips like a young J-Lo, and a waist like Halle Berry?"

Damian nodded in agreement. "Exactly. What's her name?"

The bartender smiled at the familiarity of Damian's question. "Around here they call her Odyssey, but her mother named her Keisha. She's definitely a fan favorite at the Kitty Cat Club," the bartender warned.

Damian handed the bartender another twenty for the info. He spun in his seat only to see Spoony with his distinctive limp, moving gingerly through the sea of salivating strip club customers.

Just then Spoony plopped down next to Damian with a drink already in his hand. They greeted one another with a familiar handshake, but never looked each other's way.

"I see you got your neck and earlobes glossing. So, who did you have to kill to get your money up?" Spoony spoke over the club's loud music while laughing at himself.

"Now tell me something," Damian said between swigs of his beer. "Why can't I have a job, or inherit a trust fund, or insurance policy or some shit? Why do I have to be a murderer because I got a little shmoney?" Damian asked quietly behind a hidden smirk.

"Because niggah, you can't spell job, or whatever else you just said," Spoony said, while chuckling.

"Why? Is the street saying I put somebody in a bag behind my bread or some other shit?"

Damian needed to know the word on the streets, and there was no one who kept their ear to the wire like Spoony. At least no one that he trusted anyway.

"The Wendy Williams on the street is that you've been M.I.A for a minute. Shit, that ain't nothing, cuz you've been off the radar for a while. A few people started to think you were doing a county lid or some shit."

Then he laughed.

"Come on you old fart, let's go find you some titties to toy around with," Damian said as he quickly changed the topic of conversation.

They both stood at the same time, Spoony shook his head from side to side to exclaim that he wouldn't be throwing his money away on any one of these random women of the night.

"I'll pass," Spoony said. "I've got the prettiest pair on the planet at home."

Damian looked at Spoony with the patronizing look he could muster. "It's all good, maybe next time." As they said their goodbyes, Damian passed seven-thousand dollars to Spoony in a hand shaking embrace. "There's $5,000 and an extra $2,000 for me being delinquent. I appreciate your patience."

Spoony tossed the money for his bill on the bar. "You better watch out though my boy. They've got killer pussy, and they've got pussy that kills.

And some of these females out here nowadays have them both. Let go of the lust, get you one you can trust. Straight up!" Spoony concluded with emphasis.

"I hear you, old timer," Damian replied but didn't pay any attention to what he'd heard.

"I'm in the wind," Spoony said before he started to move through the whooping and hollering crowd of men.

Just as Damian turned on his heels to investigate the Kitty Cat Clubs entertainment potential, he collided with one of the dancers.

"Damn Papi, your sparkly chain had me stuck like a rabbit caught in headlights." The stripper giggled at her own pickup line, as she scanned from Damian's chain up to his face, then back down past his Gucci belt and loafers.

"How you doing, miss butter pecan Puerto Rican. I'm Damian, and you are?"

She looked Damian over with her fingernail bitten between her teeth, taking in every detail her dilated pupils could record.

"They call me Rabbit."

Damian went in his pocket and pulled out $200.

"Well Rabbit, will this help you fuck like one." She nodded while she creased her lips with a smile.

He handed her another thousand dollars and said, "Get my V.I.P. room, and a bottle of Ace of Spades. And I'll see you in 15 minutes."

Turning his attention back to his real desire, Damian walked about in hunt for what he truly longed to capture—Odyssey. The little trope waiting for him in the V.I.P. room was a distant second, but she couldn't give him what he really craved. His lust was in full flame mode having been successful with everything else he'd wanted that day and he wouldn't be satisfied with himself if he had not added Odyssey to his trophy case as well.

Weaving in and out of the crowded booths and past the impromptu dances the strippers were performing all over the floor, dollars flew all about like debris in a windstorm. As Damian was just about to give up his search, he spotted Odyssey leaving a group of Asian businessmen. Adjusting his stroll, so as not to appear thirsty, Damian showed his interest with the utmost finesse. As he planned it, he bumped into her in a way that made it seem like an accident.

"Excuse me, sexy, but I've been on a quest for you since I noticed you earlier." What Damian said was not only a pickup line but, it was a line that was nonetheless very true.

Standing with her hand resting on her wishbone shaped hips, Odyssey snapped, "Ummm, do I know you?"

She was feisty, and he liked that.

"Because if you knew me, you'd know the only time I have for conversation, is if it's the kind where we talkin' about money. So, if you don't mind, I'd like to get back to the people I do know, who pay me well for my time," she directed at him as she called herself turning to walk away.

Just before she could turn and sashay away, Damian caught her hand.

Snatching her French-tips from his grip, Odyssey turned to face Damian as she spoke with an irritated brow, "Boy, what do you want?"

Damian chuckled at her curt behavior while digging into his pocket. He pulled out $500 and held it up next to his face. He wanted her to take notice of his flawless, arctic, white smile, just as he had done to the stripper previously before her.

"I don't have a problem paying for your time, since you don't have time for small talk." Damian kept smiling, oblivious to the fact that his plot was being counterplotted.

"And what do you expect me to do for those little kibbles and bits? Let you lock up in this pretty pink poodle? Boy that ain't close to enough dog food to send this bitch in heat. Thanks, but I'll pass!"

Odyssey turned and bounced all her thickness through the steady sea of customers.

Damian had now seen that Odyssey had her name down to the very last letter. The word Odyssey itself meant a long, hard, eventful journey, and seemingly to Damian, she had learned to exude that aura perfectly. Doing to Damian the same thing that she had done to a plethora of men, filling him to the hilt with wanton desire.

But hold the fuck up for just one minute! I know it ain't trickin, if you got it, but this fool tricking like he got Bank of America on speed dial!

It's true. I am an egalitarian and all, and I do believe that the hustlers, pimps, hoes, killers and such, should all get their fair share of blood money.

But I got more people's lives too distraught with my devious natural ability, so I'm going to need him to hold up on all this splurging.

Or better yet—

I got something for his ass, out here acting like a niggah who ain't never had shit before. Send his ass right back to his natural form.

A broke ass joke!

"So, what that bitch niggah say?" Yoshi asked Keisha as they sat tucked in a booth in the corner of the club, the whole time Keisha slowly grinding on Yoshi's lap.

"Just what you said he would, saw this ass and was fixated, then tried to play me with his laid back, I'll pay to play maneuvers," Keisha said in between the grinding rhythm she had perfected.

"I think I know how he got it, but even better than that, I think I know just how we're going to get it," Yoshi responded.

Keisha smiled at Yoshi while rubbing the back of his smooth bald head. "And how is that?" She asked, still lost in her own hypnotizing dance.

"Baby, he's just like Samson, his strength is in his weakness," Yoshi said as Keisha leaned back to look at him eye to eye.

She asked, "And what is that?"

"Let's just say, Odyssey will surely make him go blind. Just like Delilah did Samson."

Odyssey was Keisha's alter-ego, one that she used to mesmerize any man she thought had baller money to spend. Together, Yoshi and herself had watched Damian from the moment he'd walked into the club throwing money around like it was nothing. From their point of view, it was their business to get as much of their money out of their pockets as possible.

Keisha slowly continued to grind on him to R. Kelly's 'Slow Wind' while Yoshi placed a call.

"I think I got some knowledge on that business you're combing the streets for, from a week ago. I think the boy just left?"

Yoshi listened while his counterpart spoke to him through his cell phone's receiver.

"That's what's up, I'm glad I missed that money train. Because you need to recover that luggage. Straight up!"

"Cool. Well, have my dinero ready, cause when I tell you what I know, it's going to blow you out your socks," he said before letting the line go dead.

Once Yoshi finished his call, he patted Keisha on her firmly oversized rump before giving Odyssey the go ahead. "Now go lure that lame into our game. You know what to do."

Keisha kissed Yoshi vigorously, then hopped off his lap, with every step and switch of her waist, her transformation from Keisha into Odyssey grew with every switch of her hips. The more men watched her with drooling tongues, the more she turned up the quasi like fantasy that was Odyssey.

If men only knew, she thought to herself, *that the deadliest animal in the rainforest, is the prettiest and most helpless looking frog that everyone wishes they could touch.*

She smiled over her shoulder at the men who gawked at her backside, just before vanishing into the V.I.P. entrance.

Probing her way through the rooms, Odyssey poked her head in the third room that held a sign that read "OCCUPIED". She wasn't surprised in the least by the kinky private show she'd walked in on. She had known Damian had crafted this the minute he'd walked in. Odyssey saw Rabbit approach him the moment he came through the door, and Odyssey knew Rabbit would jump on anyone she thought might have a carrot. So, she decided to position herself in the corner shadows of the room's leather sofa. She figured that was the best seat for her to participate from afar.

Not once did they break the sexually fascinated stare that existed between the two of them. All the while Damian continued to move like a dolphin in water, with the motions he continuously delivered to Rabbit's inner softness.

"Ohhh Yeah!"

Moaning came from the pleasing effects his hardness was sending to her G-spot.

Damian was naked, except for his socks and alligator shoes, and Odyssey could see every muscle of his toned body. She concentrated on how with every thrust into Rabbit, Damian made his member disappear and magically reappear, Rabbit seemed more and more willing to be milked like an oil piston turning on its hinges.

And just like a piston, turning on its hinges, every time Damian plunged downward, the building fusion in Rabbit's womb caused her to squeal, "Ahhhh," in complete pleasure.

Feeling more than a little turned on, Odyssey decided to put on a nice show of her own to feed a little protein to Damian's macho.

Slumping deeper into the crevices of the sofa, legs agape, Odyssey fished hooked the cloth that covered her crotch and pulled it aside. Now, nothing restricted Damian from taking witness to all the techniques Odyssey used to tease her throbbing lotus crown.

Odyssey licked her index and middle fingers while smiling seductively as Damian looked on. She then began to make quarter sized circles around her clit.

Still eyeing Odyssey, Damian took gulps from his Ace of Spades bottle as he stroked inside Rabbit like a thoroughbred horse jockey. He poured some of the intoxicating liquid all over Rabbit's plump rotund booty before he picked up his velocity, then administered a thunderous slap to her backside.

"Ooh . . . shit . . . yeah!" Odyssey's mouth fell open at Rabbit's outcry, the echo of her ass being slapped, and the fire sensations she continued to feel every time her fingers strummed her bud had Odyssey on the verge of imploding.

Damian was simmering, and so was Odyssey. "Fuck me!" Rabbit screamed as Odyssey's hand moved in a rhythmic technique as her head flew back, she was now boiling, and so was he.

"Faster. Please. Harder. Yes, fuck me!"

Rabbit was almost there.

Damian continued to stare over at Odyssey as he clutched and spread both Rabbit's cheeks, causing the bottle to upend, pouring Ace of Spades all over Rabbit's ass.

"I'm cum-cuming," Rabbit exclaimed as Damian started to overflow like a bubbling kettle. Odyssey herself jerked with spasms along with the climax of Damian and Rabbit. The trio seemed to have erupted in sequence as if they were all one volcano full of lava.

Taking a moment to gather herself, Odyssey fixed her hair and lingerie. Then she left before Rabbit could discover that someone had sat in on their private session.

Damian leaned into Rabbit to his hilt, then dashed the last drops of the champagne remains on to her already sticky hair and back, never losing sight of Odyssey as she rose to leave, licking her own stickiness from her fingers. She then blew him a kiss and vacated before she revealed herself.

"I got that pussy," Damian said to Rabbit, but he was referring to Odyssey the whole time.

"You sure did, Daddy," Rabbit replied, not knowing his statement had zero to do with her.

Damian laughed as she voiced her clueless appreciation.

"And thanks for the assistance," Damian said as he buckled his pants and smacked Rabbit on the ass one last time for the road.

CHAPTER
7

KEISHA. YOSHI. DAMIAN.

🐱 *You ever heard of Harlot's web? Sure, you have, because Harlot's web are those repetitive tales that are told about the most voluptuously tantalizing women, those women who dupe men because they relish in the quarry of over minding and undermining the opposite sex. These are the women in those tales who have played their way into the hearts of an unsuspecting man's good grace, only to have him robbed, sent to jail, to the crazy house, or killed. And it's usually all because of her heart's heinousness!*

These women feel no greater fulfillment than when they demolish yet another member of the male society!

Prime example, Keisha, aka, Odyssey.

Ever since she was six years old, Keisha's been repulsed by the male species. Her uncle had been the first man to make all men her arch enemies for life, and though he was the first, he surely wasn't the last to violate her premature adolescent body, but he was the one she could never forget, because he was someone she loved and trusted.

So . . . I'm sure you can see how a woman like Kiesha is perfect for me!

But sadly, and needless to say, not only was Keisha's body ravished as a child, but her mind had also been fondled in so many inappropriate, unrepairable manners that it would have made a priest in confession blush.

By age thirteen, Keisha had grown tired of men forcing themselves on her for the purpose of relieving their two-minute jollies, so much so she thought it better to auction herself off to the bidders who would pay finely for the worth of her young stock. Keisha figured that since her sex was all she was good for; she might as well make some dollars for her talent.

And in my opinion, Keisha was a smart little girl!

At least the profession of prostitution was more beneficial than staying under the same roof with an uncle who molested her as frequently, as he took his next breath of fresh air. It only helped her learn quickly about the valuable impact that I, money, have over these people in this world.

By sixteen, Keisha was a full-blown scrape, who had every voluptuous tactic a rancorous woman could have. Not to mention, her resplendent looks complimented and hide her hardest bite.

And now at twenty, Keisha was the most poisonous of all spiders! She had grown seasoned in the rituals of her knack, and over time, her fangs had become educated with experience, and through practice Kiesha had learned just when to inject her venom into her male prey.

Damian just didn't know that Keisha was about to sink her teeth to the bone.

Sadly, most gentlemen have no clue that they're about to be captured in Harlot's web. And unfortunately for Damian, Odyssey was a harlot in whose web he was now entangled, merely destined to be bitten, a result that simply left her victims in a state of helpless paralysis.

And little did Damian know he was about to be crippled for life. 

He walked into the Kitty Cat Strip Club the following night. Damian was oblivious to the goon that watched his every move. Lurking in the club's shadows, secretly waiting to carry out their plot as Damian moved through the mob of the Saturday night's crowd.

Damian was anxious to play his own plot on Odyssey, one he had undoubtedly pondered on all night long. When he'd left the club the previous night, all he could think of was her nubile body and assertive personality.

Even while he attended to his extremely attractive Italian guest, who met him at the threshold of his hotel suite's door, wearing a sable trench coat with everything lace underneath it, he still could not take his mind off *her*. Damian was so boggled by her temptress spell, that he spoke Odyssey's name aloud at least twice while his promiscuous Italian nympho thrashed about his loins wildly. Good thing for him that their vigorous love making had rendered Arletha with temporary impaired hearing, which allowed the night to continue to flow smoothly, and granted them both access to the peak of their sexual pinnacle, several times.

The following night, Damian was looking to conquer a more steadfast and reluctant type of woman, one that could not be turned on by a man, but only turned on by his money.

Damian decided to be candid with her and himself, so once he spotted Odyssey moving through the crowd of men, he walked straight into her path. As they neared one another and their gazes became fixed upon one another, Damian produced a roll of hundreds snuggled in a rubber band.

Inches apart, he grabbed the front rim of the satin panties Odyssey wore, pulling the lace away from the small of her stomach with his middle finger, he showed her the knot of money, then dropped it in her panties before letting the satin laces free, allowing them to pop against her freshly shaved upper pubic. Odyssey kept her eyes trained on Damian as her hand raised to her hips in her trademark fashion.

"You know once your money goes from your possession to mine, I don't have to give it back," Odyssey said in a defiant type of tone.

Damian pulled back a little, and with a light smile answered, "I don't want it back."

They were still being spied on by almost half the club, but to him, only she mattered. To her only his money was relevant.

"So, if you don't want it back, then what do you want?" Odyssey's mouth asked what her eyes had shown Damian she already knew the answer to. That was when he knew that his deal had gone through escrow, which only made Damian turn his arrogance up to level ten.

"I want the merchandise that I just paid for," he said all while taking hold of her hand and leading her to the front door.

"Hold up," Odyssey sternly said as she snatched her hand loose. "I'm at work. I can't just walk out the front door half-naked."

Damian looked at her and raised an eyebrow, as if to say, so what's the plan.

"Look, give me ten minutes and pick me up out back." Odyssey was about to walk off, but not before saying, "And don't think I'm not on my lady shit. You're taking me to a nice spot, and the dro and drink is included, if not, then you can get *these* Franklins back right now. I ain't cheap and I ain't rat-shit, so tell me the business right now."

Odyssey wanted to know how she would be treated just in case a few thousand, and some dick is all she came out with tonight.

"Do I look low budget?" Damian asked as he stood there in his Taylor slacks, linen shirt, with diamonds cascading spectrums of colorful light around his neck, chest, and ears.

Looking him over with approval and satisfied with his answer, she was about to fall in stride just before he himself wanted to make his expectations clear.

"Leave your purse and cell phone in your locker or with somebody. We're going to my suite. And I don't need you trying to call no troopers, just in case, you know."

Odyssey looked at Damian wearing a 'boy please' type expression, but she thought to herself that maybe he wasn't as easy a mark as they had him pegged to be.

Then Damian added it before she left, "And wear what you got on, that shit got you looking S.T.D!"

Her eyes narrowed into him as if she had just been insulted in an unidentifiable language.

Odyssey snapped. "And what are you trying to say, I look like I'm carrying a disease or some shit?" Her hands back holding her hips, in a trademark, pissed off posture.

"No, I'm saying you look sexy to death."

Their smiles merged, and for the first time in a long time, Odyssey blushed, from what she considered, was a bonafide compliment.

"I've got a trench coat in the car, you'll be warm, don't worry."

At that, Odyssey dashed into the back to prepare to exit Kitty Cats stage left, with everything in order, including an abrupt talk with Yoshi. Odyssey left the building with her focus on cracking the safe.

But even if not, she figured if she couldn't get to his big bucks, she'd settle for getting to her second love in life—a big dick.

Odyssey ran out the back door in her skimpy Victoria's Secret bikini cut satin panties, and matching bra, heels clicking and clacking against the pavement, as she scurried to Damian's passenger door.

She hopped in and Damian hit the gas pedal.

"Damn, I'm feeling the Audi, leather smelling like you just drove her off the lot like yesterday," Odyssey said. She began to recline in her heat-warmed seat, all while trying to gather a little intelligence, without exposing her intent.

Thinking of Odyssey as just another exercise to his exhibitionism, he was never allowing the slightest chance to pass up on boasting about his new status of wealth.

"Nah, it's more like forty-eight hours old."

Odyssey laughed and shook her head as she relaxed against the headrest, thinking of how self-indulged the pilot of the vessel she was riding in was, as she shut her eyelids just briefly.

"What are you drinking?" Damian asked, as he reached over to stroke her upper thigh, which the trench coat had been gracious enough to reveal.

"Ummm . . ." Odyssey gave a womanly purr, as she tilted her head towards him and said, "I'm a Remy or Hennessy girl myself, but I'm not drinking by myself, so as long as it's dark, I'm down."

Damian was in and out of the liquor store in a flash, diving back in the car. He looked over to see Odyssey separating white lines on an old Rick James CD cover, with the Walmart business card he had picked up earlier that day.

He had spotted the bag she had concealed in her palm, the moment she jumped in his ride. He just did not know, until then, it was cocaine she held in her clutches with such ownership.

Odyssey snorted one of the white granny powder trails off the CD.

"So, you like that duff, huh?"

"What?" Odyssey responded after she felt her throat begin to drain.

He repeated. "That white, that girl, that fish scale, powder? You like to snort, get your duff on?" Damian was making sure she understood the point he was asking.

Odyssey sensed his sarcasm, and shot back, "Ain't it obvious, rocket scientist?" before she leaned back down to finish off the remains of her dusty trail.

After she felt her throat drain again, she asked, "Would you like a hit?"

Now Damian felt it was his turn to be curt. "Nah, keep your sack in your pocket, I don't sniff that!"

Five minutes later, the valet was taking Damian's things and the couple was en route to his suite. Once they were alone inside, Odyssey discarded the trench coat and kicked her heels to the corner, just before she flopped backwards on the king-size bed, just like they do in every mattress commercial.

Damian shed his jacket and shoes as he scooped up the TV remote. He found one of his favorite channels—the classic boxing network.

Setting the bag that held their alcohol and weed paraphernalia on the table, Damian walked over to straddle Odysseys lower body while she laid back on the bed, eyes closed.

With all the possible variations of ways this could pan out, Damian leaned over her and kissed the hollow spot of her chest just above her bra line.

Odysseys hands mechanically felt the back of his neckline. The more his tongue went southward making circles at the center of her stomach, and over her hip bone, the more she guided his head to her all-you-can eat buffet.

Whimpers escaped her vocal cords, from the sensations of Damian's tongue. Those sensations were mixed with the heightened cocaine sensitivity that drenches the body's nerves. Odyssey had almost surrendered herself over to Damian's erotic prism.

Suddenly, moving Odyssey's panties to the side and swiping his thumb over the button of the sexiest female privates he had ever seen, the most undeniable surges of pure pleasure clapped Odyssey free from her hypnosis.

"Oh, wait, hold up," she said as she went from her laying position to an upright sit. She lightly nudged Damian back as she rose up.

With no objections, Damian got up, grabbed his bag of goodies, then went to the table so he could open his fifth of 1738, and roll his blunt.

Odyssey asked, "What's your name?"

"Dame, it's short for Damian," he said while cutting his finger into the Swisher Sweet, emptying the blunts tobacco filling. Damian then popped the seal on his drink and took a few healthy gulps straight from the bottle.

Offering the 1738 with his outstretched arm in her direction, Odyssey rose from her seat, and went to retrieve the fiery substance that swished about the reddish brown labeled bottle. While standing in front of Damian showing off her curvaceous frame, she took a long deep swallow of the heated Remy. Odyssey sat there nursing the bottle until Damian finished rolling the blunt.

The blunt was rolled, and lit, as Odyssey allowed their small talk to turn into casual flirtation. She hit the bottle again and turned it back over to him. Somehow their small talk burned halfway through their blunt session. By this point they had finished a little over a third of the Remy.

Odyssey exhaled a cloud of smoke and said, "I need something out of you, then I need to do something, then we can make the walls sweat, and the neighbors know your name in this bitch."

For the impact that Odyssey had just given to his ego, whatever her request was, it was already granted. That was something she knew just the same.

"I need to get zestfully clean, and I need you to get some room service up here A.S.A.P." She paused to let the bud smoke steal her breath, then she continued, "'Cause dick, drink, and dro have a bitch on a hungry one, every time."

They both thought Odyssey's joke was comedy, as they chuckled with amusement. Damian went from his seat to the phone that sat on the nightstand by the head of the bed.

Odyssey sat at the foot of the bed with her back to him as she hit the weed, watching Muhammad Ali rope-a-dope George Foreman.

"Hello, room service . . . " Damian had made a connection on the other end of the receiver as Odyssey leaned back to exchange intoxicants with him.

"What do you want?" He handed her the almost half empty fifth of Remy Martin.

She responded, "Steak and eggs. With ass like this I can't afford to miss a good meal. Hook a bitch up Dame, damn!"

While placing their order, Damian observed the "ghetto Kim Kardashian" that sat before him at the edge of the bed, he watched the way the girl talked trashy, but tried to act classy. Without a doubt, if Damian had to bet his bottom dollar, he knew just which character was the real her.

He had seen way too many hood rats trying to play prissy in his day. They all suffered from an identity crisis, until a real niggah like Dame brought them back to reality. He decided that the real Odyssey had to be brought back to her roots, and that making her do all kinds of explicit and sexually gratifying things, all night long, would be just the right medicine to bring her right off that high horse she was riding.

As Damian gave the clerk their order, he sat there and took mental notes, all while staring at her backside, thinking to himself that this would be one for the record books.

Feeling ever so slightly turned off, but trying not to appear finicky, Odyssey was recovering the small glass capsule that was inserted about an inch deep into her womanly parts. With her back to him and her legs agape, she confiscated the tiny container. Retrieving the little vile that held five Xanax bars, which had already been ground to dust, from her womanly slit, it had been stashed there for *this* exact moment.

After sipping her Remy, Odyssey uncapped the capsule, and poured its substance into the Remy bottle. Slowly and with short circular movements, she mixed the grainy substance into the liquor. The fact that she was hiding Damian's antidote in her womb, was the reason why she had held him from having a drink of her nectar when they first entered the suite.

"Room service will be here in about an hour," she'd heard Damian announce aloud as he hung the phone back on its receiver.

After washing her hands, Odyssey turned off the sink water and left the bathroom, still swaying her ample derriere from left to right as she shimmied her way over to Damian. He was so mesmerized by Odyssey's flawless body and powerful sensual aura that he hadn't thought twice before they exchanged liquor for the weed. Googling straight into one another's eye's with only two feet of air to separate their closeness, they both then took vigorously long swigs and drags of the inebriating euphoriant they held.

She unzipped his slacks before forcing them down around his ankles. Then reaching inside his briefs, she toyed with him until he had grown semi-erect. As Odyssey began to push Damian backward onto the bed, he again took another throaty swallow of the Remy's intoxicating liquid. Nevertheless, Damian was still unsuspecting of any of Odyssey's faulty and foul behaviors.

"You tried to show me how you slang this meat with that little premier you gave on that bitch Rabbit," Odyssey told Damian, as she slowly teased him, he took another swig of his Remy as she finished.

"But a Rabbit will fuck anything. I'll bet my tongue got more grip and game than that bitch has guts." Odyssey was ready to stand behind every word she stated.

Standing before him, Odyssey playfully snatched the bottle and held it to her lips, only seeming to take a drink of the conflagrating drug fluid. Not once did she allow the tasteless grains that now mixed with the liquor to come close to hitting her tonsils.

Then without warning, Odyssey pulled Damian's shaft out, and popped it in her mouth, leaving it locked between her cheeks. She had a tongue like an unwelcome squatter who refused to leave someone's private property. The longer she held him caged in between her tongue and the roof of her jaws, the more her mouth switched into an icy hot flame. Grunts and groans were all that could be heard coming from Damian.

For the next thirty minutes Odyssey was all over Damian's manhood. By the time he grabbed a fist full of Odyssey's red hair he was in uncontrollable heat. In merely seconds, Damian's thrust became frantic and slightly off pace.

Kneeling between his open thighs, she handed him back the alcohol which now held enough Xanax to paralyze an adult bear. As Damian took yet another gulp of Remy down his hatchet, simultaneously Odyssey was also taking a mouthful down her hatchet as well.

Damian's grunts and groans only lead up to his fully grown erection, both gestures showing proper salute to her effective talent. As he arched his head back, to take down more of the fiery liquid, that's when Damian cuffed a handful of Odyssey's red hair with his hand and gave her mouth one nice long pump. They both recognized the first jerk that would have eventually led to him excreting his milk at any second.

The plight of Odyssey's plan was now past her.

She had gotten Damian to drink the drug induced Remy bottle full of Xanax, at the same time she was finishing their active encounter. Wiping herself clean, she rose to her feet so he was face to face with her, his sights completely locked in on the first and only woman that had ever held commanding jurisdiction over his body and brain.

Hitting the blunt again before it blacked out, Odyssey handed Damon the almost roach, he tilted the Remy back for yet another sip before handing it back to Odyssey.

He was hexed by the fruity peach that first beckoned him to give chase, which was now the same peach that was taunting him to have a taste. Reaching out, Damian grasped hold of Odyssey's hips and tried to pull her back down, but she was able to scamper free of his capture. She giggled as if she were a teenage schoolgirl who was overly excited about the anticipation of her first sexual experience.

Odyssey had the bottle in hand, walking away from him, headed for the bathroom. She turned the bottle to the sky, making it look as if she had just drunk more than a smidgen of a shot.

It was all falsified, Odyssey's lips had been perched together, so tightly that not a drip of the drugged Remy got into her system. Little did Damian know that he had drunk the remains of the laced bottle absolutely solo.

She walked in the bathroom and turned up the hot water on the shower knob, and steam immediately bounced off the shower walls, and out of the bathroom door. Coming out of the steamy fog filled bathroom and moving towards Damian with the speed of a snail, Odyssey again faked as if she was allowing the liquor to waterfall down her pipeline.

Stopping and peering over her shoulder just before she fled back into the bathroom, she gave Damian a smile and a hint of an incentive.

"I hope that Remy has you ready to put in overtime, 'cause I'm looking forward to working extra hours for a bonus."

She sent a smile in his direction before vanishing into the bathroom and shutting the door.

The heated shower water instantly began sending steam beneath the bathroom door, and Damian took his leisure time to roll another blunt and peel off every piece of garment that sheltered his nudity. Only his glimmering chain and earrings remained worn as showcase ornaments, but other than that, his flesh was on total display.

Some almost twenty minutes had been misplaced, and before Odyssey exited the shower, steam rose from her body as she hid her secret area behind a warm beach towel.

"You ready for round two, Daddy?" Odyssey asked in a sex infused tone. All she could hear was Damian murmuring something beneath his breath.

Standing bedside beside a sprawled-out Damian who had not moved a muscle since Odyssey had left him drained, all she could do was stare down at his sleeping body and marvel at his stamina and resilience. It had taken six crushed Xanax, a fifth of Remy, almost an hour, and for Damian's nuts to be unloaded before he was out for the ten count.

Kneeling so he could hear, she began to whisper in his ear. "Dame, can you hear me?"

A barely audible, "Umm hmm," fell from his vocal drawl.

Leaning in close enough to Damian so her breath would have tickled his ear, and chilled his spine, if only his senses weren't numb past overload.

"I just wanted to tell you, that you just been bitten."

Odyssey smiled at his sleeping face, then she went down to kiss the tip of his flaccid penis, before walking over to the hotel phone. Picking up the receiver, she called the number of her counterpart who had been eagerly awaiting on standby.

Immediately after the phone's first ring.

"Hello," Yoshi said over the phone's receiver. "You good?"

"Yes Yoshi, everything is A one. The niggah sleep like he's been hit by a tranquilizer strong enough to send a bear into hibernation," she responded after taking a long drag on a Swisher Sweet cigar.

"Hurry up and get here. The Ritz in West Hollywood, room 1200." They finished their conversation and hung up. Now all she had to do now was wait on Yoshi.

Keisha poured out a few lines, as she thought to herself, 'Why not get me a blast while I'm waiting on Yoshi's slow ass.'

Once Yoshi had arrived, it had taken but mere minutes to find the Louis Vuitton luggage bag that contained the riches he'd known Damian was hiding. And once he opened it, it was like a golden colored light had filled the room. Yoshi felt as though he had found his destiny as he stared into the bag of cold hard cash. Once he flipped open the Louis Vuitton luggage bag, "Bingo," was all Yoshi said with excitement in each syllable.

"What, let me see," Keisha had shouted as she bolted from the chair in her panties and bra with the smoking blunt nestled between her lips. It was her turn. "Oh, my fucking god!. Niggah get that shit and let's rollie," Keisha blurted out as she went for her trench coat that rested on the back of the chair in the room.

"Keisha, clean that powder off that table, wipe that phone off and anything else your prints might be on. Then, find that glass capsule I gave you at the club."

It took her about fifteen minutes to do as she had been told, and at the same time, Yoshi removed the money from the luggage case, thumbing through it to make sure it did not contain a tracker. Then he stuffed it all down his jacket sleeve.

Feeling as if he had covered every available base, just before they walked out the door, Yoshi grabbed the Remy bottle and stopped in his tracks directly in front of Damian's lifeless body.

"Keisha, get that niggah's chain."

Keisha looked towards Yoshi and nodded her head, then she hoisted Damian's chain right off his neck.

"What about his earrings?" Keisha asked, ready to relieve Damian of all his sparkle she was already trying to unhook them from his earlobes.

They eyed each other as Yoshi thought.

"Leave the right one. So, he can have him something to remember you by," Yoshi told her as she took the left diamond from his ear and they stepped by Damian's naked body, closing the door behind them.

That's when they broke into that same familiar laugh that they'd always shared right after hitting a lick, or pulling a con, or taxing a mark, or simply what they'd often done, which was make a lot out of nothing, into a little of something.

KEISHA. YOSHI. QUANAH.

After Keisha and Yoshi made it to their low-key apartment, he unloaded the money from his coat sleeves and piled it onto the coffee table, as if it was an unscaled mountain. For a few moments the two sat on the sofa, googly-eyed and mesmerized by the biggest lump sum of cash either of them had ever seen. Neither one of them, in a million years, had expected Damian to be the kind of trick who would be good for over a quarter million-dollar payday. For a good while neither of them said a word because neither one wanted to disturb the dream and what they had done.

Keisha was the first to break rank as she dashed into her room and returned with her goody box. Popping the top and pouring the last of her drug reserve stash on the table, she separated two short thin lines. Retracting a single hundred-dollar bill from the abundance of its rubber band buddies, she rolled her Franklin up tightly. As she prepared to get high, Yoshi was already splitting open his cigarillo to join her.

Before he could there was a phone call he needed to make. As he dialed the number, on the second ring a familiar voice answered.

"Hello, what's up?" James asked Yoshi as he always would with a typical greeting.

"Yeah, the niggah walked into the club and dropped five bands down my girl's drawers. He took her to some spot in North Hollywood," he said. "Nah big homie, you just keep that, this is on the love, besides I never like that fuck boy anyway. Room 1200 big bro. No doubt. Gone."

Yoshi hung up with James with sparkles in his eyes, all he could do was sit there homed in on all the green Franklins. He was hypnotized thinking on how many blessings he would soon make it bring them. Keisha also sat bone stiff, and half transfixed, stuck in fantasyland meditating on all the fantastic new things she planned to order herself on Amazon.

"Getting us one of those three-day cruises, V.I.P. everything. We're getting out of Dodge for a few days, just to be careful," Yoshi said.

Keisha popped up like a jack-in-the-box and walked over to the laptop on the kitchen table. She was still wearing her hot red Victoria's Secret lingerie, minus the bra which she had cast to the ground like a useless artifact, the minute she hit the front door.

Yoshi hit the power button on the T.V. before sneaking out the patio door for some apparent privacy. Keisha knew just what the deal was. So, she herself moved closer to the patio door to overhear the hushed tones of his conversation.

"Yeah Q, it's already there, Bae. I just got to pick it up and run it to the next state," Yoshi paused to hear Quanah's skepticism about what he had just told her.

"Just a few days, Bae. No less than fifteen racks, maybe more." Yoshi was trying to put Quanah at ease.

Just then, Keisha slid out through the patio door, half naked, and with every intention of disrupting his phone call. Immediately she started tugging at his belt buckle, her eye's revealed to him the treacherous bittersweet idea she'd had in mind.

"Quanah, look, we need it. Milk and diapers cost for Elijah," Yoshi finished with agitation in his tone.

Yoshi tried to resist but Keisha held his belt steadfast, looking Yoshi square in his eyes, Keisha warned him.

"Let go. Or I'll tell that bitch where you're really going. And you know I will."

And Yoshi did know that whenever Keisha threatened him in her half husky voice, she was not to be tested.

He had pushed his limits once before between Quanah and Keisha, only to have almost lost his fiancée and the mother of his two children.

Knowing she had Yoshi nearly in submission, Odyssey yanked with all her might and Yoshi's jeans and drawers hit his ankles in a flash.

"We need the money, Q. Milk and pampers cost. Ohhh!" Odyssey made Yoshi sigh as his shaft hit her humming tongue.

"No, Bae . . . I'm good. Something just bit the shit out of me," he said. "Yeah babe, okay, I'll call in the morning when I get off the plane. Kiss him for his daddy, all right, all right. You, too."

Yoshi hung up, daring to reciprocate "I love you" Quanah had just told him in front of Keisha. He was on the brink of going overboard, his groaning almost uncontrollable.

"Ahhhh, Hell, Nawww!"

Was all Keisha needed to hear, to taste the last drop of the only man she had ever wanted.

😼 *Before I specify how I've come to reign supreme over young Yoshi here, I'm going to dial you in on this love triangle that's been driving him with all gas and no brakes since day one.*

See, it started about four years ago when fate, and myself, brought Keisha and Yoshi's paths into a head-on collision!

At the time, Keisha was horny, per her usual, and Yoshi was in the most pressured circumstance he had ever been in throughout all his twenty young years of life. Quanah had just given birth to their now almost three-year old son, Elijah.

And Yoshi, at that time, had no job and absolutely no hustle, and to make matters worse, Quanah, Yoshi and their newborn were freeloading with Yoshi's seventy-eight-year old grandmother in what was already a cramped two-bedroom apartment in West L.A.

So, one day, I kind of dropped the idea on Yoshi that it wasn't a bad idea, or time to knock off a few Hispanic drug dealers who lived not too far from where he stayed.

I mean why not? 😈 It was time to make those drug peddling gangbangers take a loss anyway. And once I showed Yoshi just where their stash had been hidden, I knew young Yoshi had the bravado to get the job done. So, I sent him the blessing and the curse he needed to get my business handled.

On that very day, Yoshi was going to commit his crime, it had been another bright and sunny California day. He decided to make a quick stop at a crowded Walmart to steal some formula for his newborn son. After finding his son's milk, Yoshi headed directly for the exit.

Simultaneously, Keisha was on her way inside the same Walmart, and as Yoshi headed out with the milk he'd just stolen, the second he'd turned the corner with his Enfamil can in hand— 'Whammm'—they hit each other head-on.

"Excuse me, my bad." Yoshi told her while picking up his son's milk. The impact of their collision caused Yoshi to fumble and drop the milk can.

Keisha looked at Yoshi, then to the unbagged merchandise before saying, "Don't trip. If I was you, I'd be in a hurry, too," Keisha, finished with a sly grin.

With her words, their eyes finally connected. Instant fire, curiosity, and natural understanding for one another buzzed around them in the split five second connection they were able to share.

"Excuse me sir, we need to talk to you for a moment." Yoshi, knowing that was the store security, and knowing any contact with the law was an automatic violation of his parole, and a new two-year sentence, bolted!

Initially, the store security gave chase until they realized it was pointless.

Yoshi ran until his throat turned into the Mojave Desert, and his lungs were on the brink of giving out. Almost past exhaustion, he had no choice but to stop even though the sirens seemed to grow louder as they blared in the distance.

"Get in!"

Someone pulled alongside Yoshi as he was resting, bent over trying to catch his breath.

Yoshi looked into the window of the new compact Kia, and to his surprise, it was the girl he'd bumped into back at the store.

"Boy, the police are coming, will you get in?" The passenger door flew open at the word 'police'. Yoshi climbed in, and ever since that day, they've been a match made in heaven, that's gone through hell, everywhere they go, in every sense, ever since.

After the unordinary encounter, they began to associate on an almost daily basis. After a while, they eventually made each other a part of one another's everyday agenda.

Yoshi thought he'd hit the jackpot! He had a Superfly side bitch that knew about his baby mama, who helped him in any way he'd asked. Not to mention, their sex game was what he called Planet X, which meant something way out of this universe! For Yoshi, Keisha was the sweet to everything that was bitter in his life early on.

For Keisha, Yoshi was a symbol of a new start, someone who listened and supported her throughout the dramatics she was encountering in life. He was someone who knew nothing of her past but was there to lend a shoulder whenever she cried with sorrow for unexplained reasons. Yoshi was her knight in shining armor, who never judged her. Keisha loved Yoshi instinctively, and with passion from the second their bodies collided.

But I pushed them to walk the plank!

All I did was use Yoshi's desperation to seek me, and Keisha's need to appease him for making her feel meritorious for once in her life.

I'd known from the start that mixing this duo was like cooking methamphetamine.

Surely, if they merge two highly explosive chemicals out sufficiently, then presto, parasailing in my evergreen euphoria of endless paper! But, if these two potentially high-octane chemicals aren't fused together with just the right amount of care—kaboom!—reduced to fucking rubbles, in the famous words of my guy Nino Brown! LOL.

As long as I exist, between two people like Keisha and Yoshi, there will always be an atomic bomb somewhere on the countdown. I'll always impair their basic decency and better judgments.

Fact is, the power of the paper overshadows everyone's willingness to be upstanding and forthright, sooner or later. The paper essentially halo's everyone in life, into a zombie-like state, where their minds and hearts decay unto everything, but the power of this paper.

But please, make no accidental mistake, for even the power of the pussy is second-rate, and comes in a second late, when I'm present.

For my name is Almighty Paper and to inherit me, is to have the world! 😈

Instantly, after returning from the three-day vacation, which was totally intended to establish some ground rules, Yoshi wanted to devise a plan on how they'd spend, save, and invest, but things somehow went spiraling topsy-turvy.

Their entire vacation was composed mostly of sex. The whole time Yoshi encouraged his views on Keisha about how he wanted to execute more income out of their unforeseen outcome.

Whereas Keisha spent most of her vacation time with her attention focused on "powdering" her nose and bitching about how the money and timing matched up perfectly for Yoshi to flush Quanah down the toilet like doo doo.

So, whenever she started spazzing out on the Quanah propaganda, Yoshi would divert Keisha's attention from that very, out of the question conversation, with some Indian Kamasutra.

Yoshi thought he'd gotten to Keisha's mind and that would result in them getting more money. But low and behold, she'd developed her own debut that she planned to play out on the big screen, with or without the producer's consent.

Upon walking through the front door, Keisha dropped her luggage, headed straight for the safe, and took an unaccounted bundle of money they had stolen just days before. They discussed that Keisha would be refurbishing her apartment and doing some couch shopping upon them getting home.

Yoshi figured that was a fitting idea, since he was going to need a day or so to pacify Quanah, and there would be nothing better to keep Keisha occupied than to grant her some fritter time.

Giving him a fluffy lip peck, she bounced her mammoth booty meat right out of the front door to tend to her playtime affairs.

Yoshi went to tally the remaining balance and see how much he needed to subtract to present to his humble abode so Quanah would not be suspicious of his last spontaneous disappearance.

Together Keisha and Yoshi had blown ten-thousand dollars on their cruise to Mexico. Keisha herself had just pursed another ten-thousand dollars for her splurging events, and Yoshi gave himself ten-thousand dollars to contribute to his family savings. Their expenditures left them approximately two hundred forty-nine thousand.

Yoshi, being a penny pincher, felt his stomach flutter at how quickly, and without regard, they had squandered thirty thousand dollars.

Chalking it up to the expenses of parlaying, Yoshi left Keisha's apartment eager to see his offspring and huge his pot-bellied child's mother, who was soon to be his wife for life.

I've been mulling something over and over in my mind repetitively. And I'm super moody about something that's been nagging me regarding this Keisha and Yoshi scenario. Maybe you can provide some insight? Even though this story is a parable by the most erroneous character that ever was created, it still puzzles me, and I have a questions?

How can people be so unconscious that they have a once-in-a-lifetime chance to seize an opportunity to change, why don't they ever take me and use their psyche to write a true fortune for their future?

Why not refrain from all the quasi, unimportant nonsense, and formulate a self-made success plan? Why not liberate yourself from the hedonistic views that continuously place you in a self-imposed recession every time? Why not learn how to sacrifice and stop spending your life's resources on gratuitous nothings, why not re-channel your ambitions towards generating some real equity? Why not try investing in some real property, or even open a few small proprietorships, which have promising potential to maybe boom in an industry one day.

But y'all do the contrary, your most crucial ambitions flee, once you feel the leather of a car with a foreign name, or once Alexander Wang, is stitched on the tag of your shirt or slacks.

Not that I give a damn about how you abuse the blessing of having me, I just thought you would be more cautious of what the overall penalty of me being obsolete in your checking and savings really means.

But WHY is it my question?

Why is it that most people aren't fools until they possess a huge sum of me to part with? Why not emancipate yourselves from my autocratic influence by using me to work for you, instead of the other way around?

But I'm through planting seeds for your soil and dropping seeds to feed you birds. It's not my place to awake the deaf, dumb, or blind, but to keep you just that!

So, I'm going to make this the last jewel I hail on you, until I hell over you!

I just hope you caught the word play of my last epigram, because boy was that paradox sweet, just like Mama's good old apple pie.

Two long and very aching days had passed since Yoshi had been able to detach himself from his clingy and emotional wreck of a baby's mother, the more he tried to concentrate on other things, the more Keisha invaded his mind. He couldn't help feeling that something was wrong with Keisha and the riches they stumbled upon.

And the moment Yoshi was finally able to stroke Quanah into a state of repose, it gave him the time he'd needed to hit the streets for a few, which he did without delay.

Driving his Crown Victoria with Jeff Gordon-like reflexes, Yoshi swooped in the parking stall beside Keisha's Kia and sped himself up the steps to her front door with lightning speed.

Opening the door, He flew through the living room. He completely ignored Keisha, who was laying across her brand-new sofa, and went straight for Keisha's room where the safe that tucked their treasure safely away, was.

Yoshi opened the safe and began to count. He was furious at what he found there.

His count stopped at two hundred thirty thousand.

She had spent way more than what they agreed was within their spending range.

Yoshi's blood pressure began to boil and he needed to know why in the hell she had deliberately disobeyed him.

He walked back into the living room very casually poised and saw Keisha, who sat Indian style, watching the newly acquired big screen TV. Quaffing back shots of Louis 13, in a pair of her most titillating pantyless cutoff shorts, Keisha sat looking riled to her last nerve.

Trying to pick her mood before he pressed her about her belligerent defiance he asked, "How are you doing today?"

Keisha looked at him and rolled her eyes from what seemed like California to Alabama, wearing her insolence in plain view. She was definitely showing that her attitude was geared for controversy.

Getting up from the sofa, Keisha grabbed her car keys and fun bags then leaned over to the tray beside her and scooped a nice dose of cocaine onto the key's rivets. Inhaling her habit deep into her bloodstream, Keisha got up from the sofa, and tried to walk boldly past Yoshi and down the hallway as if she was in total control.

Yoshi caught Keisha by her bitty waist in passing. With both arms locked around the hollow of her back, as he peered up and into her pupils, Keisha tried her best to avoid his peering eyes.

Eventually, and with a pout, she allowed her body to lean lightly into his, the whole while avoiding Yoshi's eye contact as she let her body seem semi-lifeless in his arms. They both knew for a short time Keisha would play stubborn and pissed off.

Truth was, that's all she had really wanted in these last two lonely days was to be held and caressed, just like she was now.

"See how unattached and uncompromising you become when you're in a shitty vibe about something?"

Keisha's eyes still traveled away from Yoshi's face. She was ready to face the music. She knew that she had some explaining to do. She wasn't in a hurry to turn over the leverage her attitude had gained for her just quite yet.

He could still sense unwilling submission in Keisha's demeanor so, Yoshi decided not to let up.

"We agreed to do things subtly, and make good choices with our money, then you go behind my back and ball out on whatever, while I'm gone. Then I come home to my girl throwing shade all in my direction. How does that work?"

At his last words, both of Keisha's hands hit Yoshi's shoulders lightly as she let her palms settle just where she had thumped him before, saying in her most girlishly pleading voice.

"See, that's all you care about. You beat the fucking door down and bypass me without a high, hug, or kiss, straight to that fucking money! Like you don't trust me or some shit," Keisha's voice gradually echoed away with each word of her last sentence, as she shied her gaze away and Yoshi listened keenly.

"Come on, Bae, you know you're putting extras on it with that trust shit. But I thought we was on one accord with how we were going to disperse our paper. Then I come home and shits missing like white people on milk cartons."

Keisha popped her lips in frustration.

"See, Yoshi, it's all about the money. But now we got that, what about all the shit we agreed that we'd do once we got it? What about us buying a house and moving to the country so we could be together? What about me having a baby and us starting a family, like we planned, and you promised? Yoshi, what about me?"

Keisha again lightly pounded his shoulders as she rolled her eyes.

"You took ten thousand of our money to your pimp, so she'd stay off your ass. You the niggah that's got to pay tithes and taxes to a bitch. Just so you can be with the bitch who's helped pay her bills for the longest now."

Keisha stared sternly down at Yoshi. She could feel herself nearing the brink of attitude.

"So, while you're making faces and acting like I'm talking out of the side of my neck, don't come in here after two days without a phone call, and try to press your line on me about shit I spent."

Dislodging herself from Yoshi's arms, she continued to where she was headed before she had been intercepted and walked down the hallway, into her bedroom closet.

Yoshi followed, feeling offended by the verbally rude and disrespectful remarks that had just been related to him, and his commitment to the mother of his seeds. He still needed to be pragmatic, to avoid a flame from turning into a California brush fire. Yoshi tried to be tactful with his next few words.

"You, right", he said as he stood in her bathroom's doorway while she retrieved her phone from the nightstand and disappeared into her closet. "I ain't got no business questioning you about you spending money that you helped make. Plus, you have been down, since I've been making mad dashes with Enfamil like Percy Harvey returning Super Bowl punts."

She giggled as she rummaged through her closet. Him hearing Keisha's uncensored laughter made Yoshi feel as if diffusing the situation would be a piece of cake.

"Just tell me what I can do to make this shit right, Bae," he begged.

Keisha walked out from the closet sporting only a G-string, heading directly into Yoshi's personal space before saying, "Leave that bitch and marry the one who you've been through hell and high water with. Come be with the one who's robbed with you, stolen for you, sold for you, the one that turned her status up on bitches for you whenever hoes got testy."

This was it. Keisha had completely taken off her gloves and was going for broke as all her emotions were being put on the table. "Wouldn't a real man fuck with the woman who knows the real him? Instead of some high-strung hoochie from the hills who tries to keep her dog on a short leash?"

Keisha turned back to the closet as she spoke. But even though she was speaking from the confinement of the closet, she did not need to see his face to know her sly tongue was making her man's temper bubble.

"Keisha," Yoshi said, "We've talked about this before, you already know what the deal is with you and I—"

She interrupted.

"No, I don't Yoshi, why don't you tell me again? Oh wait, now I remember. It's because you're afraid she's going to take Elijah from you if you move on. Right? It's because she knows shit that can get you life in Pelican Bay. Right? It's because you put everything that you've worked hard to build in her name. Right? Your punk ass is afraid that if you flinch wrong when it comes to that bitch, she going to fuck you. You get pussy over here, but you are pussy over there. Oh yeah. Now I recall, it's all starting to come back to me, like an epiphany or some shit."

Keisha said her last words standing in the closet doorway perched in her famous pose, leering at Yoshi, completely ready for the revile she had been, in a roundabout way, begging for.

Low and behold, just as expected, he let his temper tantrum fly with explicit content.

"Bitch, You got me twisted like one of those braids that got stitched to that tight ass weave you're wearing." Yoshi's mouth started flying on autopilot, which was something he had never done because he knew, through experience, that an untamed tongue often slipped like a hockey puck over ice. Yet still, Yoshi could not control himself.

"God damn right, I've got things besides just time invested in Quanah that I'm not willing to give up. I've got kids I'm not about to abandon. So, if, and when, it's time to trade in that star for a piece of Odyssey's heaven, then I'll let you know when it's time to open up your Pearly Gates!"

Keisha was hypnotized by something Yoshi had just said. It stuck out like a knife handle protruding from her breast plate.

"Kids . . . ?!" Keisha sounded shocked.

He recognized that his own careless talkativeness had just turned a minor tiff into a full-blown civil war.

"Really, Yoshi, kids!?" Keisha's volume rose as aggression swelled in her muscles as if they had been charged to strike. "Kids . . . are you fucking serious?!"

And strike is just what she did.

In a blink of Yoshi's eye, Keisha had jumped into him, flailing her arms wildly and rapidly, having no fixed target, her frail knuckles connected with Yoshi's face, blow after blow, she managed to score some chin music before Yoshi was able to corral her female mittens.

"Keisha. You need to stop," Yoshi yelled as he held her arms.

Keisha yelled to the peak of the Colorado Rocky Mountains, "What the fuck you mean kids, Yoshi? Is she fucking pregnant, Yoshi?"

Keisha fought with every bit of her dwindling strength. The more her fight waned, the more her emotional valve began to turn her anger into a broken heart, even her tears began to turn into a great big waterfall.

"Really, Yoshi, please tell me she's not pregnant." Keisha's tears splashed against her bosom one after another.

Looking at Yoshi, she could tell the facts on the story all by his body language. He hadn't denied it once and it confirmed the answer to her own question.

Standing in her closet's doorway now nurturing feelings of deception and betrayal, Keisha spoke her next words to make sure Yoshi was aware that she was about to infringe on every negotiation they had ever mutually agreed to.

"It's crazy, Yoshi. It's like I knew you'd never leave her," Keisha began, "My intuition always told me at least that much. But that was something in my own way I had learned to deal with."

Keisha gave a slightly embarrassed giggle before continuing, "I knew I could never be your wife over her. That, I've come to accept. Because after all, street niggah's like you love square bitches, and there's no way you would trade in something new off the lot like her, for a used ride like me. And I get that! I understood why I would never be your mainline, so I accepted my role as your sideline, and I thrived in my runner-up spot. From jail, to putting bread on another woman's table, to loving your son!"

Hurt spilled from her every word as Yoshi stood motionless, refusing to meet her gaze.

"All I asked for was the next part of you. For you to make an attachment with me that would bind us after we both were dead and gone. For you to give me a baby because you're the only man I've ever loved!"

Keisha began to push her tears from her face with the restored courage that derived from her adolescent days. A fury that lay latent in Keisha towards every man on the face of the earth seemed to rise to the surface. That rage that Yoshi was once immune to, he was now, the sole beneficiary.

"There were no requirements or attachments that came with you being the father of my seed Yoshi. I promised I would never salt you out to Quanah. I swore to always respect your first home as long as you granted me just one wish. You swore, that if nothing else, I deserved that. You promised it was my turn to have a fat belly and swollen feet, to have late night cravings and morning sickness." Keisha cleared her throat, "But I see no matter what I show you or how hard I try, in the end, all I'll ever really be to you is damaged goods. Just proves all I've been to you is some cheap fun. You treated me like a crash dummy doing your dirty work. You've been using me since your broke ass was returning Enfamil punts at Walmart."

Keisha's eyes went cold and listless, in turn they began to radiate with what Yoshi graded as revenge and treachery.

"Now I'ma show your ground level ass, why your grandmama warned you about bitches like me. I'm going to show you how it feels to be deceived with no consideration, by the one motherfucker you thought, once upon a time, loved you unconditionally. You've played me for far too long, and it's time to show yo' ass how Keisha Brown gets down."

Keisha's last sentence was a serious mocking of Tommy in the movie 'Belly.'

Yoshi didn't know how to respond to the raw truth that had Keisha spazzing the fuck out. So, he thought his best exit would be to remain savvy and bow out gracefully.

"Lady, I'm sorry you feel the way you do. Because most of the things you said are only facts in your own little twisted world. But I'm not about to argue with your perception of things, because that's only going to give this debate more fuel for its fire. I just hope you don't mean to follow through with any of your threats. Because I would like to think if this was the end between us, that we shared too much between one another to inflict deliberate pain on each other! Opposed to what you think right now, you know you mean life to me."

For Keisha, this was the first time ever that Yoshi's words brought no solace. He could not confuse her about what he truly felt for her.

It wouldn't work tonight.

Yoshi noticed her features had not softened, and her posture remained firm. He knew in that minute that their roller coaster ride had just ended. Keisha's often feeble mind would have been distracted and softened by Yoshi's misleading word play. But noticing that her features had not numbed, and her posture had kept to its stout stance, Yoshi knew that it was over for sure.

Keisha pulled back and swatted his hand away when he went for her. Looking deep into Keisha's eyes, Yoshi searched for something that could possibly be reciprocated, all that remained in her for him was the blackness mirroring his image. Yoshi had come to grips with the fact that Keisha was done. All he could see was a horizon of hate in her eyes.

Stepping around her, Yoshi headed for the safe, opened it, and began issuing an equal split of the money they had hustled up. She stood over his shoulder like a taunted tiger ready to pounce.

"And what the fuck do you think you're doing?" Keisha asked. She was more than ready to crank up the dramatics that she had promised.

"Come on Keisha, I'm getting mine and I'm giving you yours. Please have some class and don't come with the fucking complications, straight up!" Irritation and worry echoed in Yoshi's tone.

Unexpectedly, Yoshi was about to find out about Keisha's first complication.

"Sorry Yoshi, but you're not giving me half of shit. I see now that all you care about is that money, and your punk ass didn't have a polished penny when I first met you, and that's just how your leaving! Dirt broke and fucked up!"

Yoshi looked at Keisha before bursting into a hysterical laughter. So much so, that he began to cry. Catching his breath, he spoke without even looking in her direction.

"Bitch, you got more jokes than Dave Chappelle," he said still concentrating on his calculations.

Yoshi's teasing laughter was just the straw that broke the camel's back.

"Well laugh about this motherfucker—" Keisha screamed before leaping onto Yoshi and digging her manicured nails as deep as they would go into the flesh of his face.

Yoshi smacked her fingertips free from his soft facial tissue, just as another of Keisha's claws buried itself in his flesh. He shoved her hard enough to send her airborne backward into the doorway where she had just stood. Stumbling backward, Keisha's head hit the back of the door's frame with enough force to cause a gash that sent blood immediately gushing from the impact. Blood also began to pour from the scratches on Yoshi's crimson, soaked face.

"Bitch! You crazy!" Yoshi said, as he grabbed the room's small waste basket, and began to throw his half of their revenue into the trash can.

Shaking her mind's cobwebs free, Keisha scrambled to her feet, and out the room. Holding her bleeding head, Keisha was slightly groaning from her now waning dizziness. Simultaneously, as Yoshi stuffed the rest of his money into the trash bag, he wiped the blood that was running from his face, away from his eyes. He moved swiftly out of the bedroom right behind Keisha in pursuit towards the front door. Not forgetting the pedigree of the woman he was dealing with, Yoshi entered the living room with caution, but apparently not quite enough alarm. Out of nowhere, Keisha sprang up from behind and attacked his blind side with her trademark pink custom-made pearl handled box cutter in hand. It cut an inch deep into Yoshi's muscular shoulders, ripping downward inches across his shoulder blades.

"Aaaahh . . . shit," Yoshi yelped in pain.

And pivoting on his heels, with his uninjured arm, Yoshi sent his fist flailing backward into the air where it landed flush against Keisha's cheek and lip. She was once again knocked backwards, where her footing was regained by her impact with the kitchen table.

"You muthafucka," Keisha screamed through a blood flooded mouth.

Trying to reach out with his injured shoulder, only extended the opening of Yoshi's wound another three inches.

"You muthafucka," Keisha said, for the second time, as she regained her wits. Again, she went for Yoshi in a full sprint, for the third time, with her box cutter raised high above her head. Keisha had every intention of causing Yoshi more bodily injury. In the nick of time, Yoshi sidestepped the blade of her deadly weapon and tossed his hips into a hook Joe Frazier himself would have been proud of.

The instant his knuckles brushed against her chin Keisha's knees crumbled. She was knocked out cold, like a vampire in the daytime. Towering over her listless body, he didn't know how he should proceed after everything that had transpired.

Yoshi felt torn in half, standing there looking down over Keisha. One half of him wanted to gather her in his arms and tend to her bumps and bruises. That was the part of him that wanted to apologize and tell her that he loved her. Yet, Yoshi's other half wanted to clean up the mess, and make it appear to be a break-in.

Then he wanted to strangle the bitch of her last breath.

Yoshi stood over Keisha's vulnerable body considering his next move. He was in a pickle between killing her and letting her live. Just like Quanah, Keisha had also known about shit that could get him life in prison.

Not to mention, Keisha, if she felt it necessary, would take a life herself without a blink of an eye which made Keisha a serious problem for Yoshi.

But against his better judgement Yoshi figured it was not the right time to dispose of the realest friend he had ever known. So, without looking back, he grabbed the trash bag that contained his money, stepped over Keisha, and closed the front door on her, and on his ambivalent feelings of love and hate.

CHAPTER
9

QUANAH. YOSHI. KEISHA.

Just so you know, Yoshi is a real beast! He's what they call a shooter. An active menace. A goon, or whatever names the inner-city youth are using to tag a title on those who have no remorse when it comes to collecting their currency now-a-days. And Yoshi was one of those uniquely different kinds of go-getters, he's the type who doesn't have restraints or hang-ups on how he wins me over.

Not only will he lie, cheat, and steal, but even more exhilarating to me, he'd even kill to sit on a small mound of me.

As a child, Yoshi was an imp whom I constantly pocket pressured into doing any and all kinds of stupid things. Growing up over a third of his life in foster homes and juvenile facilities only caused Yoshi to be an isolated outcast amongst his peers. And sadly enough, until Yoshi had stolen a few white T-shirts and a pair of jeans from the swap meet at eleven years of age, he had never worn anything but used hand-me-downs, which he would eventually always have to hand down to someone else.

From the beginning Yoshi was a mischievous child with nerves of steel. Because of his lack of family structure and monitored upbringing, it seemed to Yoshi as though he was alone in this big cruel world. He thought he was only here to torment and terrorize wherever and whomever he chose!

Ever since Yoshi was a teen, all he valued was the value of a dollar sign. And by the time Yoshi was fifteen, he had stolen, robbed, and even shot a few dope boys at will for a few coins. Early in his still young life, Yoshi's biggest influences consisted of people like Tupac, the real Rick Ross, and of course, yours truly.

When shit was bad, it was I who helped him meet all his necessities. But, of course, in exchange for the strings that make his body dance, and the functions of his dysfunctional thought capacity.

But hell . . . can you blame him?

When he was hungry, I waited to give him nourishment in that old ladies purse he'd snatched off her arm. When he had holes in his shoes with nowhere to go in the middle of a rainy winter, it was I who assured him that I would be there for him, if he would just wait on the manager of the local Shell gas station to come out with the daily bank deposit.

That's when I would give Yoshi the chance to knock the manager over the head, and then WE would be off to the Holiday Inn, even maybe to Fresh Fits in the morning for that exclusive Antonio Brown Jersey.

Yeah, Yoshi and I definitely have committed to a long-term obligation to remain in each other's lives until death do us part.

I can even remember the day Yoshi buckled his knees to me just as if it was yesterday. Quanah was a few months pregnant, and they were in the cold with no place to turn. So, I told him to strap up and come get me, out little Tigers house on the west side. To my word, I was there. So, Yoshi had his $2,200 deposit to move his family and senile grandmother into that apartment they once resided in.

See! I've assisted Yoshi like a pimp does his hoe! He does all my devilish dirty deeds, and in turn I keep him fed, sheltered, and clothed. Yoshi is what I would call a real 'DO BOI' for the money.

Most pitiful thing about it all is that Yoshi actually has an Einstein I.Q. Believe it or not, this guy is actually about 20 points away from being a modern-day genius.

He is no doubt another untapped potential who will forever be subservient to my cause, just like the rest of you. It's just too bad that him, and 85% of today's youth will end up becoming P.O.M.E.—Products Of Money's Environment! LOL!

Secretly, Yoshi has been praying for a small block of cheddar so he could try breaking into the foreclosed auction buyer's housing market. Something that he has undoubtedly known will change his life.

See, Yoshi was a stringent spender because he had grown up without, so he was in the habit of rubbing two pennies together to make a dollar. Which was a move he was sure would undoubtedly change his life. But at the moment, something was tugging Yoshi toward taking his chance at being an optimistic opportunist.

He believes he's been blessed with an option to go from Mr. Hyde to Dr. Jekyll, even though he knows my "blood In, blood out" motto. Even after he swore on his first stack of hundred-dollar bills to uphold the creed that I was his omnipotent Don, the one whom he would live fast and die young for. Yoshi's been doing a great gymnastic floor performance as a soldier in my military, and that will continue, unless he tries to pull a tumbling AWOL routine. 👿

Quanah did not believe the story Yoshi had fed her about his cat-clawed face and Ginsu'd back. And to add, the money he brought home appeared to Quanah to be in a trash bag, which in Yoshi's mind was more than enough money to buy some Ex-lax to make her food poisoned belly of lies feel just like new.

Still, in spite of her growing suspicion, once Quanah had seen the abrasions dressed about her man's face, neck and upper back she immediately began to dutifully and with care apply aloe vera and other minerals to sooth his scared face and mauled back.

Additionally, relying on the medical technician skills that she'd picked up from her first six weeks of emergency medical training, Quanah had known that only a thick needle and strong thread could merge the almost foot-long and two-inch-wide gash in Yoshi's back upper shoulder blade. His wounds seemed to send Quanah right into a caring wifey mood. And taking the thickest needle and thread she could find; Quanah went to work.

As the alcohol and painkiller induced slumber rendered Yoshi almost comatose, he'd managed to drift into a deep sleep. As she watched him rest, the still uneasy feelings in the pit of her stomach continued to grow until the anxiety was too much to bear. In Quanah's mind, the only way she was going to feel better was if she took advantage of him being asleep.

That option was a simple one, to go through his personal belongings. As she invaded his pockets and looked through his wallet, she did not yet know exactly what it was she was looking for. It only took a short time before Quanah discarded the wallet because it seemed to have held tedious importance to her investigation. Lastly, she thought to inspect the grocery bag full of money.

She moved to inspect the Walmart bag of money that lay at the tip of Yoshi's fingers on the floor. Quanah politely and quietly slid the bag from beneath his right arm as it dangled limply off the side of the bed.

But it wasn't just anyone's garbage bag.

Without a doubt, Quanah had concluded, in a matter of seconds, that this money had come from a spot where a woman was the leading role-player of the household. This particular bag belonged to a woman. Because only a woman who's the "H.B.I.C." of her own home discarded her used tampons in the trash, because any woman who's had a man or lived with one was not that secure. Quanah's mother had taught her that a long time ago.

She also noticed an empty nail polish, a half-eaten apple with lipstick smudges, lengthy strands of red hair, and even a few soft Kleenex make-up wipes with eyeliner stained to them merely added to the confirmation of her intuitions.

Withholding her own feelings of betrayal, Quanah grabbed the keys from the dresser, careful not to awaken a sleeping Yoshi, and quietly made her way out the front door. In her mind, there was no way they were going to keep this money in the house for another night. It was evident the money did not come from some enemy's dope house like Yoshi had so adamantly lied. That sent Quanah's mental safety alarm ringing, she'd known there would be some type of instantaneous problem about the hundred-thousand dollar handsome ransom. And Quanah refused to get caught slippin' like a broken transmission, especially in her own home. So, she decided it best to listen to her instincts and do her job as Yoshi's better half.

The morning sun had just begun to turn the otherwise dark night into a frosty light blue when Quanah had finally made it back home an hour later. Quietly shutting the house door behind her and juggling the three McDonald's bags and drinks, she motioned to Elijah, who was sitting on the floor, glued to his favorite spot in the entire house, which was right in front of the TV watching early morning cartoons.

"Elijah, help Mommy with these bags," Quanah said, as she came through the door to her son.

"Did you get me hash browns, Mami?" Elijah gleefully asked while dashing from his favorite worn spot on the carpet to help his mother like he so loved to do.

"Yes baby, I did," Quanah said as Elijah slid into his seat, more than ready for his meal.

"Yoshi . . . " Quanah called out to her man so he would know breakfast was being served.

No sooner than the stretch of the letter 'I' had evaporated from Yoshi's name, a knock on the door that sounded more like someone pounding, echoed inside the house. Quanah was frozen in a pledge of allegiance type state, her senses knowing all the while that that kind of knock only implied that an issue existed on its opposite side.

"Elijah," Quanah said, motioning with her hands for him to come to her, the whole time she held a hushed finger to her lips so that he would know not to make a peep.

"One minute please," was the only thing Quanah could think of to say to impede their persistence.

"Go and wake up your daddy right now," she whispered directly into Elijah's ear as she kept her eye on the front door. Elijah took off down the hallway as if he was the Flash himself.

"Who . . . is . . . it?" She stuttered as she grabbed the remote to lower the volume on the T.V.

"It's Officer Sanchez, Miss Thompson," the voice responded. They could now see her prying eyes come flush with the doors magnified peephole.

"Oh, okay." Quanah had bought Yoshi as much time as she possibly could, all she could do now was see how these cards played themselves. She had no choice but to open the door.

"Come in gentlemen. My family and I were just about to have breakfast. Anyone for coffee?"

"No thank you," Sanchez said with a wry smile that clearly read how much he was all about business at that moment.

As parole Officer Sanchez and the four uniformed cops entered their home, Yoshi stood at the end of the hallway, nervous, confused, and slightly bleeding from holding his son clutched close in the arm of his very wounded shoulder.

Now see, this Quanah is a similar soul to my girl, Rita, it's not that she's the impecunious type, she's just never been a fiend for monetary riches. You know, the type I hate to love, cut from that breed who has always believed that the finer things in life don't cost a dime. The type that believes that a person's loyalty and prestige should be with their family and divine creator. High strung ass, believing that one's blessings come from hard labor, giving without expecting, and all that other good-willed clean karma mumbo jumbo.

Quanah never allowed me, the real omniscient one, to slither into the core of her. She's never been a wanton of my decree, so she's been granted some type of diplomatic reprieve between her glorious and my glorified father. But don't be mistaken, it's nothing my pops can't handle, because he always finds a way to get around the clause in the fine print.

And just like with Rita, my father said, 'if we control the ones she loves, then it's just like having her all the same!' See, I don't have to get you because often it's a greater ease to puppeteer someone you care deeply for. They say more than not, you catch a fish with a fish.

How many mothers hate the lives that their sons lead but take me to pay their bills or get some groceries, all the while knowing their child obtained me from some illicit crime. Or how many fathers know that their daughters exploit their bodies from the pole to prostitution. Yet even though they're bitterly destroyed by their baby girl's lack of self-worth, they continue to open-handedly receive those extra Franklins she gives him for gas, or maybe a bottle.

Shit!

Sometimes they even watch little JoJo while their daughter, girlfriend, or even wife pulls an all-nighter at the club or on the stroll.

But either way, I'm a direct influence on somebody, or I'm an indirect influence on everybody!

And it makes absolutely no difference to me how my eminence gets you, just as long as you get got.

But I see that you still don't see that I'm the one and only true world order. You still don't understand that I break laws and have them mended, or even on occasion, have them rewritten. I can have a bomb dropped on hundreds of thousands of innocent women and children, then I can turn right around and buy those grieving and mourning family members left behind. You don't believe me, just ask the yellow man! The power I possess is so grand that I can undeniably inflict genocide on a whole race of people, then show my fellowship to their few offspring by bathing them in my doughy green substance. You don't think it's true, ask the red man! Hell, at one point, I could purchase you a whole fleet of people, those same people would ultimately build a third of this nation and all while in bondage. Almost five hundred years later to this day, there are still enterprises, corporations, and industries that are still standing and making millions of dollars because of their blood, sweat, and tears! Just ask the black man if it's true. When it comes to me, the things that are unjust become just.

But, regardless of whomever hates it or loves it, Mr. Dollar Bill is on top.

So, not the Quanahs or the Ritas, even the Pope or anyone alike can escape my wrath. In fact, I dominate over the upright who shun me in the worst way.

Oh! You don't think I'm serious, just ask Quanah in a few pages. I'm sure we'll be able to get her to tell you how persuasive and infectious I can be before we're done. Directly, or indirectly! 👿

"It's good for you that we didn't find anything," Sanchez said to Yoshi. "You've got a nice family, and you're engaged, I see, and almost off parole. Keep doing the right thing."

Sanchez closed his door and was rolling down the window as soon as his Ford's engine came to life.

Yoshi stood there, not saying a word. A fake look of interest plastered on his face, but all the while Sanchez spoke, Yoshi's mind was not registering a word.

"Sorry about the inconvenience. We were tipped. This was simple protocol, nothing personal," Sanchez was almost all the way out of Yoshi's driveway when he yelled back, "and maybe you should stop cheating on your fiancée.

"It's nothing. She's not pregnant or nothing like that. And it's over between us anyway," Yoshi said nonchalantly, not realizing that Quanah was standing close enough to hear him.

Listening from their home's patio window, she was able to hear Yoshi's confession, his words immediately sent her body as limp as a noodle. Something that felt like devastation ripped through Quanah as if she had just been hit by an electric current surged from a police stun gun. She began packing as soon as the initial impact from Yoshi's secret had allowed her to catch her breath. Trying her best to hold her bearings was easier said than done, because the moment he topped the steps and entered the front door, Quanah became unraveled all over again.

"You ain't shit, Yoshi. I hate your ass," Quanah shouted in the direction of the living room right before the tears began to stream down her face.

With her back toward Yoshi and all eight months of her condition, Quanah managed to scoop up her suitcase and head down the hall. He was stunned and totally caught off guard.

"That bitch scratched your face, cut you the fuck up, and then called the police on you? On us? You damn right you're done with that bitch! I'd be done with the bitch too if I were you. You must think I'm some kinda' fool if you think I'm staying here with you. Come on Elijah, let's go. I can't believe this shit," she yelled as she tried to make haste into the living room.

Quanah's last words let him know that she had heard everything he and Officer Sanchez had just discussed. All Yoshi could do was be upset with himself, because for the second time in a matter of 24 hours, Yoshi's own loose lips were about to sink his ship.

Catching up to Quanah as quickly as he could, Yoshi stopped her in her tracks and wrapped both his arms around her chest from behind. Her body went rigid, as she stood there holding her bags with tears falling onto Yoshi's arms. Her eyes didn't blink as she stared straight at the door.

"I've been using Keisha since the day we first met. My face and back are like this because she wanted from me what's in your belly right now." One of Yoshi's hands slid over Quanah's plump tummy. "I don't love her, and baby trust me, she knows that."

Quanah was stiff as a board, and even though she truly believed everything that Yoshi said, she knew she had to remain disciplined and leave. At least, until she was certain that Yoshi had learned his lesson.

"She's been 70% of my hustle. She sold my drugs, set fool's up, been to jail, and even turned tricks for me. Every crumb I've ever made from her ass went to these bills and on our table. That money comes from some fake player from around the way that I knew, and she helped me get this clown. So no, I didn't take her money, I took our money."

Yoshi pointed to Elijah to bring emphasis to exactly whose money he meant.

"You're my fiancée, and someday I hope you become my wife," Yoshi kissed the nape of her neck as he held her close in his arms from behind. "And before you walk out that door, I just want you to know that my heart knows but one."

And that was it. He had laid it all on the line.

Standing there flummoxed, all Quanah could do was ask herself how she could feel touched, and betrayed by this man all at the same time? How could the man she loved be so sensitive but so remotely scandalous all at once? How could the same voice whose secrets chilled her to the bone, be the same voice that minutes later was serenading to her soul? Quanah knew she had to leave before her mixed feelings caused her to renege on what she had done.

"Let me go, Yoshi," Quanah said through a trembling bottom lip.

Letting her free from the bear hug he had clamped her in, Quanah moved for the front door.

"Come on Eli, come with Mommy, baby boy."

Elijah sported his favorite Spider-man pajamas as he rose from the floor following close behind his mother. Just as Elijah was about to shut the door behind himself and his mother, he was stopped.

"Hey kiddo," Yoshi called to his son.

"Yes . . . Daddy"?

Yoshi flexed both his biceps over his head, and Elijah instantly gave back their distinctive salutation. "Bye, Daddy," Elijah said, before pulling the front door closed with a nice slam.

Something profoundly unexplainable occurred inside Yoshi as he and his first born looked into each other's faces just seconds ago. And even as he watched Elijah scamper into the backseat of his mother's car and strap himself into his car seat, Yoshi was filled with a renewed joy, as if this was the very first time, he had ever seen his son.

Peering through the blinds in his bedroom window, Yoshi watched as Quanah backed her car out and sped into the unseen distance.

Looking at his phone's screen a conflagration engulfed Yoshi. It was not his fiancée calling his phone as he had hoped but Keisha's code name Kendrick flashed unwanted across his screen.

The fire that burned inside Yoshi upon seeing Keisha's call made him feel as if the enemy on the opposite end of his phone's line was one that needed to be extinguished. He'd warned himself before answering his phone to remain submissive and allow Keisha enough rope to seal her own fate. *It was better to keep the opponent off balance and unaware of your surprise attack,* he thought. Remembering that he had learned this tactic from a book called *The Art of War* which was a book often kept in every convict's personal library as a rule of thumb when he was behind the walls.

"Yes Keisha?"

Yoshi's murmur came across the receiver as if he was almost a defeated puppy. As if he'd wanted to wave his surrender flag to call a truce, and to see just how remotely far Keisha planned to take her vengeance.

"Damn Keisha, first you slice me up like a tomato, send the police to my spot trying to get me sent back to prison, now you calling to harass a niggah." Yoshi sighed out what he intended to be perceived as exhaustion and worry as he finished speaking.

"Come on my girl. We've gone through too much for us to end beefing like this. You win, Keisha, let it go already."

The fact that Yoshi was groping for a treaty made Keisha push harder in thinking she'd had the upper hand.

"Nah baby boy, don't try to bow out gracefully now. We're just getting started," Keisha said.

She giggled before sucking air through her teeth, "So Sanchez weak-ass didn't find a thing, huh? I kind of figured that he wouldn't. Because you never kept anything at home. In fact, anything that could have ever gotten you sent back to the penitentiary you always kept at my house. But I bet they scared your ass half to death, huh?"

Keisha didn't expect Yoshi to have a rebuttal. And he didn't. So, she kept right to her purpose at hand.

"The police in your house. Four deep, tearing your shit up, just hoping to stumble onto something to send you back. I wonder what you did with the money though? Quanah probably hid that shit before they could find it."

All Yoshi could do was stand there listening, sensing all the while that there was a punchline to Keisha's bullshit rambling.

"Yeah, that's probably just what happened. Leave it up to one of us women to save your ass every time. Huh, Yoshi?" Keisha's voice crackled slightly as she spoke.

Yoshi could tell Keisha was beginning to sob on the opposite end. In his mind, this was his best time to intervene.

"Look Keisha, I know I told you a lot of lies and did a lot of wrong by you, but it's not too late to fix things." Yoshi knew everything he'd just said was nonsense, but Keisha did not have to know it. "It's not too late. We don't have to end like this, forgive me, Ma, I'm sorry." That was all Yoshi could say. He'd kept it simple, short and sweet.

That was the last bit of Yoshi's unfeigned approach, and he'd hoped like hell that she'd agreed with what he said. Sitting in her car in complete silence, Keisha debated with herself about if she should allow the only man she had ever wanted to openly lie to her yet again, and get away with it. But Keisha undoubtedly knew the rules to the game. An occasional fight, throw a little shade on his family life from time to time, even dipping a little over her limit in the pesos, she knew that Yoshi could respect. But when she'd picked up the phone and dialed 911, love immediately vanished as soon as the law showed up. And even though she had known that she did not want Yoshi in jail or hurt, she also knew she had cast too many of the wrong stones to turn back. So, she figured she might as well go out with a bang.

"Fuck you, Yoshi," Keisha shouted, "All you care about is my capability to get new money motherfucker. You got damn right you're sorry, but not as half as sorry as you're going to be!"

Behind her ranting Yoshi could make out what sounded to him like the high idling of a car's engine. Then, only seconds later, a high impact collision flared not only through his receiver, but also through his actual eardrums. Glancing out of his living room window, Yoshi was taken aback by what he'd seen—Keisha!

She had sped down Yoshi's cul-de-sac accelerating, without hesitation and almost top speed. She'd rammed her compact Kia into the tail of his Crown Victoria. She tried reversing her Kia in another attempt to crash their cars again, but somehow the two vehicle's bumpers had lodged them together.

Uninjured during the impact, Keisha exited her totaled Kia holding a baseball bat, then she eagerly prepared to unleash her fury on the rest of Yoshi's vehicle.

Within the next five minutes, every child who had skipped school and parents who hadn't attended work that day, including Yoshi, had stepped outside to see the spectacle that Keisha was making of herself.

Keisha had ejected herself from the driver's seat holding her baseball bat firmly gripped, thinking that Yoshi would be the recipient of her first World Series swing, but she was even more astonished when he did not rush after her from his porch.

Oh well, better for his ass, Keisha thought, as she began to unleash her fury on the rest of Yoshi's vehicle, her rage extended to all his windows, front fender and lights, and lastly his hood.

Most of the neighbors on the cul-de-sac were at work or somewhere other than at their homes, but the two or three residents of his community who had not been off to school or work had stepped outside to bear witness to the drama. Yoshi simply sat on his porch railing, using his phone to record every piece of live footage. By the time she was done. Keisha was out of breath and admiring her handiwork, standing on her heels as always in her trademark akimbo pose, with two black eyes and a very swollen nose.

"There, that's the best close-up of today. Now Quanah will see that you're not pregnant and obsessed. The police will know I got a stalker on my hands, which needs to buy me a new car." Yoshi said.

Daggers pierced from Keisha's eyes as dark as Satan at Yoshi as he closed his phone shut and then slid it into his back pocket, his lack of temperament only made her that much more upset.

"Fuck you! You think I'm a game, you bitch ass niggah! I'm going to show you that same money you stole can get your hat brought to this *Don Diva* in a plastic bag."

And that was the statement that changed everything.

Yoshi had known that all that other talk was just that, talk. But the threat that Keisha had just made had changed the whole scenario, her words had made their worsening situation so much more real. And before Keisha could think to blink, Yoshi had leaped over the railing and landed on his grassy lawn. Keisha tossed the bat at Yoshi before she took off in a full sprint up the middle of his street. Shielding his face as if he was a boxer, the bat impacted into Yoshi's forearms, it didn't stop his stride as he ran to track Keisha down, like a hawk would have a mouse in an open field.

About midway to the street's end, Yoshi reached out and caught her by a handful of her dyed red weave. But no sooner than he had his ex-sideline chick captured by her weave, the same new model Infiniti that Yoshi had pulled next to two days after he returned to Keisha's apartment prior to their cruise, pulled right beside them and came to a screeching halt. The gunman hung his short arm that was attached to what seemed to Yoshi to be a Glock, just slightly out of the window.

"Take it easy player . . . no need for no physical assaults . . . let's try to increase the peace."

Yoshi knew the beady-eyed fellow was only trying to patronize him, because in his hand he held the upper hand.

"Niggah do you know me?" Yoshi spat sternly at the gunman while still holding Keisha bent halfway over, her face pointing towards the asphalt as her eyes were fixed on Yoshi's shoes.

"Nope, not at all. But I know the lady, and I'm getting paid not to see her get hurt." The man's tone changed considerably before he finished. "So, if you could let her go and step the fuck back, you'll be alive, so you don't make the Channel 5 News," the nameless man said to Yoshi.

The stout gunman that sat behind the steering wheel of Keisha's car registered Yoshi's dead look, and his tight angry eyed expression showed a man who was not in the least bit afraid. But Yoshi himself also registered the dead reflection staring back at him, it was the reflection of a man who'd without question had killer running through his veins, and someone who would not hesitate to demolish again if irked enough to do so.

Releasing Keisha's head with a slight push, she hurried to the passenger seat of her car as Yoshi and her hired gunman both took mental pictures of each other.

"Hope to see you around," Yoshi told the gunman in warning of what would happen if they ever ran into each other again.

"No. You don't," the gunman replied to assure Yoshi that he would be up for the task had they ever bumped into one another again. Then, the nameless man sped down the street with Keisha shouting obscenities from her passenger side window.

About an hour later Yoshi sat at his desk plotting his next course of action. Wondering his brain almost into a migraine about how to deal with Keisha accordingly.

Flipping open his laptop, Yoshi thought it best to send the video feed he'd recorded of Keisha destroying his car to Quanah's email, hoping that would be enough proof to at least prove he was dealing with a deranged stalker. And by the time Yoshi had finished sending his email, his plan had formed a shape. The whole thing, Yoshi thought, could be ended with two short phone calls.

Dialing up the first person he'd needed to help him with his intricate scheme, Yoshi reclined in his desk chair as the phone began to ring.

"What's up my dude?"

The deep baritone voice came rumbling through on Yoshi's end, and Yoshi wasted no time being coy with his half-brother about what had transpired between Keisha and himself. However, he did use his discretion not to give Dre half the details on the extent he was about to go to be rid of Miss Don Diva.

"Dre," Yoshi said in summation, "all I need you to do is give me a holler right before she heads your way. And double up her regular supply for me, and I'll hit you off with some extra bread for your help!"

The phone went mute because Dre was no doubt weighing the extras Yoshi had just told him would come along with the deal. Even though they were half-brothers, Yoshi knew it best that Dre did not have full information on everything that was supposed to occur. The less he knew, the less he could tell. The more he knew, the more money he might want. Yes, Yoshi thought to himself, it was definitely best to keep Dre half blind concerning everything that was about to unfold. Not that the details mattered at this point, because Dre knew Yoshi all too well. He had known that just from the little information Yoshi had given, that Keisha had awakened a demon. The kind of demon who would not rest until she was dealt with. Dre could only hope that Yoshi wouldn't murder her in his driveway.

"I'll give you a call," was all Dre said before the line went dead.

While he waited to hear back from Dre, Yoshi considered his next move. Things needed to be lined up and ready because he knew that timing would be everything.

Next, Yoshi placed his second call. He was about to do something he'd never done, and was totally against, but his choices were either to play this card, or to simply knock Keisha off. Because it was obvious that Keisha's persistence in doing Yoshi wrong, left him with very few other options. Throughout the years not once had Yoshi ever felt as if he was in love with Keisha, although he did have major love for her. And because of that, he could not foresee himself being the reason behind her funeral.

The phone began ringing to the number on the card he'd pulled from his desk and dialed. The voice that answered on the other end of Yoshi's receiver was raspy and smoke ridden, but inviting, in its own sleazebag kind of way.

"Hello?"

For the second time, Yoshi wasted no time in being coy. "We need to talk, meet me in the Walmart parking lot on Osborne and Sepulveda in fifteen minutes. I'll be in a gray Celica."

"Wow, Yoshi, I never expected to be receiving a call from you. To, what do I owe this pleasure"? The bitch was trying to be funny and condescending with a question Yoshi thought to himself, he was not in the mood.

"Fifteen minutes. Walmart," he screamed before hanging up.

YOSHI. QUANAH. DRE.

Two days later, sitting in his Celica in a trance like reverie, all Yoshi could think of was the time's he and his newly acquired rival once had, and all his thoughts seemed to have him feeling more melancholy than anticipated.

Yoshi knew that if he took the next steps and violated this code to the game, there could be no form of retribution to restore his virtues. This was all for Keisha's good was the reasoning Yoshi kept feeding his conscience to justify his actions. *If I don't do this, she's gonna make me kill her,* which was also a true factor in his overall decision that was nonetheless irrevocably true.

His principles were only on the table to save her life, and in Yoshi's book, he made himself believe that was a good enough reason to break a carnal rule, a sin to the game Yoshi knew he would always have to live with.

Yoshi received the call he'd been anxiously awaiting about 40 minutes ago, he immediately called Mrs. Robinson and told her where to meet him. Just as Yoshi was about to circle the block for the second time, is when he spotted Keisha's new Infinity parked in Dre's driveway.

That was it, she was trapped, Yoshi thought as he pulled across the street to the park where he could easily watch the only two ways in and out of his half-brother's housing track.

A few minutes later, Robinson pulled into the park and parked beside Yoshi under a shade tree. She rolled down the window and cut her ignition off.

"Team one and team two are in place." There was an edge of excitement in Robinson's voice that made Yoshi sick. Robinson turned toward Yoshi and asked, "Is that them? In the green Durango."

"No." Yoshi was tempted to let it pass, to make Robinson look like a fool in front of the narcotics unit, which she without a doubt already would, because the almost 5 pounds of cocaine she thought she was about to bust, was only 42 grams. Which was just enough to get Keisha for a trafficking case.

"Is that them?" Robinson pressed again with the exact monotone as before. At the same time looking for the truth in Yoshi's eyes.

"Yes," he replied from his position, safe from anyone seeing him parked on the street with his lights off. He knew what was going to happen next.

This was for her good, he thought to himself. It was hard for him not to think about all the fun times they had shared together, the cruises, the trips to Vegas, shopping sprees and hot tubs, the clubbing, and concerts.

Robinson made the call over the radio, "Team two. It's a go. The black Infiniti. Go, go, go!"

Immediately and seemingly out of nowhere, four unmarked narcotics cars swooped in. The cops swarmed the car like bees to honey, promptly the driver and Keisha were sprawled onto the pavement.

And that was it. Yoshi had seen enough.

He started the Celica he'd first bought when he had gotten out of the penitentiary a few years ago and slowly drove off. To him, the car was kept out of tribute to the game. Never throw away the things that you were blessed to be given, before you went from trashy to classy. And for that reason, the

Celica had maintained prominence with Yoshi through all the other cars he had rolled and sold over the years.

Keisha was one of those people who helped catapult him from trashy to classy, she was his Celica. He hated to get rid of her, but it was for her own good.

...20 MINUTES LATER...

Pulling into his usual stall Yoshi cut the engine, exited the car, then took the steps two at a time. This was the master part of his master plan. After all, Keisha was right in her comment.

"It was all about the Benjamins." Yoshi thought of what she had said, as he turned the key and entered the apartment.

Reaching the safe in the bedroom, Yoshi turned the three-tumbler lock. The lock was set for the first month they had met, 7, then the date of both their birthdays, 21, and the current year to that date, 22.

The lock responded to the correct input and Yoshi turned the latch.

Keisha had managed to spend another ten thousand dollars in two days. Yoshi could not help but think that was the money she had threatened to put on his life.

Oh well, Yoshi thought while stuffing the bundles of cash down his coat sleeves as he had done before. Then, Yoshi pulled the diamond studded necklace from his inside pocket, picked a pair of Keisha's jeans up from the wash basket, and began lining the diamonds into a cut on the waistline of her apple bottom jeans. *There,* he thought, *a little something to remember me by.* Yoshi's thoughts made him grin as he walked out of Keisha's apartment for the very last time.

When I was created, envy, greed, lust, pride, wrath, gluttony, and sloth, all accompanied me, the love for money! Our creator cast us into the land of milk and honey to cause as much havoc and claim as many souls for my father as possible. Not only the seven deadly sins, but the eighth being the love for money, awarded you people with reason to steal, rob, backstab, and even kill, in the realm of everyday ambitions to gain a new dollar. Could you imagine how much simpler things would be if I did not make people stoop to their all-time low, just so they could bask in the experience of my all-time high?

Yoshi just snitched on his best friend to keep from having to kill her, that's a hell of a means to an end, wouldn't you say? If Keisha did not have the means she would have never told Yoshi, much less even thought to say that she had enough paper to get him knocked down. And the strangest thing about it all, is that Yoshi had known inside that Keisha would never have him hurt, and was only acting behind her hurt, herself. But Yoshi had come to that conclusion as he sat in the park and reminisced on their happiness.

He had also known that I was just sitting in that apartment, beckoning him to do what he knew was required to alleviate Keisha from the picture, then claim me without any type of ramification.

Yoshi had even nourished his own ego into believing that him snitching on Keisha was for the perseverance of her own life. But I know, and I'm sure you know as well, that that was just merely the best lie he could sell himself for the sake of again selling his soul.

There are times when I wish I could advocate for these insane people, times when I wish I could come to the defense of these simpletons. But the prosecutor is too sharp at condemning people to my damnation, he leaves not even an inkling of room for doubt, and the penalty for doing vile things to play with my father's favorite toy, is life. And for some, death!

Even though Keisha and Yoshi are but minor ripples in the extent of the destruction I cause, there are also other ripples just like them, ripples *that eventually make small waves, which often turn to tidal waves, then eventually into typhoons.*

But for you, the deal still stands, our offer is still on the table. In fact, we'll make you a tsunami. That's like Bill Cosby and Donald Trump money!

What do you say? Deal?

I understand, you need a little more time to think on it, but hey, it's a limited time offer, so I wouldn't take too long mulling it over if I were you.

Now, where was I?

Oh yeah, the part of our story where betrayal is backdoored by treacherous hate.

Bet you didn't see this fastball coming, all you'll hear is the umpire screaming, "strike three, you're out," just before the pitcher steps off the mound jogging ever so casually to his dugout!

Two days passed since Keisha had been charged and sent to the Lynwood County jail, and just as Yoshi had expected, his phone had rung every hour on the hour with a collect call recording for the past 48 hours.

Instead of answering, he decided to schedule himself a computerized Saturday visit under the bogus Identification he kept laying around for emergency purposes.

In those two days' time, Yoshi had done all he could to make sure Keisha's stay at the county jail would not be long, and that her abode and Infiniti would be well maintained in her absence. He figured the least he could do was to make sure Keisha didn't have to do a long stay behind bars, and that she'd have the comfort of her apartment, her car, and a little dough when she finally returned home.

"Borders . . . you're at window 18," someone announced over the intercom.

Yoshi sat there fidgeting and at times, holding his breath because the anxiety of not knowing how this conference may unfold had his palms sweating, even what he thought was a hint of nausea creeping into his belly out of the blue.

Keisha took her seat smiling from ear to ear, she was speechless at the fact Yoshi was sitting across the glass from her holding the phone. She'd thought his record would have prohibited him from ever visiting her. But here he was.

"Why the hell haven't you been answering the phone," Keisha spoke the words with the same speed as them entering her thoughts. Her second question carried off the first as If it was a run along sentence. "How the hell did you get in here?"

Keisha asked the rhetorical question to express her shock, not to expect an actual answer.

Again, her smile came back as If it was the sun peeking around a cumulus cloud, just as her mouth continued to move in sequence with her growing smile without missing a beat.

"So let me tell you what happened—" before Keisha could get her lips on automatic rapid fire, Yoshi jolted in, "—I know what happened."

They both sat there for a second sharing silence. Keisha's look reflected a boggled discernment, Yoshi's look was marked with an eccentric mischievousness, and a hint of compassion laced in its shadows.

"How did you know?" Her words sputtered like a car that had just run out of gas.

Yoshi only allowed the suspense of his nuclear bomb to build for a short moment. "Because I'm the reason it happened!"

Once his words registered, her whole face had begun to sag downward toward the steel desktop her elbows rested on. Her eyes began to water as they stared through the glass at one another.

Keisha found the strength to force it from her gut, "You set me up, you cheese-chasing ass rat!"

Tears fell as she thought to herself the man she had let play up under her skin was a charlatan. And a real disgrace of a sellout.

"You! Get on the stand, Sammy the Bull, head of the investigation, call the law, close the case ass fuck niggah!" Keisha flung her insults through the phone at Yoshi, and the more she spoke, the more his grin froze as if it was an emotionless Polaroid.

She had reloaded her verbal magazine and was just about to unload her second clip, but instead Yoshi beat her to the punch.

"See, that's just the fuck why you back there. Shooting off at the mouth with dummy rounds. Didn't I teach you years ago that you can't throw firecrackers at a real Vietnam vet, because he's gonna shoot, and somebody gonna get shot because somebody else was faking!"

Keisha looked at him annoyed. "Come on Yoshi man," Keisha spoke in almost a half plea, "You know I'd never really hurt you. You lied to me for years. I love you, Yoshi, I was fucking hurt!"

She patted toward her heart while saying her last words to give emphasis to her point. "You sent me to jail. You don't care about me none, Yoshi?"

Yoshi felt it was now his turn to snap, "Never hurt me. Huh? Well, I've got a foot long, two inch deep scare In my shoulder blade that says you're a muthafuckin lie. Fucking right I cared about you, that's why I left you with fifteen thousand, that's why I didn't dead yo'ass while I had you knocked out on the floor, even though I knew the whole time, that you were going to cause all kinds of disruptions in my life," Yoshi kept plowing ahead, "You plotted on me, called my P.O., brought drama to my home, tore my shit up, had a weird niggah pull a gun on me, and to top it off, you threatened my life. You muthafuckin right I sent yo stupid ass in here to sit down for a minute. It was either that, or I put your crazy ass on ice for good. You tell me, which would you have preferred?"

Yoshi was eyeing Keisha, she peered back just as intensely with a look that could kill as she spoke, "I would have rather you killed me, at least I would have died with some type of respect for you. At least a bitch would have died knowing that the niggah I been fucking for the last four years had some kind of dignity. Punk ass!"

He shook his head in amazement at Keisha's bravado.

"Look. This was pointless, and it's about time for me to go."

Keisha sat there motionless, staring at Yoshi as If he had the biggest piece of shit on his face. "Your car's out of the impound, so it'll be in your parking stall when you get home. The rent was paid up to six months already, I paid It up for another year. So, you're 18 months to the good. I also got you a lawyer that says he can get your trafficking charge broken down to a simple possession, just as long as you tell them you're an addict. They'll give you a program, and you'll be out within a year. Oh, and those apple-bottom jeans In the dirty clothes hamper that I bought you last year has something In them for you, make sure you check them thoroughly."

Yoshi sighed.

He was done, and this was it.

The whole time he spoke Keisha held the phone but never looked up from her lap. Yoshi could tell she was disgusted with him. Yoshi figured he'd rather her be disgusted with him, as opposed to dead from him.

"I'm sorry how we worked out, I wanted things to be different. But you're a real boss lady, Keisha, so I know you'll be just fine. You take care in here my girl!"

Yoshi had spoken his peace and there was nothing left but to walk away.

Just as he set the phone down and turned to leave Keisha behind for good, their eyes met one last time as Keisha's glare was menacing and as sable as unburnt coals.

"Thanks for your assistance. But really all you should have done was say three words, and I would have forgiven you for it all," Keisha rose to her feet as she summated, "But you couldn't be man enough to at least give me that much respect."

Keisha's next words were piercing, but all Yoshi could see was the first day they'd ever met. All he could feel was the electric current that transcended threw him the first time he'd ever seen her. Her angelic, misunderstood, innocent face begging him to jump in her car so she could help him escape from all that madness as well as all the madness that had followed in the thereafter.

In that painful second, she was perfect. During that moment, the conception of Yoshi realizing that he loved Keisha was undeniable.

"I'm going to get you, Yoshi. I promise to God . . . you're going to die," she vented. The hard plastic phone hitting hard against the glass is all that brought Yoshi back into the correct time zone. He didn't even hear the last word's she'd spoken, as Keisha strutted away a only she could, turning more and more into Odyssey with each and every step.

****

Riding down his half-brother's street an hour after his visit with Keisha, Yoshi was still disturbed about what had just happened. He knew what he had done to her was a direct violation of the street's rules. And the only way Yoshi could put a cap on his warring emotions was to dismiss them. He knew no better way to do that than to go and hang with his brother.

Dre was his soldier, his road dog, his real one. And though he did not come equipped with Yoshi's killer gene, he was still by no means a pushover, and a resource that never failed at showing the value of his worth.

"Look, hottie, I appreciate you bringing me up to speed on things, and if the shit is what you say, then we'll do business. But all this trying to bait me in with the pussy all of a sudden, like your pussy can pimp me, ain't the business! So, keep it professional, and keep in touch." Dre closed his cell phone shut as they both laughed and took a swig from the same bottle of Remy Martin.

"Looks like you got 99 problems, dog," he said to Yoshi.

Yoshi appreciated that Dre was attentive enough to notice things weren't good. But it was really Dre's street resources that gave him the insight on Yoshi's problems.

"Keisha's in jail and I haven't spoken to Quannah in a week. It's all bad, bro. Then I've been having these strange dreams, like I'm seeing people I've known forever for the first time. It's like I'm seeing them in some type of divine way that I never have before.

"Hold up, hold up," Dre interrupted, "You sound like you need a straight-jacket. Better yet, I know what you need. It's time for you to be a party hopping, panty pumpin', pill poppin' animal for a few days. We've got to power you back up my boy."

Yoshi sat quietly for a few moments in silence, letting the words of Dre sink in. "It's time to turn up!"

Dre asked, "So, are we having a function or what?"

Yoshi threw back another shot, wiped his mouth with the back of his hand, then started to bounce his head back and forth just as Dre had done earlier, indicating that it was more than time to get out of his mind.

Dre, Dre, Dre! There's not too much to be said about Dre just yet, because he only a few years ago came to be a true patriot of my money green flag. Now don't get me wrong, he has always been infatuated by my appeal since I could remember, but also since I could remember, Dre has lacked the self-indulged confidence that it takes to be front runner in the race to win me over. For the longest time not even the smallest gram of clever cunning existed in this suave green-eyed liaison of mine, though I must admit, he is converting into a money goblin quite nicely.

Yoshi was the clandestine weapon I used in persuading Dre. Whereas Dre was plain and unpopular, had no sense of style or originality, didn't even have the heart to steal a piece of bubblegum, or much less talk to a girl as a teen. Yoshi had always come along to be his benefactor and overlord.

In those years every move that Yoshi made, Dre followed, or mimicked. But to Dre's benefit every move made by Yoshi produced something new for Dre, and with every something new Dre began to pan out his own individuality!

Things shifted for Dre when Yoshi had to do his few years in the penitentiary. During that time Dre had seemed to have lost his way, as if his lucky charm or rabbit's foot had been misplaced. Dre had become aimless during those years that had passed until the day Yoshi had resurfaced, which coincidently seemed to be the very day Dre's ambitions had reemerged.

With them back together, meeting up with me was something of an inevitable fate, at least that's the way Dre saw it. Much to my surprise, but to my father's plan, I'm certain Dre's calculations on us as a trio was exact and correct.

And ever since Yoshi first clicked with Keisha and hit for that kilo of cocaine and those few thousand, Dre hasn't looked back since. Of course, the 20 oz. of cocaine and 5 lbs. of dro that Dre is worth and has been juggling for the past three years was courtesy of the 12 oz. Yoshi fronted him back in the day. 4 oz. of which Yoshi told Dre were simply his to have out of the that, Yoshi had given him on consignment.

But the real riddle to this equation, comes with a self-explanatory answer. Get Yoshi out of the picture, and Dre will self-annihilate in no time. In fact, those are just my intentions. To do away with one and annihilate the other.

It's just as the old saying goes—why throw two, when one stone to kill two birds, is all you need to get the job done! 😼

Getting Yoshi to relax and ride out the melancholy he appeared to be officially hexed with was not too hard a task for Dre. Besides, from what he had heard from a conspiring rival of Yoshi's, he had the assets it took to make some fun happen.

Saturday, after they became lightweight loaded off Dre's gallon of Remy, they began their two-man Mardi Gras by dropping Yoshi's Celica off and jumping in Dre's 1972 Monte Carlo. They decided to hit a few parks and feel the vibe on LA's Saturday lowrider scene. High riding with presidential poise is what Dre told Yoshi they were doing. And that was just what they were doing.

It was the Monte Carlos 3 color greens and California gold candy paint that was wetter than a baby's bib after it drooled down a popsicle. The engine as well as the other chrome trimmings had been dipped more times than a female salsa dancer. Its red oak wood dashboard coincided with the steering wheel and the other interior's red wood trimming to match the off-white leather bucket race car seats and head ceiling.

But it was the 180-spoke, 26-inch toothpick Dayton's, that made unhealthy hearts fill with hate. And make no mistake, there was an ample amount of unhealthy real niggah's conceived in the city every day. Hitting up a couple parks, they ran into some childhood friends who filled them in on where the night's festivities would be jumping off. From there they decided the barbershop was next before they rolled all the way to Ontario Mills to go tag popping bananas. Not once was either of them without a Styrofoam cup of Remy to keep their brains altered and their tipsy to just the right buzz.

Around 5:00 o'clock they had landed in the Staples Center— Yoshi kept season tickets every year— to watch the infamous Lebron James and the up-and-coming, young legend, Kevin Durant, do their stuff.

The Lakers won 104 to 101 and after the game they journeyed to Inglewood to get dressed at one of Dre's lady's houses. From there, it was club after club. From Pasadena to Gardena, South Central to Long Beach and more. They'd been spot to spot, and by the time Yoshi had flopped on

Dre's guest bed at 4:32 a.m. that Sunday morning, his attitudes and perspective had changed, just before, rest invaded his party, tattered body. Sunday was pretty much an equivalent replica of Saturday. It was not so much as far as the events, but the day's laid-back cheer is what showed that it would be a refreshing day.

Dre rocked Yoshi awake around ten that morning, with a glass of 1800 Tequila thrust in his face. "The only thing that beats morning breath and a hangover, is another drink, dog." Dre spoke his last words in his Tommy voice, of the Martin Lawrence show.

Yoshi took the cup as he rolled to a sitting position, then with a cat's agility, Yoshi snatched the blunt that dangled loosely from Dre's lips. Dre shrugged as if what Yoshi had done was null, then he reached behind his ear and put the fresh cigarillo he had pre-rolled in his mouth. Flopping on the couch beside Yoshi they sat in front of Dre's 64'in flat screen Panasonic.

The late Young Dolph latest music video flashed across the screen as they both took drinks from their morning alcohol and then puffs from their weed. Dre fiddled with his laptop that rested atop the couches' armrest.

"What we got up for today bro, I can't do another one like the other one?" Yoshi was referring to all the ripping and running they had done the day prior.

"Shit I know that's real," Dre responded to Yoshi between drags of his blunt in a way that told Yoshi that Dre supported his notion. "Today we just going to barbecue and get white boy wasted, fuck off in the pool, and see if we can put a few things back on track."

Yoshi didn't quite understand the last of what Dre meant, but before he could inquire, Dre said as he headed for the kitchen, "My Armenian peoples got a few nice new foreign cars he is trying to dump for cheap. I didn't ask about anything brand new for you because I know you think shit like that draws heat. They're right there on the computer screen. You can check them out if you want," Dre said in summation.

Looking over the pictures on the screens monitor Yoshi had to agree that the prices were right, and they all looked pretty much brand new to be two and three years behind the year to date.

"When cars look this good," Yoshi began, "with these kinds of low miles and price tags on the market as a grade 'A' steal, the first thing I think is refurbished."

Yoshi spoke aloud to Dre who was in the kitchen microwaving their breakfast. Dre returned and handed Yoshi his French toast sticks, assorted fruits, and syrup, as he answered.

"Yeah, I would think the same thing if I didn't know the guy," Dre pointed to the screen while chewing his own French toast sticks, fruit, and syrup all at once. "They're imports straight from China. He buys them dirt cheap from those rent-a-car places overseas. Then he manipulates the system on their end, so the car companies' insurance covers the price of it being imported, and somehow gets the company to refund a kickback on the vehicle. I think the companies sell him the cars for the low, rent them out under an Alias and then report them stolen. Of course, they're never found because they're in America. Once they're here, he twerks the serial numbers through his DMV connection. And Shazam, he's got $15,000 three-year-old Beamers with 30,000 miles on the dash. Niggah can you buy that?" Dre summated, this time using his Goldie voice from the movie, *The Mack*.

Taking another peek over at the monitor a surge of pride began to inflate Yoshi's chest as it expanded to his smiling face and now twinkling eye. "As a matter of fact. Yes. I. Can." Yoshi said his last words imitating *The Nutty Professor's* Sherman Klump.

Their laughter spread between the two of them hysterically, one choking on his food, and the other on his weed smoke.

After morning had moved on and the afternoon had settled in, it was around three o'clock when the shindig began to come alive.

Yoshi happened to be outside, standing up against Dre's garage, as the short Armenian man pulled up in Yoshi's new luxury sports coupe. The very moment he saw the sleek black paint on black leather sports luxury car bend Dre's corner, Yoshi was a sold customer.

The short Armenian man, parked, exited the car, and introduced himself, "I'm Mike. You must be Yoshi."

"Yeah. Hey bro, your homeboy's here," he hollered into the backyard.

"He told me a lot about you. You like it?" Mike pointed toward the sleek black paint on black leather.

"It's definitely everything you advertised it to be," Yoshi said as he stroked his chin and nodded his head in approval.

Mike in that moment did as every good salesman does, he made good casual small talk all while going over every intricate detail about the 2020 Beamer he was certain Yoshi was about to buy. Eventually the two men shook hands and Yoshi signed the papers on the dotted line.

"Mike . . . what's good my niggah," Dre said as he walked out his front door. He met Mike and they embraced.

"Please excuse me gentlemen, but I came to this good gathering for three reasons, to sell a car, to eat me some barbecue, and to knock me a bad bitch."

They all began to laugh.

"The car is sold, but the bitches and barbecue are inside," Dre said.

"So, I'll see y'all in a minute!" Mike headed for the inside as they laughed while he departed.

Dre's phone rang as they stood there, lusting over the Beamer's elegance. Immediately, Dre snatched the keys from Yoshi, and headed towards the driver's side. "You comin'?" he asked as he opened the door to get in.

Yoshi snickered to himself and began to open the passenger's door when his cell phone also began to vibrate in his pocket. Yoshi was about to chase Dre, but the number on the cell phone was of way greater importance than retrieving his keys. Looking at the number before he answered it, he took a deep breath.

"Hello?" Yoshi said with care into his phone's receiver.

"Hey, how are you doing?" The voice he heard came back at him with just as much tender concern.

"Hey, you comin' or what?" Dre asked as he started the engine. Yoshi motioned for him to leave without him.

"I'm better now, how are you?" Yoshi asked, wanting to tread this water as lightly as possible.

"That's not what I've heard. Somebody told me you've been weeping to them for the past week, like somebody did you wrong or something." Yoshi was glad to hear Quanah's mood had changed. She sounded so nice. He could tell that she wanted him to reciprocate her playfulness.

"Somebody did do me wrong," Yoshi teased Quanah.

"Who?"

"This female. She took both parts of my heart with her, too," he responded.

"You at the bar-b-cue?" She asked.

"Yeah . . . how'd you know?"

Dre backed out the driveway in his Beamer waving bye. Yoshi did his hands as if he was an old man shoeing away his grandchildren.

"Dre called me and told me you might be there, and that I should come through. You want me to come through?"

Yoshi felt on top of the world. "Yeah, come through ma," he said. Not to mention, his buzz contributed greatly to his sudden sprightliness.

That's when he felt Quanah smile, and that's when Yoshi knew they would be all right. She told Yoshi that Dre invited her to the barbecue that evening, but because she did not want the atmosphere between the two of them to be awkward, they decided to make a date for the following night. That only gave Quanah the time she needed to get her hair and nails done before they met up and went to the cinema.

Aside from the couple hashing out their differences and Keisha being behind bars, Quanah decided it best to bring Yoshi's money back home tomorrow evening. Hearing she had not done anything foolish with the money that Yoshi had schemed so earnestly for, was not only a relief but a weight lifted from his shoulders. Once everything had been established and the phone was hung up, Yoshi felt elated and on top of the world.

Moving through the house gingerly so as not to fall or spill a drop of his 1800, Yoshi found Dre talking to a couple of young ladies wearing bathing suits in Dre's jacuzzi. Tapping his half-brother's shoulder, Yoshi who was half drunk started to speak before Dre even spun to acknowledge Him.

"Bro. I don't know what you told her, but thank you," Yoshi said.

"I got you bro," Dre responded. His broad smile brightly showing for Yoshi's appreciation.

"Hey! You're my closest loved one, and I would stay and tell you that same thing a lot more times but, I gotta take a serious leak." Everyone in the jacuzzi began to laugh as Yoshi stormed off.

Coming in from the backyard Yoshi teetertottered down the hallway toward the bathroom. The phone in his pocket began to vibrate again. Not paying attention to where he was going, he picked it up thinking it might be Quanah calling him back.

No one answered at the same time he opened the door to the bathroom; he had already unzipped his pants.

"Do you mind if we help you with that?"

The two bikini clad young ladies Dre had just been getting high and speaking with were now looking at Yoshi's exposed appendage flapping in the wind.

Without giving it a second thought Yoshi responded, "As a matter of fact, ladies . . . yes. You. Can!"

THE FOLLOWING DAY

This weekend started off in the worst way," Yoshi said to Dre across their late Denny's lunch. "But somehow you worked your magic and really helped me to put my game back on track."

"Don't even trip, bro. That's just how we do," Dre replied between bites.

"You helped me tighten up my whip game, Quanah ain't trippin' no more, and you pulled me out of the mud and dusted a soldier off."

Yoshi continued as they both chewed on their thick ranch bacon cheeseburgers. "I appreciate you, bro, in a real way."

"Nah, keep all that sentimental shit over there on your side of the table, bro, we don't do the touchy sensitives around here," Dre joked as he bit into another chunk of bread, beef, and bacon.

Yoshi was setting down his soda pop as he countered, "I just recognize real niggah moves." He wiped his mouth with his napkin and lightly tossed it onto his plate.

Dre avoided eye contact as he wiped his own mouth and discarded his own napkin onto his empty plate.

"Well, I'm just paying homage. You pulled me out of a hell of a lot of trenches," Dre looked over to his brother as Yoshi summarized. "Even kept me in new clothes."

Yoshi gazed across the table with a modest expression, Dre looked back expressionless.

After they concluded their modest meal together, it was time to go. They'd planned to meet back together at Yoshi's house later that afternoon, and then from there they would figure out what to do with the rest of their day.

Yoshi was driving to his house when his phone began to buzz.

"Hey, babe," Quanah started to giggle. "What's up boy, what you doing?"

Yoshi teased affectionately, "Dang Double-O-Seven. You're going to change your profession from housewife to secret agent?"

"Boy, shut up," Quanah spat back playfully before she added. "Look, I'm here at the Shell gas station around the corner from the house. I'm too fat and lazy to get out and pump my gas. If you're local and you really love me," she was pouting in Yoshi's ear, "if you're local and you really love me . . . ," Quanah did not ask what she was obviously hinting towards. She was simply in a roundabout way letting him know that if he took the initiative to do what she wanted, then she would take the initiative, "come pump me now." Quanah said as she finished with her come on punchline.

Yoshi started dying in laughter as he quipped, "Well you just happen to be in luck."

"And why is that?"

"Look in your rearview mirror," he said as he pulled in behind her. He stuck out his tongue when he saw her looking in the rearview mirror.

Opening his door and exiting his car, Yoshi then headed into the Shell station to pay for her gas. When he came back out, he had a pack of Mambas and some change. He walked over to her car and put the pump in her tank. By then she had rolled down the window.

Quanah with her head out the window joked, "Boy, which one of them hoe's cars are you driving?"

Yoshi looked back and grinned before saying, "Don't you worry about all that, you just get ready to give me my pumps later."

As they ate their candy, Yoshi leaned into Quanah's driver side window, so they could talk.

"You look good, baby," he said as he hunched in and gave Quanah a kiss.

"Ummm," Quanah chimed after their lips parted. "You look good and taste even better."

He peeled the wrapper off a strawberry Mamba and fed another to her. "Where are you and my little one coming from?" Yoshi asked, while looking at his sleeping giant slumped almost grotesquely in his car seat.

"Well, he's been at his uncle Jeremy's all day playing with his cousin Ra'Shawn, and I've been in the street doing big girl stuff."

Yoshi caressed the back of Quanah's hand. As he did, the emotional avalanche that he had been running from finally caught up with him—he really did love *this* woman. She had been a ride or die through thick and thin, plus she was the mother of his children.

Her tenderness, in that moment made him realize everything that he had in her. With the brush of his fingertips, he was almost overwhelmed with an emotion that overcame his usual tough exterior. They talked for about fifteen minutes rekindling, forgiving, promising, admitting, and saying the things that needed to be said. They were two people who loved each other and desperately wanted to salvage their relationship.

"Baby, don't cry," Quanah said as she wiped the tears that rolled down his face. Then she grabbed his strong jaw and began to kiss his pain away. Each kiss bliss, each kiss solace, each kiss strength, and each kiss imprinted on his heart. "I love you baby."

"Look," Yoshi said, wiping the tears from his face, "I love you back." His voice reciprocated the same validations. Their foreheads rest together, but their eyelids remain gazing into each other's, as she gave one last parting kiss, before he pushed away from her car door.

"I'll meet you back at the house later, okay?"

Yoshi then opened the rear passenger door, leaned in to kiss his son, and on his way out of the backseat, leaned in to kiss the back of Quanah's neck. She popped the trunk as he shut the door, "It's in your favorite bag. See you at five. Don't be late Yoshi!" Quanah reminded him about the matinee as he shut her trunk and headed to his car after returning the pump to its holder.

She watched Yoshi in her rearview mirror as he walked back to his car and climbed in his driver seat. He could sense someone holding their prying eyes on him. He looked up to see Quanah peering in her rearview. They were the most beautiful eyes he had ever seen.

Yoshi blew her a kiss, and Quanah smiled with cheeks full of blush.

Then she pulled away, and so did he, headed straight home. As he drove, he couldn't stop thinking about her, she was his heart, and he would wait for her forever.

He drove home, collecting himself, while he recapped on how his soon-to-be-wife had just mollified him with her delicate affections. Yoshi pulled away feeling every bit illuminated. So much had transpired in the last two weeks that Yoshi had yet to process, but the short encounter he'd just had with Quanah had him thinking about all that had happened.

With those thoughts whirling around in Yoshi's mind, on his short ride home, he had come to the final realization, about more than one thing. The first was that he would be moving his family out of Los Angeles, and he would also make some investments for his boys, while opening some kind of lucrative small proprietorship.

Yoshi decided that those would be the next two endeavors that he would begin to accomplish. He walked through his home's front door, giving it a kick with his heel to secure it behind himself. Carrying his duffle bag, with his dirty clothing from his stay at his half-brother's, in his right hand, the soul trendy Gucci backpack was locked over his shoulder like a harness.

As he walked into the front door, he instinctively held tight to the Gucci backpack that held all the money. As he made his way down the hallway to his bedroom, for some reason Yoshi's senses seemed unnerved, but he shook the notion off as paranoia just as quickly as it had come.

Taking in the familiarity of the aroma in the house, creaking wood floors, and the chiming of his grandmother's grandfather clock, he moved down the hall to his room, still thinking about all the memories his family would be leaving behind once they had gone. Setting his duffle bag down, he picked up his television remote, turned on the TV, and hit the BET channel.

Flinging the remote on the bed, Yoshi walked over to his dresser and kneeled kneeled in front of the enormous oak wood drawers that held small mirrors aligned as décor, along with his huge heart-shaped wood-framed mirror on top. There was a picture of his fiancée and their son, where his gaze lingered.

Again, but this time with ringing alarm, the same leery feeling from earlier jumped deep into Yoshi bones. Except this time, it was more than a feeling, it was a fact, and that fact was standing in Yoshi's doorway with a pistol aimed at his back.

It was Dre.

From, the very day Yoshi came home Dre vowed, not to me, but to himself, to use Yoshi like Yoshi had used him all those years ago. As a footstool, errand boy, crash dummy, a yes man, and every other tool Dre could think of in the shed that a peasant was used for. Until this very point, that's exactly what it's been. At every turn, Dre has played on Yoshi's goodwill, brotherly love, charities, and loyalties. So, who better for me to send to get Yoshi, than someone who is in his debt? Who better than someone he'd trusted, fought for, lied for, and even went to jail for?

To the naked eye, you would think that Yoshi was the conductor between these two brothers, but in all likelihood, Dre's been the orchestrator of their symphony for some time now. If Dre needed clothes, Yoshi stole them for Dre until he taught Dre how. If Dre needed money, Yoshi would split what he had down the middle, or Dre would look out, while Yoshi snatched a purse or clipped someone's chain. If there was somebody who didn't like Dre, Yoshi would fight for him, until Dre had started to build up enough nuts to fight for himself. Even Dre's first sexual experience was courtesy of Yoshi, amongst all the other things on the extensive checklist as to how it's been Dre using Yoshi from the very get-go.

But those things are no longer here nor there, my only concern is that Dre is ready to dissipate their brotherly ties, all for my capital power. This whole while, Dre's been looking for any opportunity to unleash his vengeance, a perfect impromptu situation to alleviate Yoshi from it all. And what better time to serve a plate of treachery than when an exorbitant sum of cash is the desert that should follow. 😈

"Man . . ." Dre said, sounding half astonished as he sat on the farthest corner of Yoshi's bed, still pointing his gun at the back of Yoshi's head. Once he was comfortably seated, he started up again. "I thought the bitch was gassing me, trying to send me on a dummy mission because she figured out, I really couldn't stand your ass," Dre said.

Yoshi's brain turned on the switch.

And that was the point when Yoshi understood his mind had been sufficiently distorted by the drinking and women, something else Dre had banked on. He silently cursed himself twice now for his stupidity.

"I also thought because the bitch wanted you dead behind the fact you turned informant on her, that she'd say or do just about anything to get you in a bag." Dre gazed over at the money that lay beside Yoshi's dresser on the floor.

Yoshi was frozen with shock. He couldn't believe that Keisha had the ability to turn his own blood against him. But he also knew that Dre was a simple-minded soul, someone easy to control.

"That slut, Odyssey, wasn't lying at all I see. Actually, the bitch was probably telling the truth for the first time in her life," Dre added as he continued eyeing the money. "God bless her shitty soul for that."

Yoshi was still on his knees, staring into the dresser drawer's mirror, at Dre who kept going.

"The bitch wasn't going to get me to be the long arm of her revenge, not when I've been waiting for the right time myself to inflict my own big payback."

Their staring eyes were intense reflections of one another's own face.

Dre held his gun fixed on Yoshi with a cocky smirk on his face. "But what she was saying was worth inspecting, and if it did turn out to be real then I figured this would be the best time to get rid of you."

"Can't stand me? Pay back? Niggah, what is you sayin'?" Yoshi asked.

Dre gave a chuckle and a slight shrug of his shoulder.

"I'm talking about getting your hand-me-downs and leftovers, always being in your shadow but not being big enough to fill it. I'm talking about not being able to find myself because you stood in the way, because if I wasn't like you, then I was a nobody to everybody. You treated me like I was a tag-along dog, more than a brother."

Dre's voice cut into Yoshi's thoughts. "When I was just headed to your house and pulled up to the stop light across the street from the Shell, I was surprised when I seen you getting that favorite bag of yours out the trunk of Quanah's car, the same bag Keisha told me you only kept big money in, that shit was too good to be true. Then I saw how heavy the bag looked, I just knew it was a hundred or better," Dre said, pointing to the Gucci backpack that sat open on the floor.

"She pointed me to my destiny and sealed yours bro, because like I said before, I wouldn't kill you over old grudges, but I would for sure over a bag of green."

Raising his head and glaring into the mirror, Yoshi's half-brother's true face was revealed to him for the first time in his life. The hatred in his eyes, and greed, and his crooked smile, the underhandedness of his jawline and envy in his eyebrows. It was apparent that Yoshi's most villainous adversary was his righthand man, and only family.

Making his atonement with God through quick prayer, Yoshi felt his internal clock was nearing its end. Picking up a stack of bills with his right hand, he examined the hellacious idol that was about to cost him his life, all while his left hand eased for his Gucci bag.

"Besides, you've been my cash cow. The only way I planned to check you out, is if you were cashing out," Dre laughed. "And, ironically, life has led us to this."

Yoshi was speechless. It's like he didn't even recognize him anymore. He didn't know the person he had just earlier had breakfast with. He silently cursed himself twice now for his own stupidity.

As their eyes were locked and both their pulses raced rapidly, Yoshi asked, "Keisha told you about my money. What else did she tell you?"

He tried to swing his hand from the inside of the Gucci bag and raise his weapon, but he was a fixed target in desperation, they both had known that he would try.

Pock, pock!

The 9-millimeter hit Yoshi on his left side as he slammed his back into the dresser, and the second shot just inches under his heart left him automatically panting with short, hurried breath.

"Yes, she told me about the gun, too," Dre finished the question Yoshi didn't get to finish asking. Yoshi's handheld onto the money with a deadlock grip before he was shot. The pain made his hands dig deep into its papery substance. Yoshi's head went from Dre to his bed's nightstand, where their family pictures of Elijah, Quanah, and himself, all set in frames.

Dre picked the money up from the floor before it could become soaked with Yoshi's blood. He never looked once at his brother, as he lay there bleeding out the last of his life.

His breathing became shallow and slowed with short gasps, his life evaporating yet still managing to smile at the picture of his son and fiancée. A warmth passed through him as a chill set in around him.

Lying on the floor, Yoshi's breathing became more uneven and faint. He struggled to get to his feet, but he had no strength and very little breath. He knew the end was near, as his life of crime began to flash before his eyes. He saw the face of Quanah and Elijah, as his field of vision began to collapse from the corners of his eyes.

"I promise, I-I'll wait for you."

That was the moment Yoshi's heart could beat no further. He died with open eyes gazing upon his family, and with the very thing that sealed his fate drenched in his blood and locked between his fingertips. That vision continued to collapse until there was total darkness that accompanied the last labored breath from his body.

CHAPTER 12

DRE. CHARLES. TONY.

re had planned every detail of this evening with the precision of a surgeon.

The first thing he did was to make sure no one saw him entering or leaving Yoshi's house. He was counting on the fact that not many people came in or out of Yoshi's area, which would have allowed him to go unnoticed or overlooked by any looky-loos.

Mostly, all the bases had been covered, Dre thought, as he played and replayed all the details of how he had murdered his brother in cold blood. He was very meticulous about his entrance and exit to the scene of the crime. He had even wiped his prints off the front doorknob before he exited out the backyard and hopped their fence.

Even having left his car around the corner was an important move in getting away with his sweetest two-faced taboo. Making his way out of Yoshi's housing community and across the street to the bus stop all while towing Yoshi's Gucci bag over his shoulder, Dre called his most reliable.

"Charles, I'm over on Dexter and Mahogany, sitting at the bus stop. My bro just got me caught up with some niggahs. They tried to jack me, but I got away. Hurry up, I'm like a fucking duck in hunting season. Come and scoop me up," he said before he hung up.

Ten minutes later, Charles eased up to the curb at the bus stop, careful not to scuff Dre's 24-inch wire rims on the curb.

"The Mustang would have been way more low-key than the MC," Charles spat as soon as Dre jumped in. "But when I got to the garage it was gone. So, I figured that you were in it."

Dre had no intention of leaving his car around the corner from Yoshi's house, he told Charles in response. "I was driving it, it's around the block, take me to get it."

They'd gotten the Mustang and made it out of Yoshi's neighborhood undetected. Once they had made it home, Dre went directly to his room, tossed the Gucci bag on the bed as if it was a pillow, then immediately returned to the kitchen to have a drink.

"So, are you going to tell me what happened?" Charles asked Dre in between his second and third shot of Louis XIII.

Dre fed Charles his version through a bullshit skit, and by the time he was concluding his lie, and firing up his weed, some of his eeriness had vanished. Even his thoughts of being discovered had subsided or were suppressed was more like it.

"The AK-47 is in the back house. Let's go handle that," Charles stated as he rose from his seat once Dre had finished his fabricated spiel, again reminding Dre of the lie he had just composed.

"I just told you there was a shootout and the police are probably swarming like bumblebees and those fools definitely ain't standing outside."

Charles sighed heavily, so his irritation could obviously be heard, and then he settled back in his seat and poured himself a shot.

Either the weed had brought on an alarming panic, or Dre's conscience had kicked in, sending him a warning to take a few extra precautions to ensure he remained an emancipated man. Springing from his chair and running to his room, Dre returned in an instant and handed Charles the murder weapon. It was scrubbed clean with alcohol by Dre before he handed it over.

"Break this muthafucker down like a kid does syllables in a spelling bee," Dre finished. "Bring me the firing pin and the barrel. And I need this shit done A.S.A.P"

Charles noted but said nothing. The edge in Dre's voice emphasized the eagerness of his request. Charles downed another shot, then immediately took the gun, and left.

Dre sat back and opened the Gucci Bag full of money. He was beginning to feel much more comfortable with the day's events. He went to his room and stripped before setting all his clothes aside so they could be burned out back. As soon as Dre was naked, he went for the scalding hot shower water to wash away anything that may have linked him to the crime.

After a refreshing shower, Dre tried to put his thoughts back on his usual business. He called his bookie, who handled his bets and the fighting events he was usually interested in.

The phone rang as Dre waited patiently on his bookie. "Yeah, my 75 lb. Red boy, $15 doggy bones. You got anybody who can match his weight for that kind of money the day after tomorrow?"

The man on the other end gave a tight-lipped whistle before saying, "Boy, that's a pretty penny. You must have faith in that one, because you never go over a rubber glove." He continued, "I say, it's your dough, so it's definitely your show. Same as always, I geta $1,000 off every 10 and everybody's pat down before they enter the establishment. But anyways, you've already won enough money here to know that."

Randy, his bookie, paused, Dre could hear the turning of a rolodex. Then he returned, "Here we are. Got a ranch in San Jose who's got a 75 pounder that he swears drags barrels of hay."

Dre chuckled at what he'd just heard. "The card says no less than 10 and no more than 25. The card says he put it in his résumé less than a week ago."

The bookie finished in his Midwest timbre, almost managing to sound dubious. "I'll call you back before the night ends if possible, but I hope that puppy of yours is ready to go the distance, Dre. I know you got some killers on leashes, but I've heard a little something about this Rancher fellow, something about him raising baby lions. I'll call you back with the details partner."

Dre hung up his cellphone with Randy and headed back into the garage, all the while pondering on the information Randy provided him. He fired up another blunt as he sat in his lawn chair.

Taking a brief moment to watch Charles and Frank's tactics on approaching how they would hoist and remove the motor, Dre handed Charles the weed and told him he would be right back.

"You can stay and help if you want, a little oil and grease may make a better man out of you."

Dre looked over his shoulder grinning, "Nah, Imma let y'all handle that. The ladies say my chest is too hairy as it is."

Charles laughed as Dre disappeared around the side of the house, not five minutes later. "Randy talk to me, bud, tell me it's good?"

Randy exhaled the toxic fumes from what had to have been a Marlboro light. "We're on countdown like a NASA spaceship. Showdown Monday at 6 p.m., be here an hour early for the wash down and inspection. Wire your two-thousand security deposit, if you forfeit, the money goes to the opponent and vice versa. See you Monday at sundown." The dropped signal told Dre that Randy had disconnected his call.

Standing in front of Zeus's cage, Dre pulled out a piece of sirloin steak that was raw and bloody. The sirloin came into view, its stench activated their senses, tempers flared and made them antsy, their jaws clamping wildly at air as the prize passed their cages in plain sight. Zeus is where Dre stopped.

He was gnawing at his gate with such determination, that his gums left red blotches spotting across his fence.

Opening the floor trap, Dre tossed the bloody steak inside as Zeus chewed viciously while regarding his master. He had known that he had been called on. So now that he had received one more blood-soaked delicacy before he went into battle, he was ready. All of them had known, it was the same ritual replicated that they had seen on numerous occasions. First you eat blood, and then you draw blood, the routine was set and Zeus was now ready.

One more call to make, then everything will be handled, Dre said to himself, as the phone rang lightly.

"Hey, Dre my friend, how's it going?" The deep Hispanic base tone of the voice did not match the gaunt, 5-foot 4-inch man who answered it, and it made Dre smile every time.

"It's going good, Tony, better than ever." Dre hesitated for a moment allowing Tony to catch his significant meaning. "I'll be upstream doing my usual fishing in a few days."

Tony cut in on cue. "I'll be glad to see you my friend, let's have a drink then. Same place, no?"

Tony was crafty, Dre thought to himself before saying, "Yes Tony, and tell Carolyn and the kids I said hi."

Tony shot back cheerfully, "Will do. See you soon my friend. Take care."

That was all that needed to be conveyed as both phones went dead.

Dre thought the best had been handled, and figured his agenda was clear for Sunday. He planned to drop the Chevy at the paint shop, shoot some dice, and then catch up on his night top. That's what Yoshi and Dre had always called *fellatio*.

Not basking in Yoshi's memory for a minute too long—*why should I?*—Dre thought It was his time to shine, and boy was he ever ready for the spotlight.

😈 *Sad to say, but that almighty dollar that Dre had anticipated to flow so freely, is about to start depleting almost right before his very eyes. Lol.* 😈

48 HOURS LATER . . .

"Charles! What the fuck is this?" Dre asked.

Charles took a taste of the white grainy half hard block of cut open cocaine that sat in the middle of a kitchen table.

"Whatever that shit is," Charles stated after he had rubbed the rest of the substance that was on his fingers into his pants leg, "It ain't what you thought you were spending thirty grand on."

As soon as Charles had finished, the phone was answered.

"Dre, my compadre. How's it going my friend?" Either Tony was playing dumb or thing's had went bad somewhere amongst his ranks.

Catching himself before he'd recklessly said something he would regret, Dre cleared his throat, took a deep breath, and said, "Tony, have I done anything today or prior that could have caused our friendship to go bad?"

Hearing what sounded like accusation, tension and a raised tone, Tony told whoever was in his company to give him a minute. Then he returned, "Dre, we have had a very lucrative friendship for some time now. Which, I believe, neither of us would risk jeopardizing. So, why would you assume there to be something unsatisfactory between us? Is that the impression you received today at the bar?"

So, it was a fuckup on his end, Dre thought, and the pressure that escaped Dre's chest once he exhaled was close to a drowning victim being resuscitated.

Of course, he and Tony never *really* met for drinks or even much less laid eyes on each other that day. Wherever Dre called for drinks, Tony would automatically dispatch one of his employees, and like always, that would be their rendezvous point. Dre would always go to the bar at the appropriate hour and have a few drinks, and shortly thereafter one of Tony's mule friend's or cousins-in-law who could use the cash and had the time would show up with his product.

"Well now, Tony, I didn't perceive anything was wrong at the bar, but when I got home and was able to sit down and dissect our conversations. It was apparent that things were not right."

Again, Tony went mute. The dope was fake, you fucked up dick head, is what Dre's mind was screaming, but he managed to keep his mouth shut while Tony carefully appraised Dre's words. Always the businessman, he came back on the line with lull words for Dre's ear.

"I am sorry if the message I tried to convey did not come across to you properly my friend. I've been having unfortunate household issues lately." So, it was a thief in Tony's organization, Dre thought to himself, he kept his ears open as Tony continued. "But I believe your call has shed the spotlight on my family's latent issues. You've given me a solution to my terminal problems. Thank you, friend."

Somebody's ass was grass, Dre thought to himself this time. "I will be coming that way before the week has ended."

Dre had severed Tony's train of thought by interrupting, he understood what Tony was saying loud and clear, "And this time it is I who will buy the drinks when you arrive."

Tony's voice held glee that showed he was more than happy to sterilize this shitty situation, "Thank you for being so civil with my carelessness. You are a good friend, see you soon." They both hung up in unison.

"What did he say?" Charles asked, wondering about the conversation's outcome.

Dre was wrapping up the flawed cocaine as he spoke. "Motherfucker talking like he knows he's got to straighten his face up. He made it seem like somebody's been stealing from him for a while now and I just helped him find out who It was. He'll be down here sometime in the next three or four days. Which, when I really think about it, might be a good thing."

Charles nodded his approval before saying, "Tony's a fair Paisa and his word is law. So, at least if nothing, you're good on that end."

What Charles had said sent Dre's mind flashing back through the last two days. First, he'd spent 12 thousand getting his Chevy in order, then he lost another five thousand at Red's house on Sunday night before that Monday's dog fight and cocaine pick up. Zeus lost him fifteen grand and died in the process, but he fought like a champ. The "Rancher" had phoned Randy after that evening and reported that his red boy by the name of Lion, had died also, on their way home. Even the penicillin, adrenaline, and pain medication shots that the "Rancher" administered to Lion only sustained his life for an hour. Now, the 32 he had spent on what he thought was booger cocaine sugar, turned out to be booger cocaine without the sugar coca. Dre was over 60 thousand dollars in the hole, and more than pissed about it.

"Well," Dre began as Charles poured two shots of Patrón® and handed Dre his blunt, "I guess It can't get any worse." They clicked their shot glasses together and said, "Here's to shit getting better."

Then they threw their heads back and swallowed their liquor, both of their glasses banging hard and echoing against the countertop.

"Ha-ha, you can't bite the hand that feeds you and think everything is just going to be peachy keen. You can't kill off the people who have been responsible for your pathetic livelihood behind some pointless hate-filled reason and think you're going to be done with me.

My father and yours truly, are the autocrats around here, you, simply wait to fulfill my wishes, then you wait on the alms to come. And that's if I decide to throw you scavengers anything at all.

Don't you get it, or should I say, don't Dre get it?

When he crossed his own flesh and blood for my party 😜 green, was the moment I could care less if he lived or died, and that's when I became his utmost sanctity. That's when he became my expendable vanguard. The authority and governing of his own life was handed over to me the second he gave in to my correction, but this fool thinks it can't get any worse.

LOL! Sorry ole buddy Dre, but It don't work like that. And little does he know, it can get worse, and I think it's time to show Dre just how much worse it can get. 😈

Every minute, of every hour, since Dre had spoken to Tony almost two days ago was pure torment. He had sat in his home depriving himself of the outside world with his cell phone in one hand and the quarter of cocaine he had been heavily snorting from in the other. He was pacing back and forth like a worried parent over their missing child.

Dre's subconscious was picking at him all the while, convincing him that Tony was ridiculing him for his gullibility. The only thing that kept him from feeling duped, was the boost that revisited him every time he inhaled a line of *white girl*. He had also been counting his money so often that paper cuts started to turn his fingers a bit raw.

Sunday night Dre had pulled his dough from that hidden trap door in Knockout's doghouse. Figuring that if Zeus did somehow lose, he would be short on the currency he needed to purchase the whole kilo.

Too many mishaps had occurred like a chain of falling dominoes since, and Dre had become too busy and complacent with the idea that his money was safe where it was. Stepping into a pair of 501 Levi's and a white T-Shirt, Dre grabbed his Dodgers ball cap just before sliding into Gucci flip flops. Pushing the 5 grams of powder into the miniature pants pocket, he gathered up his keys and a half ounce of weed. Then, he was on his way.

"If anybody stops by, call me. I've got to get out of this house to get my head right. This waiting shit is driving me crazy," was all Dre had relayed to Charles as he pulled out his garage, leaving Charles sitting in a lawn chair on the porch smoking a Camel cigarette.

Driving like a turtle through his neighborhood, Dre was almost tempted to go back to Red's to shoot some more dice. But as fast as that notion had arisen it had subsided, recollecting on how bad he'd lost just days ago at one of Red's daily dice games.

Dipping his pinky nail in his tiny cocaine bag, Dre pulled up to the neighborhood liquor store in pursuit of blunts and a bottle of Remy. Taking notice of the few teenagers loitering between the beauty supply shop and the liquor store, Dre recognized amongst the young brothers one he'd known.

"Ain't you Patricia's son?"

The kid nodded but didn't attempt to advance into a private conversation as Dre had anticipated he would. Stepping from his car and into the store, Dre couldn't help but to reminisce on the woman who was like a mother to him. As an adolescent, if it was food, clothes, or shelter that Dre needed, Patricia would do more than her best. Or'leana and Patricia were close friends before everything had transpired, back then, Dre had even had a crush on Patricia's oldest daughter growing up, but of course, Dre was too repugnant to be anybody's boyfriend back then.

Exiting his neighborhood liquor store with his bag in hand, Dre sat in his car with his window down with his music playing low.

"Hey Tonka!"

Dre half shouted in the direction of the still loitering teens, but only one of the young men knew exactly to whom Dre was referring, and as everyone else looked to and from each other cluelessly. The same young man Dre had previously spoken to made his way over to see what he had wanted.

Leaning down into Dre's window so they were eye to eye, the curly head teenager asked, "What's up big bro? "

The kid's skepticism subconsciously revealed itself in his uncontrolled side to side rocking, "Calm down, my dude. I'm a friend of your mothers, my name is Dre. You might not remember me."

Dre stuck his hand out sensing the younger brother's weariness, Tonka stuck his hand out to shake Dre's but countered with a lie.

"Naw, I'd be lying if I said I knew who you were." Dre nodded his head in slight disappointment before pushing the conversation forward. "So they still call you Tonka, huh?"

Dre smiled as he asked, which made the kid a bit embarrassed as he glanced over his shoulder at his peers before answering. "Only a few."

"So, how's Juicy?"

At the mention of his sister's name, the young man's eyes grew wide, showing Dre both surprise and protection. Dre laughed aloud as the youth thought over how to best answer Dre's question.

"It's not like that kid. Your sister and I are just old friends is all." Dre dug into his bag and handed the youth a few blunts, then he dug into a sandwich bag he had hidden in the car's center console and handed the young brother a few grams of weed. The young man's face showed just how elated he truly was.

"Good looking, at least now I won't be so stressed the fuck out," the youngster joked as he waved the $10 bag of stress weed he had bagged and intended to sell.

"One time! "

Someone shouted just as the blaring siren's seemed to surround them from every possible exit. Everyone who could, ran for their freedom, but Dre was already boxed in by two unmarked undercover police cars, and the officers did not hesitate to jump from their cars and draw their weapons, giving him the impression that they'd rather shoot than make an arrest.

"Stick both your hands out the window," the undercover policeman yelled through his microphone.

No sooner than Dre had done as instructed, his cell phone began to buzz with an incoming call, "Ain't this a bitch," he muttered under his breath.

There was only one reason why Charles was calling, Tony had sent someone to deliver his product, and Dre was not in a position to receive it.

"With your right hand, reach across your body and open the door from the outside. Then slowly step out of the car with your back to me!"

The John Wayne look-alike roared over his car's loudspeaker for the second time. And once the officer's had Dre apprehended, they went through the extremities of three car searches, then two body searches, before hauling Dre in the rear of their narc car with two pending charges.

Possession of narcotics and possession of a firearm. Not only did the officer find Dre's three grams of cocaine, but he also managed to confiscate the compact 9mm Dre had stashed in his car's pop off door panel. He needed his phone call, to get bonded, then a good lawyer.

In just that order.

Leaning his head back into the hard plastic police car seat, Dre could only think to himself yet again, the same haunting feeling from earlier made the words slip from his lips without thought, "This shit can't get any worse!"

CHARLES. TONKA. DRE.

eah man! You just asked me that question ten different ways, you badgering me like I'm some punk star witness on somebody's jury stand!" Charles had become fretful and inpatient with Dre's hundred and one questions, being hammered with the repetitiveness was one of Charles' pet peeves.

"My bad, Cap. I just feel like my ship may be sinking like the S.S. Minnow. And if I don't hit land soon, I'ma end up lost somewhere at sea, like unfound pirate treasure. Look. I talked to my bond lady already, and she said if I bring her ten thousand, she can spring me like a W.W.E ring mat."

Dre hadn't come up for air because he wanted Charles to keep his ear tuned in. "Go through my dirty clothes hamper, the money will be there. The number to the bond company is on the refrigerator, ask for Candy, she'll walk you in, just let her know you're my Unc." His sighing indirectly told Charles just how overwhelmed with the bullshit he really was.

Charles could tell Dre's spirits were down, so he tried to give Dre some reassurance that he'd always have some insurance as long as he was around.

"Alright, baby boy. I'ma call Tony while I'm walking to the store to get the Mustang. Then I'ma take the money to Candy so they can free yo'ass. I'm something like, All-State baby boy, you just sit back and try not to eat too much County jail bologna or peanut butter, that shit will have you with more gas than Chevron and Texaco put together."

They both laughed which seemed to sedate Dre's nerves, even if only for a split moment.

"You just hold your head down for a few more minutes and we'll have you out of there in no time," Charles said, but there was no reply, just the dial tone from a disconnected caller.

Thinking it best to get going before laziness settled in his old bones, Charles rose from his chair gingerly, his big frame only permitting him limited short steps until his knee could tally his bulk. He moved through the house and into Dre's bedroom with measured strides.

Clothes were sprawled out all over Dre's room, except for the tiny hill of crumbled up designer pants and shirts that sat obliquely against the room's corner wall. It appeared to be Dre's dirty hamper even though there was no basket insight.

Average 24-year old, Charles thought to himself, "Totally opposed to cleanliness.

Charles then gave a smile to his parental judgement as he dug through the laundry that smelled more of compost than clothing. Once he reached the middle, he'd found exactly what he'd been looking for. Bracing himself along the side of Dre's headboard, his brain seemed to go black like a Las Vegas power outage. His fingers grew numb, and he started to sweat for the first time in life, like men his size typically do.

"Fifty thousand dollars!" Charles said, trying to get over the initial shock of what he was holding. "Fifty thousand dollars!"

The shock slowly departed, and the second time he said it, he gave in to the amazement of what lay firmly in his palm.

These kinds of puppets are the best of the absolute worst. They're like the jackals and vultures of my animal kingdom.

They don't possess the will to attack because they feel deprived. Such as the envious do!

They won't undermine other power pieces or even plot on the weaker marks, for the sake of thinking they owned it all, like the greedy picture, this world.

They're not predators who have come to feel the beauty they were given as a blessing, was also a horrid curse. Which is often the way of today's lust driven harlot and philanderer.

Their objective is not laced with a personal agenda to come out on top from the initial contact, they don't bait you in with acts of trust, that's the mechanics of the prideful betrayer.

Nor are they against all odds. They don't possess interior resentment or the willingness to destroy because of their bitter heartlessness. That could only be the wrath of a hater's hatred.

Those five deadly sins can be commended. They can even be praised by my father for the calamity they evoke. Those five deadly sins require you to eventually do the deed and show your true colors. And We like that.

But see, the deadly sin of sloth has no color, it takes on no shape, it even has no reflection that can be gauged in the eye's, tongue, or actions. They appear indifferent to it all, so as not to expose their indifference from it all.

Now Charles . . . hmmm . . . I've had this serpent slithering backwards on his back since the dinosaur days. And he's still the same round-faced Doe boy begging for change, just like when he was a kid. The same Charles who convinced the people at the disability office that he was a diabetic hemophiliac. Which was also a lie and a play for him to sit on his lazy ass. That was when Charles was in his mid-thirties.

Hell, the only reason I allowed him to touch the little money I'd privileged him to in the 1980's was because at the time his 'the white man owe me' mentality, contributed to the dynamics of furthering the oppressed state of the African American community. With my junior scout Ronald Reagan supplying the nation, and slugs like Charles, whose only plight in life was to sit on their ass, is what made the 1980's a perfect place for a demon dollar like me to shine. I simply used people like Charles's lack of education and natural ability throughout the decade to spread epidemic amongst the black and brown communities. You think I really cared if a few self-indulgent mothafuckas came out of the ghetto with a few messily million . . . .naw . . . It didn't make one bit of difference. Especially when I could always come back and pluck them off like "Sue Lin" does your girlfriend's excess upper lip hair.

See . . . 99% of those people who were moving drugs and had copious collateral during that time, I made certain they fell victim to the very master they were pushing. Charles tried not to be a crack statistic like so many had during that time. So instead, my father just substituted cocaine for far more harmful vices, and Charles no doubt took to them like a fish to water.

Now even though money, dollars, me, is the stump of it all, even though I'm the biggest entity, my father has ever sent to turn man against man! But please, don't get it twisted. My father also has other tools that he's coerced man into creating for man's own demise. Such as drugs, gambling, and other carnal desires.

And sadly, for most, If these three results are one in the same, you'll be vexed beyond damnation. Something like our good old friend of indolence named Charles, or as I like to call him, the slithering sloth.

"On a serious one though, Tonka," J.T and Reese both cackled at their friend as he leaned over the pool table, Tonka managed to throw them an askant look that displayed his fretful dislike for his family nickname, a nickname that they'd now began flinging in his face at every leisure opportunity. "Ain't that the old head from earlier at the liquor store who came to pick Dre's Mustang up?" Reese asked.

The three teens watched as the hulky older man teetered his way through the dimly lit smoke fogged room before finding a set at the bar. And for the next hour as the trio subtly kept their eyes on the big fellow, who only seemed to be drinking a bit of alcohol while chatting with the bartender named Jeff. Tonka could tell that whenever the bulky man wasn't logged in a discussion, his attention was locked on a small piece of paper he left lying on the wooden bar top. Alternating from his paper to the ESPN network the huge older man after an hour's time, gave himself a satiate smile, just before calling over the bartender as he fumbled restlessly in his pocket.

And that's when it hit Tonka like a kid batting at a piñata, "He's placing bets," Tonka mumbled to no one at all.

Betting was a nightly thing at the bar, so it was really nothing unordinary. But the oddity of it wasn't that one of the locals had come in to place a bet. What made this situation so intriguing to Tonka was not only the amount of money in which the bet was placed, but the swagger the bulky man continued to possess after counting out $2,000 in one hundred bills. As if the habitual affair of possibly losing 2,000 bucks in one day had been a routine thing in his life, all his life.

Finally emerging from the back room, Jeff gave the carbon copy receipt to the older black man who looked like a Sumo wrestler. The old man seemed to be a bit less antsy as he sat relaxed and sipped on a drink that was relatively dark.

About two minutes later, the co-owner, Max, stepped from his back-room which he only did if there was big money on the line or, if the club was having a problem.

"Capone. My guy," Max said boisterously as he smiled before he took a seat next to the old head at the bar. As they made small talk, Max waved the bag he held between his index and middle finger slightly around in the older man's face. Eyeing it wantonly, Cap tossed a small mound of bills on the counter in front of Max, who then tossed the bag onto the bar top in front of its purchaser. A few more words were exchanged between the two before Max patted the older man on his back, then rose to leave.

"They're only associates. Max don't fuck with washed up junkies," Tonka again spoke aloud to no one at all.

Rising from his stool, the old man seemed to flounder a few steps on his way to the front door, then he was gone. Tonka watched as he seesawed his way to Dre's Mustang before speeding out of the parking lot.

Instantly Tonka's brain began to work. He began to wonder why now that Dre had gone to jail, the man who looked as if he was Dre's father was driving around gambling away his money and, apparently also using some type of hard drugs. As Tonka mulled it over further in his mind, he'd also figured Dre had caught a serious case that day.

"Everybody In the hood knows you're balling. But I know two things about you, Dre, that most people don't and now that you're in jail and your flunky riding around spending up all your money. I think it's no better time than the present."

An epiphany seemed to strike him, like a hard metal object falling unseen from the sky would strike anything in its path. It came to him like a downloaded message that only his encrypted brain could decode, and without question Tonka was certain that this was how he would pay his debt to his family like he'd secretly promised. Tonka felt it in his spirit, that his great god had sent him a sign that this was the right way, and he'd be damned if he didn't take it, there was too much at stake for him not to..

****

The fire that burned the unfit chemicals from the once white chalky but now brown milky liquid, always made Charles's stomach churn every time he backslid back into his addictions. Filling his syringe and making sure no air remained in the vile, Charles set the loaded stick on the table as his eyes lay glued to the TV.

"Come on, baby." Charles coached the team on the TV that he had wanted to see victorious. "It's only a 35 yard chip shot, in your dome. You do this every day. Come on, baby."

He undid his belt and began wrapping it tightly in the center section of his elbow crease. At six to one odds, if Dallas made this field goal and won the game, he would be 12 grand richer.

Concentrating on the ball after it left the kicker's foot, Charles watched it begin to sail end-over-end upon its initial take off. Midway it seemed to be aligned to split the uprights directly down the seam. But the more it seemed to climb the more it veered from its trajectory.

It was wide right. The kicker had missed. And Charles instantly turned raucous.

"You punk son of a bitch! You no good, overpaid, weak ass bum!" He yelled at the TV. Then, sinking back into the sofa he picked up the needle and inserted it under his skin. The grand celebration was set regardless of if he had lost or not. He had made his decision at the bar during pregame, that if he'd won, that's how he'd party. And if he lost, getting high would be his pick me up.

"No harm, no foul," Charles murmured as his body began to slouch forward. Within minutes, he had hit the floor face first, and as he did so, he vomited, defecated, and passed out all at once.

****

Awaking that next morning with a terrible headache and vomit dried on the carpet and against his cheek, he smelled like week old grass clippings and knew that he was going to have to take a long shower.

The phone was buzzing like swarms of bees that began to buzz between his ears, but the friction was not as unbearable as at first. On second thought, the buzzing was more annoying than painful. Charles looked to his left at the floor where his cell phone jittered in intervals. Picking up his phone and pressing the talk button, Charles put his arm on the sofa, then catapulted himself to a sitting posture.

"What's up my guy?" Charles asked while he centered himself.

"I can't call it Unc," Dre uttered with hostility and a ping of disappointment. "I was supposed to be out this morning but they're claiming there's a hold on me for an assault from 2011. That shit is super bogus. They dropped that case months after it happened." Dre was talking faster than a Twista rap verse before he sighed.

"So, when are you on the calendar?" Charles asked, knowing that the issue was minor, but none the least, only something the courts could resolve.

"In a week." Dre fell silent at his own words, seemingly subdued by what he had just heard himself say.

Charles sat there pensively while holding the phone, figuring the best he could do in this predicament was to reassure Dre that he had ample support.

"Look," Charles started, "It's just the week. At least you know your bond has already been handled and as soon as you hit the court line, you'll be home. Look around." Charles was about to say something he was hoping Dre would take heed. "There's a lot of dudes standing beside you in that county jail who will never touch the free world again. Count your blessing, my boy, and be man enough to let the babies cry."

Charles could tell Dre was musing over all that he had said.

After what had to be a calming minute, Dre came back to the line with more spark in his tone. "You know what cap, that's thick loogie spit. A lot of these brothers ain't gone never hit them streets again." Dre had now sounded undaunted. "My little situation is good. I ain't got no words."

Charles felt good for making Dre see the broader side of things, but bad because nausea had his stomach in tight knitted knots.

"All right, well look, it's 6:30 in the morning and my stomach is bubbling like some KFC grease. You hold your head up my dude. Call me back later," Charles said.

Dre gave a light chuckle at his reason for his dismissal as he replied, "Don't clog up my toilet pipes."

Charles responded quickly, "Drop one, flush one, baby boy. You know how it goes."

Dre laughed and then said in summation, "Alright Cap, hold yo head, 100." Then the line went dead.

Making sure to grab his drug paraphernalia from the table while in a rush to the bathroom, Charles shimmied free from his clothes, adjusting the shower water, and took a seat inside the tub.

Setting his utensils on the toilet stool which was bolted to the floor just at arm's reach from where he'd sat in the shower, he began to perform the process of cooking his dog food.

His body during it craved to have its viral venom crawling through his system, which would wane the nausea and loosen the knots—Charles knew from experience.

Once the syringe was loaded, he roughly snatched his belt from the floor and tied himself off. Plunging the needle's point about a half inch into his veins, he then eased the perilous dependency that he had once rehabbed from, into his bloodstream with slow fondness. Again, his mind and body levitated to a gratifying dimension. Again, his head dropped as if his neck muscles were elastic bands that possessed no tautness, and again, his internal organs could not be restrained.

This time, he drooled as he grinned all while his bowels ran from his body. He thought to himself, 'old junky wisdom. Can't shit yourself if you're using it when you're in the shower.' That's when his consciousness faded and he began to doze off, as the belt and the needle remained dangling from their once lost, but now found again home.

CHARLES. TONKA. DRE.

onka was stooped down, between the Ray's barber shop and the pool parlor. He was sitting in a lawn chair that was hidden by the darkness and the lack of parking lot lighting. All of Tonka's customers had known this was one of his late-night sell spots. Everyone who was a customer had known that Tonka and his .357 always sagged deep in the intimidating unseen night. He was lurking somewhere deep in the shadows, waiting to make a sale as always.

Word had spread behind two unsuccessful robbery attempts that Tonka would dispel the conflict just as fast as he would sell a tenth of crystal.

"Business as usual," he said quietly to himself, after making a $20 sale and watching the crystal head scurry into the clammy, still night. Taking a swig of his Patrón ® to warm his blood, Tonka nearly choked in mid swallow at what he had looked up to witness.

"What the fuck is he doing here again?" Tonka said quietly as he stepped back slowly, not wanting to arouse any attention.

Scanning the scene, he saw Charles waddling with eagerness from the Mustang into the pool parlor, seemingly unaware of the eye's fixed on his every movement, as his feet moved in a rush to his objective. Just as quickly as he had dipped inside, the big fella casually exited. Even though he had a tad more reserve as he left, Tonka still noticed his uneasiness quite easily. Once the Mustang damn near fishtailed out of the parking lot, Tonka became full of urgent inquiries that he needed answers to. In his favor, he had known exactly just the right source to go to.

"Yo, Big Jeff?" Tonka said confidently, as he leaned over the bar just enough to make himself conspicuous through the onslaught of waiting customers. It was 11:00 p.m., on a Friday night, and the pool hall was crowded as usual. Jeff moseyed over while drying his hands on his apron, his face showing a joking mockery as he began to speak.

"I thought I pay you every week to sit outside and watch the pool hall, yet every time I look around, you're sitting in that same stool watching me." Every time Tonka was off his post, his older cousin, Jeff would say something of the sort just to make him aware of every time he was out of pocket.

"I got two questions," Jeff leaned his weight on his hands that rested atop the bar, then gave Tonka a look that implied that he should get on with his asking. "Who's the big fucker that's been coming around the last two days, and what's he about?"

Jeff gave a look of mild concern as if tending to his barkeep was more important to him than worrying about his little cousin's need for information.

"His name is Capone. He's a throwback old head. He's been around here all his life," Jeff answered.

Filling Tonka in while he made the nearest customer a double of Grey Goose, he continued, "He had a little crack money back in the late 80s but lost that shit when he started using heroin, heavy. He's been one of Max's consumers since I can remember. I thought he'd kicked that shit, but I guess he ran into some money because he's back exercising his downfalls." Jeff shrugged his shoulders and turned to go back down the bar to take care of his customer's thirst.

Stepping back into the brisk night air, Tonka went back to his post, pondering what he had heard, and affirming he was barking up the right tree and that the tree was also ripe for the picking.

****

A barking dog and the blaring 11 a.m. weekday kitchen alarm clock snapped Charles from his coma. He hoisted his sluggish bulky frame to his feet then stumbled over to the kitchen clock and slammed his hammer-like fist into it and immediately the sound vanished into thin air.

Shifting his weight on the countertop to veer over his shoulder at last night's indecency, Charles then turned toward the sink to retch. Only a dry up heave responded to his contracting stomach muscles. That's when it dawned on Charles that he had yet to eat a thing in the past four days.

In fact, except for getting higher than Oprah Winfrey's credit score, and gambling as if he had Floyd Mayweather Jr. money, he couldn't recall much of anything.

Thinking to himself that he couldn't even recollect on how much money he had lost, is what sent Charles in a panicked half skip from the living room to Dre's dirty clothes pile. Digging frantically through Dre's dirty clothes, Charles was dumbfounded that in four days he had managed to spend 25 grand. Charles thought he was hallucinating even though he continuously blinked to make sure his eyes had not been playing tricks on him.

"This boy is going to kill me."

His own words beckoning him to realize the severity of his actions.

The way Charles saw it, he had any of four options. Turn and run for the hills. Try to do something to get the money back, illegal. Taking 5 grand of the remaining 15 grand and pray he hit a winning ticket. Or face the music, as you should when you make a mistake. After a short time of weighing all the variables, Charles elected at that moment that he would pursue all four possibilities.

He laid out his plan, wishing all the while if things didn't turn out to his liking, in the process, that the streets would take him from his misery.

"That way, my son won't have to," he said tersely out loud to himself.

I presume you have a better outlook on these indolent types now? Well, you should, because it's two of them to every one of those other five deadly characters I'll expose you to. Rambunctious Prix are spreading like Covid-19, and the worst thing about it for me, is these damn slothful sinners dwell outside the umbrella of my deity. Which means they're more than likely primarily vowed and dedicated to the pipe, or powder, or pills, and in this fat boy's case, the needle. These stagnant types are subordinates to my father's drug campaign first, then they subsist secondly under and in my terrain.

You've seen them numerous times, in fact, you got a few in your family. LOL. Tell me I'm lying?

Tell me you don't have loved one's who would rather have a pop, blast, or a drain, before they have some shelter and a decent meal.

Yeah, you're acquainted with their kind, and I despise them like a child despises unflavored cough syrup. No honor or self-worth I tell you, but they appear to be angles of fortitude. That is until they get ready to go on a binge, they're the most vanilla bean people in the world, until their habit allows them to be their true selves. It's like Dr. Jekyll and Mr. Hyde with these degenerates. One minute they've got your back like Allstate and the next minute they're shooting up more shit than a Rambo movie.

Just like fatso!

Now that he's fucked up the church's money, he wants to assemble some hair-brained ideas in hopes of redeeming all he'd lost. All I've got to say is, he'll be more upset than the Republicans who tried to fight Obama and the Senate over abolishing the Enhanced Integration Act, because I don't have eye water for him to wet his tongue if he was about to die of dehydration. Damn spineless pest wasn't born with enough courage to man up to his fuck ups. Lazy bastard doesn't have the guile in his DNA to make 25 grand out of a meager start.

Makes me wonder just what he's going to do? Oh, you too?

Well, how about I give you a clue? Slow as molasses and still as glue, beat a sloth will move fast if it's scared of you! 😈

Dawn had just broken through the seal of night, to spread itself like a curtain over the early skies in a soft blue blanket. Charles has risen about 20 minutes before daybreak, standing pensively in his kitchen as he watched his coffee pot percolate. He could only seem to prepare and stress over the very thing that had denied him a peaceful sleep for the past three nights.

****

For the last three days Tonka held a hawk's eye fixed on Dre's house and Charles' whereabouts. It was Wednesday. The day before something had nudged him to pull it off before it was too late. Something had warned Tonka that if he had not done it soon, that his opportunity would be lost for good. Guesstimating that his chances would be best during daybreak, turned out to be correct, and to Charles's benefit. They broke into Dre's home about 30 minutes prior to sunrise, and just as he suspected, not a peep of suspicion had been aroused. The bad thing was that they had been tearing that place up for the last 30 minutes and had not found a dime.

Tonka watched him pull out in the Mustang around 1a.m. in the morning. When Charles had not returned until 5 a.m., Tonka started blowing up J.T and Reese like he was a female in dire need to tell them she was pregnant. Unbeknownst, Charles had left his keys with his friend named Wild Al.

Al had always stayed around the corner. They were old partners who partook with the same drugs of choice. And when Tuesday night merged into a restless Wednesday morning, Charles decided a good shot of dope and some affable company from an old friend would take his mind off his current dramas.

Tonka never saw Charles stumble through the backyard side gate, he had no idea that he was in the back house unloosening the persistent nausea of his stomach into a flower bed at the very minute he was pre-warning his friends to keep in mind the possible danger. Rushing through Dre's belongings in a thorough fashion, Tonka had known that the intended reward could be great, but the risk of being caught red-handed held the promise of a disastrous chastising.

The closet, bed, dresser, TV, and even the carpet had been scrutinized thoroughly by Tonka. Even though his effort had so far left him empty-handed, something still seemed of a premeditated déjà vu, as if he had been pulled to that place and time, as if this very room itself was a crossroad.

It was as if Tonka's senses came equipped with a money detector and if he left Dre's room, the strength of the signal would grow faint. But when he stood within the room's four walls, the signal would go from rhythmic beats to a solid flatline sound.

Only the clothes that lay gross and filthy looking against the room's back corner wall or left to be inspected, and even though Tonka was appalled that he had to ransack Dre's piss-stained boxers. He reasoned with himself that he had come too far to leave any stone unturned. He moved sordid clothing articles to the side as he felt in pockets for anything of value.

Tonka's search had been suddenly abated by what he found. A stack of bills hide inside a dingy pair of slacks. Picking up the money and sliding into his cargo pants pocket, Tonka then with a newly found vigor, began to soar through the remaining clothing.

Nothing, Tonka thought to himself as excitement post-dated through his body as if he had popped a Molly.

"Think like Dre," he tersely told himself repeatedly as he reached up and hoisted one of Dre's hats that hung overhead from a small nail. There were at least 40 hats that hung high from the room's four walls, all held fast by an inch long nail. Removing the cap and placing it on his curly head, something heavy fell, from the cap's cup, landing solid against the room's floor.

Looking at his feet, a smile spread over Tonka's lips that seemed to stretch the edges of his mouth.

"You slick motherfucker," Tonka muttered as he bent down to retrieve a duplicate of the stacks he had just found in the clothing. Again, he pulled another ball cap from the nail it had been hooked to, and again a small bundle of money thudded softly as it fell to impact with the room's carpet. Stuffing the money into another cargo pocket, Tonka looked around the wall at the 40 something ball caps, the thought that invaded Tonka's mind seemed to loudly burst from his tonsils once he had overturned another hat and a replica of rubber banded bills descended to the earth surface yet again.

"Bingo," he said aloud so J.T and Reese could hear.

J.T was shouting excitedly, "How much is it?" as he appeared in the doorway of Dre's room. By then Reese stood in the doorway, beside J.T, just as Tonka was tossing the money over his shoulder. J.T. caught it, they both began to marvel at the money in sheer enthusiasm, slapping another hat from his position high above the wall, again a bundle of US currency fell. Tonka again pinched the doughy green paper. This time it was a Pittsburgh Steelers hat, and as before Tonka threw J.T. the stacks like a Drew Brees to Michael Colston touchdown pass. There was a startling sound of a sliding glass door that caused their body parts paralysis.

"What the fuck!"

Charles had grumbled with concern as he stepped through the mini-detector sliding glass door into the house. Closing the doors behind himself, Charles was immediately stupefied by the unkempt way the house had been turned over. All he could think was that Dre had returned and instantly went into a frantic uproar upon noticing that his money was amiss. It returned panic and queasiness to his stomach as he anticipated Dre in his worst possible state.

"Dre?" Charles's voice cracked as he called out with as much prowess as he could manage. And not until Charles began to walk through the kitchen did an oddly unnerving feeling take hold of his instincts and force his body and mind into defense mode. Cautiously moving through the living room, Charles rounded the corner toward the hallway when two crouched bodies ran past him as if they were NFL running backs breaking into the open field.

He leapt back in dismay as the two bodies rounded the corner and finally found their disordered way out the front door. Charles looked in the direction of their retreat while his heart pounded as if he himself was the winner of the Olympics 100-yard dash. Starring at the backs of the two fleeing burglars, something again grabbed ahold of his now heightened sense of excessively beating heart toward the third intruder, whom in seconds time he would be face to face with.

Checking to either side of him for an object that could possibly help to mangle this nightcrawler only awarded the flogger the advantage. Charles was still glancing to his left for some form of weapon to fight with. Then Tonka came into his view and tried to sprint past the wall where the gigantic man stood.

Tonka almost squeezed completely past Charles before his handy reflex shot out a vise-grip to capture a handful of Tonka's hooded sweater. Charles was in a George Foreman wind-up as he spun Tonka in a full circle to face him. But Charles yielded his punch as Tonka spun and produced a chunky dispute closer, with a 2-inch barrel.

"You look like you've got a few more years left in you, Cap," Tonka said with a tough look as he peered down the length of his arm into Charles's face, the tip of his gun's steel almost touching Charles's chin.

"So, I'll be leaving so you can stay breathing. Right?" The Tom Cruise question was more of a confirmation of how this episode between the two of them would definitely unfold.

Charles never blinked, only trained his eyes to the circumference that held the reddish copper bullet that could have taken his life. Tonka slowly began to take steps backwards as Charles's vision seemed to go from tunnel to a broad expansion. His lungs finally forced him to inhale fresh air.

Charles could now see the culprit with an unmistakable recognition. Then, Tonka turned and ran, leaving only the pullover rain cap from his hoodie flailing in the wind behind him.

Even though his legs felt wobbly and rubbery, like an astronaut who had been in space but was now nagged by gravity, Charles could only feel relief at the fact that he was still alive. In his mind, which was merely a warning that had come before destruction, a warning that made him consider the damage his own son may incorporate once he found his home in shambles. Not to mention the thousands of dollars that were now unaccounted for. The perilous predicament that Charles had just encountered, could not be ignored. It was more or less a sign that left him with the inclination to submit his resignation. His shame gave him not the intuition, but the premonition, that Dre would pull the trigger, and that left Charles helpless.

It took all of 40 minutes for Charles to pack his things, load them neatly into Dre's Mustang, and leave a missive in relation to his unannounced departure. Then, he burned rubber out of the driveway like he had just won the Talladega Speedway, all the while, wishing he could recant his mistakes and wishing the best for his one and only son.

Scared of you. LOL. A sloth will move fast if it's scared of you! There's the sloth's true repertoire ladies and gentlemen. If they can't contrive a way to rescue themselves from their self-inflicted calamity or, they can't find cause to grant themselves reprieve for their crafty behaviors, then they flight. As cowardice tend to do, whenever the outcome doesn't appear to be promising for them.

These despicable people or fungus who live to monopolize on my unsuspecting understudies. But more than most likely, these types usually die lonely. Their shenanigans usually cost them family ties and bonds with close friends. These deficient maniacs will bite the hand that feeds them for one good night of getting high. Then their disgraceful actions apply so much guilt to their own conscience that they can't face the ones they have victimized.

It's a dog-eat-dog world my boy, can't you see? The gank, the beat, the swindle, the come up, and even the get over seems to be the world's mindstate when the mighty dollar bill is involved. Fathers cross mothers, mothers play sons, sons backstab brothers, and the unprecedented attempts to acquire wealth have no liable limitation.

One in a million abdicate against me, and only the real elite supersede my kingship to bask in their life's true purpose. But I pity those who waste their time seeking life's real meaning when I'm the most laudable thing known to man. I am the only true suzerain that should be sought out all the hours of your days.

I am who your knees should touch the ground and worship to, for what better master Master should you call to Collegiate your pointless existence to, than I?

Everyone Is brainwashed by the power of my dollar, why should you be alone? You won't get anywhere trying to refute your need for me?

Those who don't abide by my regime are homeless, jobless, always in debt, not to mention, seem to always lack simple stability. Don't you agree?

Why not join my squad? I'm the way to go, just ask family and friends if I'm the first beloved in their lives? And if they lie and dispute in claims that I'm not their first beloved. Then I'm definitely their mistress. And to me, surely, they're addicted. Don't you agree?

So, whenever you're ready just come home kiddo, you haven't been neglected or disregarded in the least.

Just come home, we're here waiting with open arms, and lots and lots of cold hard cash. 😼

Dre, exultantly shouted to release his pent-up aggression into the sharp coolness of the winter morning, as he began his journey with eager strides. He was determined to put as much distance between himself and the LA County Jail as possible. With every large step that carried him away from the previous week's confinement, inadvertent thoughts invaded his mind because the stress of his short incarceration was now bombarding his mind.

Something was unraveling Dre more and more as he dialed his uncle's number, and it went straight to voicemail. It had done this every time he had tried to call in the last few days. Charles' disappearance had made him worried, but now that he was back on the other side of the fence, his apprehensions on his uncle's whereabouts left him feeling downright bamboozled. Dre's next call on his phone's contact list was his child's mother—Theresa.

"Boy, it's six in the morning. Your son is at his grandmother's and I'm getting ready for work. What'd you want?" Theresa sounded agitated and, in a rush, but Dre was not concerned with her attitude or engagements, he was in need of a ride home and in an anxious hurry to get it.

"Why don't you come through and bring me some of those goodies. I was remembering how you used to love to get you some first thing in the a.m. before work. I got another *Kadar* in me right now if you got nine months to spare."

Dre snickered under his breath knowing he would get shot down. He knew that Theresa was not casually promiscuous by any means. She was the most modestly preserved woman that Dre had ever known. She was his idea of what a real woman is.

"Dre," Theresa said, "I'm hanging up right now, bye." Leaving her ear to the receiver a split-second longer, giving him a chance to extract from his childishness and approach her with the real nature of his call.

"lght lght. Look hottie, I'm up the street from the county jail. I just did a little over two weeks for some off-the-wall bullshit. I'm out here looking homeless. Can you come pick your baby daddy up please?"

Theresa sighed with contempt. "In contrast to everybody you know, I have an honest job, Dre, one that requires me to arrive every day, on time, or I could be fired. Where's Charlie?"

Theresa was furious by Dre's unexpected intrusion on her daily program. He knew she would vent her discontent, but he had also known her difficult rejections would soon fade to his liking.

"Shit's been crazy. I've been blowing Charles up for days now and his phone's been sending me straight to the box."

The phone remained mute for a short time.

"Ughhh," Theresa snapped loudly. "I'll be there in twenty minutes." Then the line abruptly went dead.

Always punctual, Theresa pulled up exactly twenty minutes later. Dre was standing curbside and jumped in without delay. Theresa's black and honey-colored Lexus had looked to be in the same mint condition as the day he had helped her get it off the dealer's lot.

"You're taking me to work," Theresa told him immediately as she pulled away from the curb. They rolled in light chitter-chatter without tension like old lovers and good friends, flirting gradually as they often did out of retro habit.

"You look thicker than my grandma's cornbread with a pinch of butter in that skirt, let me find out you're sexing one of those goofies at work, and I'm going to kill you and kick his ass," Dre said as he tried to sound sincere, but he was only half serious.

"Your papers to this pussy have been revoked, big boy. So, if you want the right to be jealous, you better ring me up before somebody else does." As Theresa spoke, she ejected herself from the driver seat and out the car.

Dre was headed around to the driver's side.

"Be here at 3:30 p.m. Dre and don't have your buds riding in my car," Theresa pre-warned as she reached the telephone company's back door.

As he worthlessly mouthed 'I love you,' and a kiss that he had blown to her in the wind. Closing her eyes tightly and using her jaw muscles to clamp her lips firmly together, Theresa disappeared as the door closed behind her.

...40 MINUTES LATER...

Dre pulled into his driveway, revisited by his unraveled wit just as he had shifted the keys ignition off. Something was more incorrect than an Anglo-Saxon couple coming out the delivery room with a mixed newborn. Something forewarned him, giving him the incentive to expect the absolute worst, but even his mind's preparation turned into an absolute nothingness as he stood motionless in the doorway of his tattered home. Dre's eyes flared as he walked through the rubbish that was once his home. Furniture, electronics, appliances, paintings, and other interior decorations had been tossed about like a non-essential heap of trash.

Dreading the unavoidable, he went down the hallway and around the corner to his room. He saw his clothes flung about and every last hat scattered across the floor. The need to investigate was pointless, he had known without question that someone had robbed him blind. The tornado effect that was Dre's room left him defeated as he moved back into the living room. He slouched onto the couch, put his head back, and his eyes were affixed to the ceiling.

"Muthafuckin cross artist. Imma kill you when I catch you," Dre said as he pushed from the sofa, something inadvertently passed by Dre's vision as he stood to his feet. It was a letter that looked slightly rumpled. It was an epistle written in Charles's handwriting. Dre began reading in full curiosity.

What's good young one? Shitter then a field of fertilizer if you're reading this, I'm sure.

Well. I know you're probably asking yourself how you can find me, but I'm long gone, and probably won't be returning anytime soon.

I know you most likely won't believe this because frankly I was there, and I don't believe it still myself! But what I'm writing is all facts, it's up to you to take heed.

On Wednesday morning three young punks broke into the house. When I walked in on them in the act, this tall curly head little fuck drew his gun on me, and that's how they got away. The curly head one was Patricia's boy. I can't remember his name, but I'm more than certain that that was him. Needless to say, they got away with the money you had stashed in your dirty clothes. Lol, and by the way, invest in a dirty clothes hamper.

Sorry how bad luck struck you at a bad time, but I figured you killing me if you didn't believe me would have only made your situation worse . . . I mean, after all, it would be fucked up if you killed your father like that boy did to DMX in that movie we watched.

What was the name of that movie again, son—"Never Die Alone"!?

But yeah, you're my son! All the way down to that extra chin you're starting to develop. Lol.

Wish I could have told you. I should have told you. I actually thought about it many times, but with your mother being a rolling stone and you already thinking I was your uncle, I just thought It best not to confuse thing's any more than they already were.

Hope someday you can forgive me, son!

Keep your chin up my boy. And may the plots of their demise be the intervention for your success . . . Much love & Respect..

Cap AKA Your Pops.

Different emotions circulated and crashed into one another inside Dre like a bumper car ride at the local fair. He'd felt as though his heart had been broken and mended all in one complete gasp of air. But not wanting his feelings in limbo, he swallowed his emotions and filed them deep into his subconscious to be later digested.

Wanting to grant his father some form of reprieve solely on the pretense of what he'd just read, Dre's anger instinctively skirted from Charles to Tonka. Without giving a second thought to the authenticity of Charles's letter, Dre went to his room, changed his clothes then grabbed his 9mm and Los Angeles Dodgers baseball cap from off the floor. He headed out his front door, in pursuit of who his father had said robbed him.

TONKA. DRE. JUICY.

Fishing through the closet, Tonka finally found the cream box that was lined with burgundy edges. The tip of the box that held his great-great grandmother's Holy Bible was trimmed with gold and held a picture of Jesus in his natural color and ancient Hebrew garb. This was one of the sentimental antiques that had been passed from generation to generation.

It was also the resource his late mother used in one of her lively Bible studies amongst Juicy and himself. Removing the cover of the historical piece of family history, its familiarity jogged Tonka's memory the instant he laid his eyes on the all-white leather cover. He hoisted the large book that held such spiritually potent inscriptions to his lap as he sat cross-legged on the floor. He looked over the labeled bookmarker that hung loosely from the Bible's inseam and over the purple trimming at the top of the page.

Tonka's pupils brightened just as his lips parted slightly, recalling vividly, a specific tutoring his mother scolded him concerning the ten commandments—thou shalt not steal. Shaking his head in contempt of himself at how he had adapted such a rebelliously impressionable outlook on life since his mother's accident.

Sweeping away the stringy pieces of coiled wood pulp that protected the book's vintage from one side, he then removed the stacks of money from his cargo shorts pockets and began to line the Bible casing. He placed the scented wood shards back throughout the box to conceal the money he had hidden, before he set the good book back in its snug position. Tonka then recapped the box before returning it to the spot it had occupied in the rear of the closet. Giving a vivacious grin at the way things had worked out, he turned out the room's light and shut the door behind himself.

A stricken post-puberty voice stopped Tonka in his tracks, "Oh what do we have here?" The inquiring little person looked devilishly big eyed at Tonka, standing stiff still yet delighted at what she was bearing witness to. Tonka tried to make light of it, but remained in his strong position with his younger sibling.

Tonka replied harshly, "You need to mind your business, Chick Chick." What was intended to be a threat was demoted by the child's sassy adolescence.

Rolling her eyes in defiance, as if his words held as much harm as the tiniest of gnats, Chick Chick responded with her hand on her hip and her lips in a pout, "I'm telling."

His urge to bend this pert little girl over his knee was almost irresistible, but Tonka knew that if he spanked her behind so she could not sit for a week, then there would be repercussions that were greater than the reward.

Instead, he decided to use the oldest political tactic known to government parties that enhanced them a step closer to their goals when all else failed—bribery.

"How about you keep your mouth shut?" Tonka began as he pulled a twenty-dollar bill from the inside of his cargo pocket. "And maybe get you a new CD or something?"

Chick Chick's eyes gleamed at the proposition she had been offered, and just like in politics, the powerful penny prevailed as always. He handed her the bill and she stuffed her hush money into her back pocket and ran away a happy camper.

Needing to make his getaway before he could be confronted like the grandparents did Kane in the movie 'Menace to Society,' Tonka headed briskly for the front door and began his journey. Towing his .357 in his coat pocket, he took to the streets, ready to buy himself a nice shiny thing or two, just like he'd seen Hood Starz and Ballers do on TV.

Another misunderstood youth who was gifted with enough intellectual capacity and physical skill to play his own way out of the slums and into anybody's Division 1A University. Another soul lost by its own misguided ambitions of wanting to soar in the skies of pecuniary values before its time. You impressionables always want what's already coming to you, but for some reason patience is their worst virtue. Though my father doesn't give a damn, it's perplexing and even a fraction disappointing to me to see a kid, such as this with decent upbringing, be led astray. True enough, my job is to claim souls and lead people astray, but when a gluttonous impressionable kid in a rut of a circumstance gets caught up in my money trap by technical default, it should be something mourned by the whole nation.

Of course, no one of importance cares what happens to the impoverished and middle-class masses. Why a teenage boy with such a promising future would risk robbing a convenience store for a hundred bucks doesn't matter, or why that 18-year-old girl is selling her body so she can buy Pampers® for her newborn is of no consequence when it comes to the uppity.

That's why I am allowed to roam and rein over all of you without any toil, because I keep the minions under lock and key. That's all the houses on the hills are really concerned with. And contrary to popular belief, no one's innocent. It's just a sad mishap that the insignificant ones have to fight a battle they have little chance to win. While others sunbathe on yachts and sip daiquiris without a worldly care. And you wonder why these impressionable gluttons want to taste a little bit of all the riches.

They've always been hungry and deprived. They don't know what it is to feast at the round table. So, they stuff themselves whenever they can.

What did you say? You're surprised to hear me talk like this? Well, like I told you when I first began this story, I'm not all bad!

But don't get me twisted. There's been plenty of occasions when I tried to consult with my father about how a great many of our followers are immature young adults who are simply charmed by the flamboyance we allow our temporary carriers to falsely flaunt. What our regal handler contends is that just like the rat, if those youths are enthralled by the sparkle of someone else's cheese, then they should be caught without sorrow in that very same rat's trap.

Tonka's turmoil is a product of the pressures of everyday worries, and the 'I want to be just like them' syndrome.

See, Tonka is the definition of the new glutton, but now-a-days we call them the impressionable. They want fruit from everyone's tree, but they themselves are unwilling to plant and grow for their own harvest. And we all know when your fascinations intertwine with your life's troubles and solutions are presented to your problems then shouldn't you shoot your best shot to better your quality of living?

Still not you, huh? Here you go again, with all that pompous bullshit!

Look, in life, we've got to do what we've got to do to survive. Right? Sometimes for the sake of excelling in this world we may have to compromise certain integrities, morals, and principles. Right?

There, he still did the wrong things for the right reasons, which is completely chivalrous, if you ask me. Too bad that in this life of askew karmas, the bad seems to have a way of catching up to you almost instantaneously. Making this the wishful cliché for everyone who makes good reasoning out of their wrongdoing in order to possess me. But there's always a plus to that two-sided coin. When the good from someone's work floats about unseen, to later arise as someone's deserved retribution, it's a formidable setback that leaves my father with pent-up rancor. So, the rewarded will feel our wrath, they will still genuflect from the terror we bring to their doorstep. Then we will be ungrudging, because the reward will be minimal for their lengthy price of reimbursement. 😈

The Fox Hills Mall on a Friday evening was oftentimes more like a Saturday night Chris Brown concert. Even In the thick of the winter season, young and middle-aged women sauntered about the Mall in small packs, keeping what appeared to be one eye open for the best holiday deals, while the other eye examined the grooming of their sexual counterparts.

The trio that was Tonka and his friends, J.T. and Reece, all sat in the food court receiving flippant admiration of the women who bypassed as they sat chewing avidly at their pizzas.

"All these boppers have been checking our portfolio all day," J.T. addressed them before taking a thirst-quenching gulp of his pink lemonade. "I got more listed numbers then the Yellow Pages."

"Buying new bags while I bag new bitches," Reese followed J.T.'s train of thought as he pulled out the new IPhone he'd just purchased. "I'm on like Steph Curry from the 3, I got like 9 numbers in 2 hours. Niggah these hoes been chosen like I'm contestant number one, two, and three." The trio laughed as J.T. and Reese gave one another the military salute from across the table to show respect for each other's egocentric antics. Even though Tonka joined in the laughter he was secretly annoyed by his friend's chauvinistic rhetoric, so he decided to put an end to their ridiculous buffoonery.

"I see y'all out here looking like y'all got that Rolls Royce money, like y'all got money trucks. I see my niggahs, all big bank Hank out the game!"

There was teasing mockery in the postponed exaggeration of Tonka's last words. Words that seemed to be completely overlooked by J.T. and Reese as the two continued smiling widely at the insult they obviously mistook for praise.

"But there's only two issues with that my dudes." Tonka spoke as If he was about to reveal some mystical inscription that had been stowed away in some holy shrine for thousands of years. J.T. and Reese looked flummoxed by what the problem was Tonka was referring to. "One. Niggah we don't just have 'throw-it-in-the-bag' money!"

Tonka made It apparent in the dramatic way he spoke so they now clearly understood they were lost in a mirage of being ballers. "This pee-wee money . . . I've got 8 thousand after the 2 racks I just spent. Bro, you got niggas out here spending 8 racks on rim and paint."

They peered over the table at Tonka all while musing over the reality of what he was saying. He'd stolen their attention, and that was all he'd needed.

"And secondly," Tonka threw up two fingers in a peace sign fashion, "these curvy women aren't choosing on us because our charisma Is a perfect 10!"

J.T. seemed to take light offense at the fact his closest road dog just informed him that his swag was not responsible for the ladies sudden paramour Interest.

"So, if it ain't for my rugged good looks, then why are these birds landing on me like I'm the only telephone line in the city?" asked J.T.

Again, "Dumb and Dumber" clapped one another before saluting the air.

Tonka was agitated then said, "These ain't Hefty Duty trash bags we got piled around us folks. Birds only land for two reasons, to rest and to eat. Right now, we definitely look like bread to these L.A pigeons."

He leaned back as he checked his surroundings before saying, "Just look. Every woman that walks through the food court smiles at us or bats her fake eyelashes in our direction. I bet a hundred bucks to a bucket of carbon dioxide, she checks these bags either before or right after she acts faintly persuaded by your suave good looks."

J.T. and Reese gazed around to see if Tonka's prognostication was accurate. And sure as shit stinks, the droves of women were showing their beautiful white teeth to be noticed, either just before or just after they sized their pockets by every purchase they had made that day.

He was right. The droves of women who smiled at them either just before or just after they saw the designer bags they'd purchase while shopping.

"Thirsty bitches," J.T. mumbled as he watched the third woman who had flirted openly with him show her cynicism by assessing the value of the materials that were at their feet.

Reese intervened, sounding slightly disgruntled said, "Looks like we only good for what it is we got, my dudes." He pulled his chair closer toward the table. He was evidently embarrassed for assuming himself more apprised than he had been.

"Don't take it to the butt, loved one," Tonka began his pep talk under the pretense that what he was about to say would rally his troops in the right direction. "These ladies are just like the rest of the world, their dividends come before their health, their sanity, and their souls. Longevity without that long green makes no sense to the women and these 2000's. They want finances, then they want fun. And the only way they're going to have fun is if we have the finances."

Tonka sucked up the last of his pink lemonade through his straw. Then, turning to his left, he shot his empty cup into the trash container, when the cup hit the rim and slid into the pits unseen bottom, they all saluted the air in unison.

"Well, I like having my finances up, and I righteously want to have fun with the floozies. So, I guess that means we've got to keep getting this dough."

Reese chimed in, "How exactly are we going to keep getting this money."

"I'll tell you how," Tonka said to them as he looked back and forth between them.

"We've got to let this old money go and use our dough to make this new money grow. No more selling stress sacks, it's time to kush it up. That way our clientele and prices will come up. Plus, we need to invest in another hustle, too. That way we'll have our hands in every market these streets have to offer. If we're going to be street vendors, we might as well have all the streets merchandise. Assemble our dream and attack it as a team, and we'll be winning like Jordan in the NBA Finals."

Tonka again leaned back in his chair and folded his interlaced fingers over his hot dog bloated stomach. This was one of those moments he needed desperately to be mentored. It was one of those times when his unoriginal ideologies placed him in, way over his head. And this was one of those situations where his personal imposed idiosyncrasies could potentially envelop them in troubles. But, in this trio, there was no one to oppose his opinion with enough brains to make a difference, so ultimately, his doctrine would lead.

Turning his attention to something that had rendered him diffidently speechless, Tonka watched Reese's eyes as they followed the person who wandered over Tonka's shoulder behind him. Reese's response had shown Tonka a glint of timorousness.

"What's wrong bro, you okay?" Tonka asked with his hand under his shirt, alarm radiating across his face.

"It's that niggah, Dre, bro," J.T. answered as he kept Dre fixed in his sights. "That niggah looking like he on some testy shit too, bro."

Tonka leaned back with his hand still under his shirt gripping his blue steel. Turning his head to follow the trail of his friend's eyes, he could just make out the Dodgers jersey and fitted cap that passed out the mall's doors and into the chill, damp air. Taking into account, he recognized the familiar Dodgers ball cap that he had slapped off Dre's wall and onto the floor just the day prior.

He exhaled while simultaneously wiping his sweat beaded forehead. He released his pistol as he looked over to his partners. J.T and Tonka gave each other an assured look that disclosed loyalty. Then, he glanced over at Reese, who was in some form of reverie, which left his mouth agape and eyes bulging, focused on the door Dre had exited. Balling up his napkin from his meal, Tonka again leaned back and fired his shot across the table. It bounced off Reese's lips and fell to his lap as he jumped in a startled gesture.

"Close your mouth, fool. Sitting up here looking all scared to death and shit," Tonka said with conviction.

J.T. looked over to Reese who sat beside him, speaking his disapproval of Reese's inability to respond under pressure.

"Yeah, my dude, you looking like that crying ass niggah on that movie *The Wood*. Freezing up when shit might get real. Come on, Tonka, we outta here."

They rose together as Reese followed their lead.

"And just like that niggah in *The Wood*, you riding your scary ass in the backseat," Tonka said.

Reese's lips clamped tightly together as he followed closely behind J.T. and Tonka, thinking to himself that he had lost his courage in the face of their adversary. Reese felt emasculated as he trailed them quietly out of the mall to the car, where he dove without complaint, into the back seat.

****

Dre's mind exploded as his hands slammed against the steering wheel causing the dashboard to vibrate and a painful sting to shutter his hand.

"Mother Fucker." He shouted but was muffled by the clamped shut window, looking right and left as he sat at the corner's stop sign debating if he caught sight of someone he was hoping could assist him in his endeavors.

"Check baby out, still head turning, heart throbbing, and full of something inside that makes a niggah like me want to stick to her like a magnet," Dre said aloud as he threw his playful remarks out his passenger side window while pulling to a crawl beside this young man's fantasy and old man's dream.

The vixen gave a smirk smile but never allowed her head to swivel.

"That was cute, do I know you? " The question was asked by the female maverick. She kept marching with only her bean pole waist to carry the hips and ass that sailed flag-like behind her.

"You might know me if you took the time to look. I know I changed over the years, but I could never get rid of my Irish side."

Stopping in her tracks just as Dre hit his brakes, his car signals making a constant blinking noise in the car.

"St. Patrick's Day, is that you?"

The young woman loomed over the window while still standing on the curb, bent at the waist with her hands resting over her knees to get a better look.

"Every day but on St. Patrick's Day."

That was the same answer he had always given her years ago when she had asked him on the other side of her mother's front door. Juicy would always say his green eyes reminded her of Irish St. Patrick's Day, which she had henceforth nicknamed him Saint Patrick's Day over 15 years ago.

"Boy, pull over and park so I can holla at you one time," Juicy said.

Once Dre had pulled back on her block and parked, she jumped in and they talked like childhood friends who had not seen each other in ages. In truth, it had been forever since they had seen each other, but their reunion was not by coincidence. Even though that's what Dre would have liked it to have been and said so to Rita without batting an eyelid when she asked.

Gossiping over the past and present for about an hour, Dre expressed his deepest sentiments for Rita's mother, Patricia, right before he skillfully guided the conversation to his intended destination.

"How's Tonka? I saw him for the first time in years about a week ago, same lanky little curly head niggah he was when I last saw him. Who's these little dudes he's running with though, they rotten like an open can of month-old unrefrigerated tuna."

Rita looked at Dre with creased worry lines stitched on her smooth forehead, but the time wasn't right. "Something in my conscience had told me we needed to have a sit-down, and it's been fucking with me since that day."

Her lips tightened, "Tonka ain't no bad kid, he's just looking up to these ghetto fabulous niggahs 'cause this place we live in is empty when it comes to good role models. Seeing the Dre's with the money, Lexuses, and all the hood rats had him thinking that lifestyle is applicable because there ain't no real men out there to tell him no different. But inside, he's really good folk," Rita added, then looked back out through the windshield at the cars that zoomed past on the Main Street.

Wearing a look of disagreement with her prejudgments, despite her assessments of his kind were correct, Dre played as if her assumption of him had been asinine.

"So, it's like that, huh?" Dre sounded both shocked and offended all at once.

"I would have thought that you, of all people, who have lived in the systemic struggle would give brothers like Dre the benefit of the doubt."

He had stretched the emphasis of his name to show Rita that she had personalized him with them.

"Don't get touchy," Rita had picked up his sarcasm. "I didn't mean it like that. But in general, when most of these brothers out here are doing all the wrong things for all the wrong reasons. Then you see a half legit kid who's simply enticed by their unproductive open-eyed lifestyle, and don't encourage him to do otherwise. They're helping our systemic struggle to reincarnate itself and our next generation.

Rita gave Dre a once over from head to toe before she added, "And you with your diamonds and Lexus seem to fit the bill. Living like you shopping out of the Robb report with no job. Yeah. You are definitely part of why we're still deteriorating culturally."

Rita gave Dre the sexiest austere look he had ever seen, which left him temporarily paralyzed with a loss for words. It was so noticeable that his crush on her had sprouted from the past at just that second.

Clearing his throat, Dre charged forward with his refute. "Saint really ain't the anti-christ you trying to make me out to be with such determination, Rita. Nor am I excused from doing whatever it is out here that I need to do in order to get mine. But I do see the catch-22 that you're talking about, like the barrel of it is just inches away from my face. And that's why I want to talk to Tonka, might be able to say something to open his third eye."

He tapped his forehead for effect.

Rita accommodated Dre with a smile and approving nod, a nod that revealed her newly found respect. After moving through other Important topics and more gossip, 20 minutes later, Juicy was pulling herself from the Lexus leather seats and shutting the door behind herself.

Before she had a chance to chase away in all her self-confident sex appeal, Dre rolled down his window and shouted, "Yo Rita?"

She spun at the mention of her name. "What's up, Saint Patrick?"

Dre was making one last attempt at achieving his plot without seeming suspicious, "Tell Tonka holla at me. It matters that I get a chance to talk to little dude before anything happens. I owe Pat at least that much."

Hearing someone, much less Dre say he needed to try and get through to her little brother in the name of their deceased mother, touched her spirit deeply.

"How about you tell him yourself. If he isn't at the mall at this time, he's ain't nowhere but at that damn Bar and Pool Hall. Same place you and all your day ones used to hangout back in the day."

Dre thought to himself, *bingo.*

As Rita again turned to leave, Dre keyed in on her backside, "I see you're still walking around with more inartificial pulp flavors than the Welches Corporation!"

Rita laughed aloud at the uniqueness of Dre's compliment regarding her body in coalition to her childhood nickname, she simply put more attraction into each throw of her powerful hips now that she knew he was watching.

As Dre pulled off, he watched the one he felt like got away in his rearview, fantasizing as a grown man on his childhood dream girl. Dre spoke the old Pimp's proverbial his late brother Yoshi used to recite aloud as he left the curb, "Bitch can't help me get rich, she can only help me stay broke. Thanks, Rita."

Dre left Rita in his rearview forever, with intentions on putting a bullet in her brother's third eye.

****

"$3800. That's all you spent?"

Tonka nodded his head with his lips sealed tightly as his cheeks lifted in a proud grin.

J.T. took in the clean upholstery and smooth body frame of Tonka's blue B.M.W 326I.

"It's kind of small, plus It's a 2017. But for the price, mileage, and condition, you in pocket."

Tonka knew that whenever J.T. mixed his hate with his props, it was his way of showing he was jealousy happy for you, which was an oxymoron that Tonka was all too familiar with when it came to his friends.

Upon leaving the mall, J.T. and Tonka instantly took Reese home. They felt Reese had exposed himself in the mall by showing just how very shocked he was at the very sight of Dre. They'd known in a tight situation that he would clam up and could not be trusted, so there was no need to put him in waters they were certain he could not swim In. The moment Reese was out J.T.'s car, they began to laugh about how he was acting like a buster from every state on the United States map. After their 15-minute laugh on Reese, Tonka told Dre to drop him off at some location that J.T had never heard of or been to before.

Though it raised J.T.'s curiosity, he didn't question what his friend had up his sleeve because he himself had more important business to attend to further their cash ventures.

An hour later, Tonka was telling J.T. to come outside his home and see his new ride, and after about ten minutes of gawking over Tonka's new car, they jumped in and drove to the place that was their everyday agenda—their neighborhood bar and pool hall.

It was now 7:30 p.m. and the sun had fallen into the early darkness of night. J.T. and Tonka sat on post as usual in his new whip as they waited to serve their regular clientele, who they knew would soon come stumbling through the darkened night looking bug-eyed for a hit. Earlier when they separated, J.T. managed to gather all the different assortments of street pharmaceuticals they agreed to purchase. Now it was time to open up as vendors and entrepreneurs of the small drug game.

At least that's what these jackasses thought. They thought it was time to be small-time drug lords. But I'm about to teach these kids a very important lesson. Most times our perception never seems to align with reality. Because whenever Mr. Money Bags is in the picture, you could be here one minute and gone the next. Just one second, you'll see exactly what I mean.

"Once these go-fast heads, put it on the wire that we got powder, pills, and kush now, we're gonna be sitting pretty good," J.T said to Tonka between long lung crippling drags of the top shelf Sativa they were smoking.

"Yeah, my dude, as long as we stay in grind mode, shits going to come together like two titties In a push up bra."

As Tonka passed J.T. the blunt, J.T. laughed at his friend's metaphor. That's when it came to him to ask Tonka a question he'd wanted to ask for years.

"My dude. Since we were young you stayed coming with the metaphors when you talked. Now don't get me wrong, sometimes that shit be lit, even though half the time most muthafuckas can't keep up with the punchlines, you still be maken hella sense. And I just wanted to ask you bro. Why is it, you vibe like that?"

Tonka wasn't caught off guard by the question. In fact, it seemed like a question he had already rehearsed himself to answer.

"Well, bro, it's like this. Ever since I was 11, I've been about my bars like a Klondike®. Even when I'm in the streets, or class, or whatever, my mind is always in the booth. So, I work at it daily, even though I don't get wages or benefits right now. Imma still keep working until my dream pays off."

They both shared a second of silence then Tonka finished, "Plus, the ladies love when my words shoot like that little fat white baby in the pamper with the arrow!"

They both chuckled at Tonka's high cap.

"Aye . . . it's been awhile since I heard you go. Gimme some of that gangsta shit one time bro?" J.T. asked Tonka, as he turned the beat a tad bit lower in the car so Tonka could be audible over the playing background music.

Bobbing his head in sync with the beat, J.T. looked away from his friend while grinning at how easy it always was to get Tonka lost in his element of rhythm. The parking lot was completely dark as cars swished up and down the street. J.T. could make out a lone figure in the near distance crossing the street as Tonka began his flow.

"Pop's didn't want me- step dad taught me crack- moms was daily with the 9 to 5 just short of brakin' her back—"J.T. could hear the lyrics but was more focused on what appeared to be that same man entering the pool hall parking lot—"Part of the felon gang- real bids under my belt- no need for you snitch niggahs- just this choppa and myself."

Tonka was just getting warmed up when J.T. began to tap him lightly against his shoulder, "You see who I see?"

Tonka was already pulling his blue steel 9-millimeter from beneath his drive seat just as J.T. was simultaneously cocking his 11 shot 10 millimeter.

"In the famous words of the Ghetto Boys, 'If It's going down, let's get It over with!'"

They got out of the car and shut the doors behind themselves. They then both walked to the back bumper of Tonka's BMW, both steadying themselves close to the ground with their hands firmly clutching their coat pockets.

Stopping his advance about two parked cars away from the stone-faced teen's, Dre clutched the 17-shot-40 Glock he concealed in his jacket pocket. Standing beside a Chevy Camaro rear left fender, he established in his mind the car would be his cover once things got hectic.

"Damn, my young dude . . . you seem a bit standoffish. Like you ain't happy to see me or something?" Dre intended to interrogate while he played the cat-and-mouse game to get them to lower their guard.

"You don't look like a messenger of good news. Plus, you've got to stay on point in these city streets, the surprise element is a killer. You feel me?" The cat-and-mouse games were obviously unnecessary as they knew exactly why Dre was there, and the duo felt there was no need to be coy about the matter at hand. But it was their ballsy cockiness that told Dre they were in preparation for a duel. Straight forward with what he'd known before he'd proposed a common ground solution, then, if they thought he was a game or toyed with the concept, he would entertain them with all the drama they were looking for.

"90 racks is what you flocked from my spot," Dre said as he caught a glimpse of Tonka's comrade who was standing behind the back passenger door staring at the back of Tonka's head, as If Dre had exposed something voraciously unknown.

Dre smiled and said, "Guess the little homie standing behind you didn't know It was 90 bands." He nodded his head in the direction of J.T.

Tonka never took his eyes off him as Dre picked up from where he left off. "So, here's my deal. Give me back 60-thousand, y'all keep thirty, and there is no harm no foul. You young goons got to get money, too, and I respect every hustle in the game. After all, y'all didn't jack me directly. And I'd like to think even though there's something telling me differently, that y'all didn't even know whose house y'all was breaking into."

Pausing, Dre looked from one to the other.

"So, what do you say, my dudes. That's the best I can do, and as sweet as it's ever going to get."

Dusk had just about set in, but the awareness that encircled Tonka made it seem to him like his vision had turned cat-like. The stipulations he just heard were more than fair, and they also sounded a tad bit better than potentially dying or killing someone. Any man and his sane mind would have signed that dotted line.

The smallest technical difficulties remained.

"We don't have 90 thousand because you didn't have 90 racks! It was more like thirty thousand. So, whatever that fat filthy motherfucker sold you was damaged goods. Bet he didn't tell you he was riding around making heavy bets and buying more heroin than that ex-Preacher Eddie what's-his-face. You go to the jail and that sloppy washed-up dude was riding your whip like it was his and spending your money like it was his to blow. We just seized an opportunity and it should be that punk ass niggah you riding up on ready to make holy like a Christian congregation!"

All Dre could think to himself was that Tonka was lying.

"Patricia, I tried for you." As the last of his thoughts fell from his mouth, he said, "You know . . . that punk ass niggah you was talkin about," Tonka gave Dre a smirk nod that told just how ready he was for anything, "that's my Pop's you bitch ass niggah!"

Dre shouted his disrespects just as he came up with his glock in hand.

Plock! Plock! Plock! Plock!

Dre discharged four shots from his gun solely In Tonka's direction just before he dove behind the car for cover.

Tonka dove for cover just as Dre was firing his weapon. With his gun snatched free from his coat, Tonka's heart pounded heavy.

Pock! Pock!

Dre heard J.T.'s 10-millimeter bark twice from the opposite side of the BMW. Poking a quick peek around the front side of the Lincoln he was leaning against, Tonka fired around at the front of the Camaro where he had seen Dre crouched.

Pop! Pop! Pop!

Dre lowered his head for safekeeping as Tonka's bullet tinged into the car and whizzed by him.

"Aye, bone . . . watch the backside of the Camaro. We got cuz boxed in," Tonka shouted loud enough for his friend and foe to hear their plan.

Plock! Pock! Pock! Plock! Plock!

Tonka heard the forty Glock and ten-millimeter exchanged punches, which he knew would ultimately give him a chance to sneak one car closer to Dre.

Rounding the front of the car, Tonka was barely able to get his head down and sink to his knees before—*plock! plock! plock!*

Dre had sprinted between the open cars and fired shots in the direction where Tonka was coming from. Rising over the hood of the Lincoln Town car, Tonka fired twice.

Pop! Pop!

He noted in his mind the deep shriek that escaped from Dre's mouth at the sound of his fleeing feet.

J.T. stayed low as he crept behind the backside of the Lincoln.

"You swing wide around the parking lot, and I'ma make this fuck boy come out to play."

J.T. looked diffident as Tonka could read his best friend's skepticism.

"Bro, we should do what, J.T.?"

"We should do what, Bone? Let this fool regroup and catch us slipping another day or somethin'. He's wounded, and on the run, and in our neck of the woods, I'm ending this shit now!"

This was the finale, and as J.T concentrated on Tonka's unyielding expression, he'd realized just that so, he nodded to Tonka before ducking low and running the length of the parked cars before disappearing.

Night was now blanketing the parking lot like a black wool cover, and only the lot's lights contributed to helping the obstruction of Tonka's vision. It was deafeningly silent outs, just as it always was after a hail of bullets penetrates the night's air. Walking down the very row of car's which Dre had retreated to, Tonka confirmed by the trickling line of blood that Dre had been shot. Tonka followed the steady red drips of blood as he crossed over two rows of cars. He moved fast from cover to cover with his head low and pistol ready to blaze.

Standing behind the back tire of an old model Thunderbird, Tonka went to one knee to look beneath the row of cars where Dre's trail led. No legs were in sight as he rounded the car and continued to follow the cherry-colored specks. Three cars and to the right between an Expedition and a

Mercedes, kneeling to peer under the car, again Tonka saw nothing of any shoes or movement. Trying to stay as low as possible, he duck-walked to the back of the Mercedes, and that's where the small prickles of blood seemed to instantly be cut off like a tightened sink faucet.

Panic and alarm trembled through Tonka half a second before he realized he was bereaved of his life. First his ears registered something heavy landing on the hood of the expedition beside him, just as he heard—*plock! plock! plock!*— over his left blind side shoulder.

Spinning to face his fears a quarter of a second too late, the slugs entered Tonka's left shoulder, lungs, and small intestine. He managed to shoot one last shot as his body flung against the Mercedes back finder. Tonka's single shot struck home but was not enough to be a kill shot. The bullet hit. It landed atop the car's hood which he had just stood, all while sending his body flying from the car in the opposite direction.

He crawled backward as the tears streamed down Tonka's face just as he felt his life begin to drain onto the pavement. He struggled to drag himself away from "the reaper" he knew would soon be in pursuit. He tried to push to his feet from the ground's coldness, thinking to himself that he'd rather die on his feet versus laying on his back. But trying to hoist himself onto the rear of the Mercedes bumper, only made him more dizzy and stifled with defeat.

Tonka's hand never turned his .357 loose. He could feel blood saturating his coat and pants, and the night breeze mixed with the dampness of his clothes caused him to shutter, just before his teeth began to lightly chatter.

Closing his eyes and propping his head against the car's rear bumper, Tonka inhaled as much oxygen as his depleting lungs would allow his abating body to intake. His life demoted with every inhaled breath.

"For the sake of your mother," Dre began as he stepped around the other side of the Mercedes rear end, limping from the bullet that initially winged his leg, and now nursing a slumped shoulder that was also dangling loosely, "Imma make sure your casket stays open."

Glaring up into his persecutor's eyes, Dre angled his glock from Tonka's cranium to his chest plate. But before Dre could completely make Tonka a dead situation, scorching hot pellets were heard before the impact exploded through the breastbone of the unsuspecting Dre.

Pock!Pock!Pock!

The shot's pushed him back first to the concrete, sending him flailing and his gun flying in the distance. Dre's body would never move again, he would be outlined in chalk right where he lay.

Sirens blared meekly in the far night's darkness. J.T. kneeled beside his friend despite the commiseration stretching tightly across his future.

"Damn, my dude. You looking at me like I'm a memory already or something."

Tonka gave a laugh that immediately turned Into a cough that had him heaving for air. "Fi-fire up me a blunt bro." Tonka lips trembled uncontrollably as J.T. took the titan from inside his jacket pocket, lit it, then held It to Tonka's lips.

As Tonka used the last of his lung capacity to draw in the cigarette one good time, they both could hear the sirens nearing closer.

"You gotta go my dude, they-they're getting close-closer homie." Tonka warned his friend after exhaling the small intake of weed smoke.

J.T., without worry, pulled the blunt from Tonka's mouth, took a hit, then placed it back to his friend's mouth.

"Tell my sis, she-she can find me, in the same place she still looks for our mom." Taking another pull from the weed with all the strength he could muster, Tonka then handed J.T. his 357 just before motioning his hand for J.T. to hand him the murder weapon.

Tonka was making sure the murder weapon would be attached to his soon lifeless palm once the police arrived.

J.T. handed his gun to Tonka. Simultaneously hugging his closest friend who in that moment, they both realized, was more like the only brother neither of them had.

"Get on oh, my day one. Take my ca-car."

As the volumes of the sirens grew closer, these inseparable two shared their utmost respects with a solemn tear. Wiping his face clean and stuffing the gun in his coat pocket, J.T. stepped over his closest friend without looking back, he jumped into Tonka's car to flee the scene. J.T. smiled in his rearview mirror as he could hear Tonka empty the clip into the cadaver that was Dre's already dead body.

That's when his last breath slipped from his chest and the gun fell to his side.

Tonka was dead

CHAPTER
16

JUICY. GWUAP.

That was the second funeral Quanah and Rita had attended in a little over two weeks. Except this time Quanah lost her child's father and fiancé in Yoshi, and Rita had lost her little brother and a childhood friend and homeboy which they both were still in the earliest stages of grieving over. It had been pretty much a mystery as to who killed Yoshi, until Rome's death produced the murder weapon with the same shell markings and distinct groove pattern In Yoshi's murder.

Everyone thought Yoshi's murder would go unsolved. But when Rome and Dre were found dead at the scene, and the gun that was covered in Dre's fingerprints matched the shell indentations in both Rome and Yoshi's homicides, Quanah's heart finally felt it could move forlorn to a modicum type healing.

As Rita sat in all black at the cemetery, knowing this was the moment she would have to relinquish her Yoshi forever, Quanah now hugged Rita with all her might, just as her friend had done her just weeks ago. Rita was lost behind this disaster, even though she was a God-fearing woman who firmly believed that whatever be God's will was what was best. She still could not help but to question why such tragedy had raided her life twice in such a short time. Raised by her mother to have unmeasured faith, Rita never once questioned the act of her supreme Father.

Except for today.

This day her dissonance showed, and she demanded answers as to why she was being stripped of her loved ones.

After the casket had been lowered and all who had come to say their farewells had covered Rome's casket in roses, only two remained present with Rome's chariot.

"I'm sorry, Tonka. Rest in peace little brother. And give Mom my love." Rita spoke her last words as her tears splashed the rose petals she held to her chest. Then she released her thorned rose into the hole atop the casket where her brother lay to rest. Another rose followed hers into Rome's personal drop slot. It landed across her own atop of Rome's resting chest.

Looking to her left to see whose hand had found its way to holding hers, she wanted to see who's touch held such mourning and remorse for these two quickly claimed lives. Rita was greeted by someone whom she knew loved Rome dearly, someone who tried but was Ineffable to speak of the lost his heart felt wept.

Rita could only shelter him in her arms as he wept

"It's okay J.T. It's okay."

Once they were both able to gather some emotional reticence, J.T. walked to Quanah's car with Rita while they talked along the way.

"You were with Rome when he died?" Rita asked J.T. as they strolled along slowly.

He nodded to Rita's question.

"Dre pushed up on us with the bullshit. He tried to press us like some little boys. Then he tried to bust on us like we was easy slaughter. Tonka wasn't backing down."

Rita took inventory on what she'd just heard. Rita shook her head as she wiped her crying eyes. "Whatever ya'll did to make Dre come after y'all don't even matter now. Because it ain't gonna bring your friend and my little brother back. In the end J.T. I just hope It was worth It."

His face was a clear reflection to Rita that whatever it was worth, it surely was not tantamount to Rome's life.

Reaching the car, J.T. opened Quanah's passenger door as Rita and J.T. hugged goodbye. Rita slid in as J.T. shut the door behind her.

Once the window came down J.T. decided to speak his last respects, "Yo, sis . . . like, whatever you need whenever you need it big sis. Even though one of your brother's is gone, you still have a brother left."

Rita was touched because she'd known every word J.T. spoke he sincerely meant.

"Oh yeah," J.T. snapped his fingers as If to remember something, "you can find him where you find your mom."

Rita looked clueless at J.T. as he stared back into her face hoping he could open the door to whatever this riddle was. A riddle at that moment, shot well over Rita's comprehension.

"That's what he said to tell you, you can find him where you find your mom." J.T. gave a slight shrug after he'd finished his relayed message.

Not a thing seemed to remotely register in Rita's face from what J.T. had observed.

"Don't worry. Whenever the time is right, whatever he means, it'll come to you. Just when you least expect It."

J.T. paused.

"Don't forget what I said, Rita. You girls be safe." Then with a salute, J.T. patted the top of the BMW's hood, and turned to make his way to his car.

Rita's mind had been tormented by what she'd heard well after she'd heard it, and as she sat in her bed that night oblivious to sleep, she thought pensively on the meaning of her brother's last words. Out of the blue, Rita seemed to recollect the memory vividly. It was as if she had descended in time, to the very moment before her mother had passed. She remembered Rome and herself standing at their mother's hospital bed, all the while Rita cradled God's book in her arms. Praying that her mother would recover from what had broken most of her bones. Amongst more severe injuries that threatened to sever her away from the world. Miraculously, Patricia had come to, her vision barely visible through the swelling that surrounded her lids. Seeing that their mother was conscious, Rome and Rita both began to weep with joy and sadness. In Patricia's last feeble strength, she touched lightly to her heart with her right hand, reached over and patted those same fingertips alongside Rome's temple. Then their mother extended her arm a bit further and patted Rita's heart. With her last muster of life, Patricia laid her hand over the family heirloom, which Rita held possessively to her chest. A smile that showed her love for them both spread across their mother's face, it held a warmth and admiration they had never seen In Patricia's eyes before that moment. A second later, Patricia was gone, her hand dangling lifelessly over the hospital bed rail as nurses and doctors came storming, in in a frantic rush.

Rome and Rita had often, in they're more mature years, discussed the symbolism that their mother tried to convey to them both in her last minutes with them. After years of analyzing those last precious moments the trio had together, Roman and Rita had agreeably concluded that their mother was inferring she would always be no further than their hearts, their heads, and their family Bible. That's when Rita snapped free from her daydream, leaped from her bed to a sitting position on the floor, then slid the box which held the antique family Bible from beneath her bed. Struck by a revelation as If someone had hit her over the head with a Heineken bottle in a bar fight, Rita grinned as she realized the meaning of her little brother's message. It was a sour piece of something to realize, it immediately turned her grin into a watery eyed melancholy. Lifting the lid and removing the Bible that was surrounded by the carved coiled wood chips, Rita set the holy book between her Indian style crossed legs, then she opened the family Bible and began to read over the familiar passages just as she had done so often before. First,

Rita flipped through 1 Corinthians 13 which was her mother's favorite verse, then she moved on as the tears formed. Next, she scanned over Luke 3:16. She remembered that it was her favorite verse as if it was the first day she had been taught it. Its moral importance still etched deeply in her memory, amongst the other memories that would forever remain of her mother and brother.

With her mind jogging through memories, Rita subconsciously thumbed through the Bible until she finally turned to Psalms 23. This verse was always Rome's, Rita's, and Patricia's most prized prayer In the Bible. It was the only verse the three of them would recite in unison every time after they studied. Once Rita reached the page she sought, there was a folded letter creased between the pages with her name scribbled on the outside. Seeing her name caused air to pressurize in her chest as if her lungs were a vault about to be sealed. Emotions paraded around in her like little girls holding hands and spinning circles in their barrettes and new dresses anticipating a trip to Disneyland. Pushing away the tears were rushing down from her face; Rita began to read her letter word for word.

"So, you figured it out.?! I thought you would, seeing as how you've always been the smart one in the family." Rita smiled at her brother's compliment all while still using her index finger to wipe away her sorrow. *"I bet you're wondering why and how this letter found its way into our families most sacred possession, lol, the possession you hide quite nicely in the back of your closet. Lol."*

Rita shook her head and smiled.

"Just because Mom and Dad made you the smartest, didn't mean they didn't bless me with a little brain to think with. Anyways, I just wanted you and little sis to know that regardless of whatever hand we're playing at the very moment you're reading this letter, I love you both. Infinitely! Sorry you missed this semester, but you needed a break anyways. But fall semester you won't miss, even for the life of me . . . You take care Super Woman . . .

P.S . . . It's at the bottom of the box, and when you see your gift just know God answers prayers. Go make me proud.

Love always, Rome. AKA . . . Tonka!"

Pushing the wood chips away from the center of the box that held a mixture of pleasant aromas, Rita covered her bosom with Rome's letter that she still held tightly clenched. She was taken aback by the three rows of big face Benjamin Franklin's that Rita could have undoubtedly sworn winked at her after she removed the wooden planks from their paper faces. Pulling the three separate stacks from the box and pressing them glued to her chest as she rocked back and forth with her eyes clamped shut.

Tears rained down her face like rain on a windshield in a wet winter storm. And in that moment, something seemed to ease into Rita's spirit and soothe her soul. She no longer asked God why her brother had died so vainly. And as she sat there in prayer, crying and swaying back and forth, she reasoned that her brother's senseless fate was an intervention for her little sister and her own security of a prominent future.

How she loved Rome for loving her but despised him for loving her just the same. For if not for his love to see her prevail, her brother would not be buried under the stump of money's gratuitous claim.

😈 *Everyone pays what's corvee to the paramount one in the end! Because like I said, I'm too prevalent to be cheated, tricked, or eluded by any means. Even the innocent are touched by the disorder that's caused by my iniquities. Just take Rita for instance. Young, inexperienced people living just like Tonka are cut into shreds on a daily basis under my dogmatics, all so they can bathe in my shine but for a limited time.*

Granted Tonka's contribution to something greater while serving under my deity was significant to someone the good Lord had destined to be an overachiever. Tonka just slipped and lost his way trying to ensure stability for his family. Yet little did he know all the while, it had already been prophesied by the real God that light would shine on his family and himself just after the darkest hour. It was his impressionable young mind and impatience to get the bag that handed him a compromising and Insolvent debt to yours truly. A debt the young lad obviously could not pay. And since he couldn't compensate, I simply got my pay in blood.

Too bad for Tonka and all the other influential kids out there whose plates are never quite full at supper time. Because little do they know, our regal master and myself can't wait to prey on those of you who are eager to be saviors without knowing any better.

On my behalf, you've got to give me some form of credit. I mean, I allowed Tonka to pass me on so Rita could excel using my usufruct revenues. And that's gotta earn me a gold star or two on the awards board. So you can never say I wasn't true to my word, cuz like I said from the Jump Street, I do good by those who do good by me. So, in essence I'm really not all bad. But don't get me fucked up. I'm watching Rita like black folks do when there's grease in the frying pan and the fire is lit. And when she slips, I'ma be the concrete floor that catches her ass.

She won't get away just like you won't get away and you be sure to remember who told you so!

Hell, I'm money . And there isn't a soul on earth who can do without me. You either work and break your back or steal for the greater gain of ME. And eventually, you just like the rest, will commit one of these seven cardinal sins. All so the eighth and most deadly sin in my father's toolbox can put the whole world on strings, just like Geppetto did ole Pinocchio.

Eventually you'll be my puppets. And your children also. Even your children's children will be my slaves.

Once I get you, I'll be a curse on your family lineage for generations to come. My father and I will make your offspring love material things. We'll make sure we turn them into greedy little pigs. Then after that, I'll be sure to turn their offspring into those envious-hearted people who hate others who have more material things then they do. The ones who are lost in their lust and wrath. I'll be certain to use your bodies and beauty disposingly. But for those of you who are full of wrath, I'll make sure you do my dirtiest works, like killing and robbing.

That shouldn't be too much for you idiots who only have vengeance and destruction on your little bitty brains.

As far as pride, sloth, and the gluttony sins, well, let's just say I've already infected over seventy percent of the world with these three sins that lay latent in your DNA. These three sins are the easiest for the false hearted to hide from the good people of this world. These sins are the sins I commonly use to get to those I can't get to.

That's of course unless I get to you first.

So, it's simple. I use pride, sloth, and gluttony to imprison you, and you, in turn, imprison those who love you, that I can't get to. Whereas they take on the burden of your sins because they love you, which simply makes them a slave of a slave.

Either teach your youth, teach your women and children, teach humanity, or I promise on my papery green 🤪 fibers that I will take precedence over ethics, code, and morale, all over this planet. Hell . . . soon enough, I'll have enough power around here to eradicate words like loyalty and love.

🤪 Maybe before long, I may make mentions of words like loyalty and love a treason punishable by death in my new world empire. Really soon, the almighty dollar is going to rule all the land, and there's nothing anyone can do about it.

So please, just keep bathing in all my sins, and I'll continue to use the almighty dollar to push start your wickedness. And I'll keep driving you just like Johnny 5 did the Mach 5. But unlike Johnny, before you cross the finish line, I'll be sure to make sure you crash and burn first.

As long as I— 😛 denario, 😛 peso, 😛 yen, 😛 moolah, 😛 shmoney is around, you and your brainwashed civilization don't stand a chance. And once you see that, I'll be here, waiting patiently with a contract to grant you whatever you wish, the moment your bloody ink hits the X on that dotted line.

Until them, we'll be here, waiting with open arms 😈.